# REST ASSURED

# REST ASSURED

## Nicholas Rhea

This first world edition published in Great Britain 2005 by
SEVERN HOUSE PUBLISHERS LTD of
9–15 High Street, Sutton, Surrey SM1 1DF.
This first world edition published in the USA 2005 by
SEVERN HOUSE PUBLISHERS INC of
595 Madison Avenue, New York, N.Y. 10022.

Copyright © 2005 by Nicholas Rhea.

British Library Cataloguing in Publication Data

Rhea, Nicholas, 1936-
  Rest assured
  1.  Insurance agents - England - Yorkshire - Fiction
  2.  Yorkshire (England) - Social life and customs - Fiction
  I.  Title
  823.9'14 [F]

ISBN 0-7278-6222-7

Except where actual historical events and characters are being
described for the storyline of this novel, all situations in this
publication are fictitious and any resemblance to living persons
is purely coincidental.

Typeset by Palimpsest Book Production Ltd.,
Polmont, Stirlingshire, Scotland.
Printed and bound in Great Britain by
MPG Books Ltd., Bodmin, Cornwall.

# One

*'I left my Austin 7 outside the house and when I came out
later, much to my surprise there was a Morris 10'*
From a claim form

"What do I do now?'

Evelyn and I were sitting in our car, which was stationary beside a lonely and little-used road high on the moors. The engine was running and we had swopped seats – I was now in the front passenger side and Evelyn was at the wheel. It was a fine dry day and Betsy, our Austin 10, was gleaming with all her chrome highly polished and her black bodywork glistening in the strong light. The L-plates to front and rear were prominent but Evelyn was not immediately concerned with the appearance of the car. She had other things to think about. I had explained about using the gears, and demonstrated how to use the clutch, and she was wondering what to do next: this was her first driving lesson on a road and I was tutor.

I was aware of the oft-quoted conventional wisdom that a man should never even try to teach his wife to drive – it was a sure way of building up to a blazing argument at the least or a divorce at the worst – but the nearest professional driving instructor was nearly fifteen miles away. That raised the question of the cost of lessons, to say nothing of the petrol we'd use in travelling there and back – it was still rationed and I had to conserve sufficient to do my job.

Taking all things into consideration, we reasoned I should teach Evelyn, with the possibility that she would receive three

1

or four final lessons from a professional. That expert tuition would provide an additional means of getting her through the driving test. This Saturday afternoon, therefore, baby Paul was with his Aunt Maureen and we had a couple of hours to ourselves. I did not anticipate any difficulty teaching Evelyn; after all, her childhood had been spent helping on her father's farm, which also doubled as a public house, which meant she was accustomed to driving the tractor around the premises. Car driving was just a case of adapting her existing knowledge while learning how to cope with traffic, the rules of the road and the Highway Code. The actual mechanical aspects of knowing which pedals to depress to make the car go forwards and stop were familiar to her, as were the questions of steering, reversing and changing gear. Despite that, she was clearly nervous.

'Always beware of other traffic,' I cautioned her. 'So before you move off, you must signal your intention before pulling into the road and you must always check your rear-view mirror. Turn your head to look behind as well, as a double-check.'

She flicked the direction indicator switch – sometimes called a trafficator – which was in the centre of the steering wheel above the horn button – and the little orange-coloured finger clicked out from the offside central doorpost, like a flat carrot with a small light inside. I saw her check the mirror. Nothing was coming in either direction. We had the road to ourselves.

'Depress the clutch and select first gear.'

She did so without any apparent problem.

'Fine, now release the handbrake as you let out the clutch very smoothly. You'll feel the car start to go forward. As you do so, take it on to the road and gradually build up speed, always wary of what might be on the road.'

'I don't want to go too fast . . . I'm nervous . . . it's not anything like the tractor . . .'

'You know where the brake pedal is, keep that in mind if you have to stop in a rush. We've a flat road ahead for about

a mile, no steep hills or bends and probably no traffic . . .
Right, off you go. When you get to eight miles an hour or so,
change up into second gear . . . into third when you get to
around eighteen and top at twenty-five . . . but check your
mirror every ten seconds or so . . .'

And so began the first of Evelyn's driving lessons. She
learned quickly thanks to her experience with the tractor and
as she became more confident and proficient I took her to a
village on the southern edge of the moors, Stonethorpe, where
there was a disused airfield, the old runways of which were
ideal for a beginner to get more practice in basic skills. Then
I took her into the villages and eventually into town to cope
with people and heavier traffic. We were a regular sight as we
toured the villages of Delverdale, usually on Saturday afternoons, Sunday afternoons and several evenings per week.
Sometimes we had Paul on board and sometimes we were
alone, but I began to realize, from comments I received during
my rounds, that we were considered very modern in outlook.
Certainly, some women were drivers, just as they had been
during the war, but the sight of a young woman, a young
mother no less, driving a car on public roads, was still compar-
atively unusual in the moorland villages and the masculine
attitude to this became evident during the weeks which
followed.

'Is that Matthew's insurance?' a deeply masculine Yorkshire
voice shouted into my recently acquired telephone.

Other than business people or those with money, not many
people on the moors had a telephone and those who were
fortunate enough to afford one tended to shout into the
mouthpiece even when making a local call. Certainly, you
had to shout when making or receiving long-distance calls,
but there were times I thought some callers did not need
such a sophisticated instrument to convey their messages
locally – their shouting must surely be capable of being
heard over a considerable distance without any kind of
amplification.

'It is; this is Matthew Taylor speaking.' I was delighted that people were beginning to refer to Matthew's insurance rather than calling it the Premier. It indicated a very reassuring trust in me and my work.

'Aye, well, mebbe you could pop in and see me when you've a minute,' he bellowed.

'With pleasure,' I responded. 'Who's speaking?'

'It's me,' he said.

'Yes, but who are you?'

'Who am I? I'm very well known around here, you know very well who I am . . . oh, aye, I see what you mean. I'm not really used to this thing yet. It's Henry Noble, Noble's Haulage at Ingledale. You're not likely to know that, at your end of this line, are you?'

'Well, I do know of you and your depot, Mr Noble.' I recognized the name. 'But you're not one of my clients, are you?'

'Not yet but I might be if you get yourself out here,' he boomed with just a hint of mischievous laughter in his voice.

'So you need to talk to me about insurance?'

'Why else would I be ringing you? You're t'local insurance man, aren't you?'

'I am, so when can you see me?' I was mentally checking my commitments for the following few days. Quite a number of my clients lived in Ingledale, a former industrial community, one of only two such villages within my agency. The other was Crossrigg, further down the dale, with its brickyard, railway junction and back-to-back houses. Ingledale was due for a visit from me in a couple of days' time but I did not think Henry Noble would wait that long. I gained the initial impression he was not ringing for the kind of financial advice or help I gave to vulnerable people; he was probably more interested in what the Premier could offer by way of insurance for his haulage concern.

I wondered if his existing insurer had increased the premiums – if so, Henry, being a thrifty Yorkshireman, would be looking for something cheaper but just as good if not better. I thought I could rise to that challenge, so if this meant new

4

business then I would call on him tomorrow morning. He'd
be my first customer of the day.

I knew very little about his haulage activities except that it
was a rather small concern which specialized in quarried stone,
and there was no doubt he would be well insured. From knowledge I'd acquired through living in the district, I knew Henry's
business depended heavily on several freestone quarries in that
part of the upper dale; the high-value stone was used for building houses, bridges, churches, office blocks and even mansions
and he had the contract for transporting it to nearby ports or
goods yards from where it was taken further by ship or rail.
Petrol rationing continued to restrict very long distance travel
by lorries but we were well served with ports on the north-
east coast, and a good railway network.

In the past, thousands of tons of stone had been carried to
Whitby from these quarries, from where it was shipped to
London for use in the construction of city centre buildings;
lots of famous London buildings are built with freestone quarried from Delverdale. Freestone is a type of sandstone which
is easily worked and which hardens on exposure to the air. Its
colour varies between a dull tan to a dark brown, and in some
cases it can be stained purple from the heather amongst which
it is found; this combination of colour variants and usefulness
makes it very popular.

Noble's Haulage was a long-established family business
which had been founded by one of Henry's ancestors some
time in the late 1800s. At that time, the stone had been transported to Whitby on horse-drawn vehicles; I believe it was
just after the First World War that Noble's Haulage eventually
became completely motorized. Progress of that kind was
considered quite daring and innovative – after all, lorries were
more expensive than horses, they needed constant maintenance
and had a habit of breaking down at the most inconvenient
moments. The perceived thinking in the dale was that horses
were cheaper to maintain and did not break down; besides, you
could talk to a horse and it would respond with affection.
You could develop a partnership with a horse, too, something

you couldn't do with smelly and unreliable lorries. But progress was inevitable and there was no doubt Henry, like his forebears, was regarded as a man of vision and an innovator. That knowledge hinted at an intriguing reason for my prospective visit. If it was just a case of renewing his existing insurance he would not want to talk to me. I guessed that something had gone awry and scented a victory!

I had assured Henry that I would make him my very first call tomorrow morning, an indication of his importance to me, and so it was that I parked outside the green and yellow painted wooden building which bore a large legend – NOBLE'S HAULAGE, EST. 1882 – and a small sign saying OFFICE.

A green and yellow five-ton lorry was parked outside bearing the company name on its doors and rear panel. I could see a large stone house behind the complex, evidently the family home. There was what appeared to be a parking area in front of a large corrugated iron building which looked like a garage; I noted a petrol pump which suggested the company had its own supply – quite a common feature in these remote parts even if petrol was still rationed – and there was the assorted paraphernalia of a small but busy haulage company, such as piles of stone, spare tyres, petrol cans and vehicle parts. There was even a disused horse-drawn wagon, complete but deteriorating rapidly through lack of attention. I thought that if I had had the space, I would have liked to buy it and have it restored. The office door was closed but a sign said KNOCK and ENTER, so I did, to find myself in a dusty office with a man sitting behind a big roll-top desk. The place seemed thick with stone dust and I guessed that all efforts to keep the place clean would be futile.

'Yes?' He rose to his feet with something of a struggle and I saw his right leg was covered in plaster below the knee. He was wearing a pair of old trousers with part of one of the legs cut away to accommodate the plaster. A large sock adorned his toes and there was a metal fitment beneath the foot. There was a pair of crutches standing against the wall near his desk.

'Mr Noble?'

'That's me.'

'Matthew Taylor, from Premier Assurance.' I held out my hand and he shook it warmly with a strong grip, then indicated a chair beside his desk.

'Glad you could come. Coffee?' he asked.

Coffee was not usually offered in such places, tea being the preferred beverage, but I indicated my pleasure and he pressed a bell-push on his desk, then flopped back on to his chair with a sigh of relief.

'The wife will hear that,' he said. 'She'll fetch it across in a minute or two; that's my house just behind us. Very handy, not far to travel to work, like you, eh? Working from home. Not a bad thing when you've bust your leg like me.'

'Sorry about that,' I said.

'My own daft fault. I fell off a ladder when I was clearing the gutters on the house roof. Stupid really, but it could have been worse. I might have landed on my head, eh? With a hard head like mine, I might have cracked the concrete!' And he laughed at his own joke.

'I hope you're insured!' I returned, trying to match his joyful attitude.

'Not for breaking my leg . . . mebbe I should be.'

He was a thickset man of slightly less than average height and I guessed he would be in his late forties or early fifties. He had flabby cheeks and a thick neck, but he had kept all his hair, which was light brown and inclined to be wavy; clean-shaven, he had a good set of natural teeth and his flesh looked a healthy pink. He was wearing a comfortable sweater and shirt and I got the impression he'd rather be outside driving his lorry or doing something in the yard. He didn't look the sort of man who'd enjoy being restricted to working at a desk.

'Is that why you want to see me?'

'I'm not insured for being off work if that's what you mean.' He adopted a serious look now. 'I have life insurance in case I drop dead or get killed, but I never thought about getting insured for being off work . . . my agent never suggested that.

I've allus reckoned that if you're off work you don't get paid, as simple as that.'

'Well, is that what you want to discuss? I can certainly arrange that kind of cover, Mr Noble; we offer a good range of policies to cover most eventualities including personal injury, with specially drafted schemes to cater for sickness and accidents which affect the self-employed. We can tailor our policies to suit a particular small business, although I can't back-date a policy to cater for that leg injury . . .'

'We'll talk about that soon, but that's not why I called you. I want to discuss another sort of insurance, but I'd like Brenda to be here. It affects her, you see.'

My immediate thought was that he wished to arrange some form of life insurance or perhaps an endowment policy for the benefit of his wife, so I lifted my briefcase on to the desk and opened it to hunt for the necessary literature. Then Mrs Noble pushed open the door and walked in with a tray of three cups and a coffee pot along with a jug of milk and some chocolate biscuits. A rare treat. The coffee smelled delicious. Freshly ground, I thought. Far better than that coffee essence out of a bottle that most people used. She placed the tray on the desk, pulled up a chair and, without a word, began to pour. She was around the same age as her husband, thickset like him and wearing a red blouse and a skirt of many colours.

'Brenda, this is Mr Taylor from the Premier. Mr Taylor, my wife, Brenda.'

'Hello,' I said.

'Morning.' She didn't sound too pleased to see me. That was my first impression. I wondered if there was some kind of battle going on between them, a marital row, perhaps, or a dispute over something. But it was not my concern. I would try to ignore her grumpiness.

'Sit down, Brenda, and listen to what Mr Taylor has to say.'

Like an obedient dog, she settled on the chair next to me, handed out the mugs of coffee and biscuits and waited for him to speak.

'Mr Taylor,' he began, 'you can see what my problem is – this!' And he tapped his leg. 'I can't drive, not until my leg's back to normal. I could be off another six weeks, so the hospital tells me. Mebbe longer. And that's costing me money. It means I've only one wagon on the roads instead of two. I've only got the pair of 'em and to be honest I don't want any more, but I need to keep both vehicles at work to maintain my income and cover expenses. There's enough work for two wagons day in, day out. There's work to keep this firm going until I retire, so you can see my problem. If I don't deliver the stone, the quarry masters might find somebody who can. It's been a week now and stocks are piling up and naturally they want rid of it.'

'I follow. Things are getting urgent?'

'Urgent, yes, but not quite desperate yet. I got a call just before you came, asking when I was going to get back to work and get it moved. Things start to back up if recently quarried stuff's not shifted out of the way to make space for the next lot of fresh stone and I don't want to let any of my competitors in. These jobs are mine, Mr Taylor, and I intend to keep 'em. My job's at stake, the business I mean, that's the bottom line in all this. The firm's at risk if I don't deliver.'

'So how can I help?' I began to wonder why he thought I might be able to help him overcome this operational difficulty. 'You'll have drivers?'

'I've two drivers, one's out on the road now. That truck in the yard is the one the other driver normally takes out. That's me, I'm the other driver. I'm not an office man, Mr Taylor, I like to be on the road, not stuck in here pushing pens and shuffling piles of paper. That's Brenda's job.'

'Ah, the company secretary?' I risked a glance in her direction and she just nodded, although she did produce the faintest of smiles.

'Right,' said Henry. 'So you can see, Mr Taylor, that while I'm out of commission my truck's idle and we're not earning money. My income's been halved, in a manner of speaking. We're not operating at our full potential while I'm stuck in here and it's that truck's job to earn money. There's wages

9

to find, maintenance to pay for, fuel, tax and so on. We can't afford to let it stand idle. We've got a Public Carrier's Licence, the 'A' licence that is, so we're all above board, all legal.'

'I understand.' His plight was easy to follow but I was still wondering what my role was expected to be. He seemed to be a long time getting to the point he was making. 'So how can I help?'

'Well, this haulage contractor's business has been with the Demetrius Insurance Company for as long as anyone can remember, certainly from the time we had only horse-drawn vehicles, so you can see how far back our links go. Back to when we were established, I reckon.'

'A long time, Mr Noble.'

'Mebbe too long, Mr Taylor. You see, they haven't changed much in that time, not kept pace with modern developments. I know they've graduated from insuring horse-drawn vehicles to modern cars and lorries, and they are pretty good where small companies like this one are concerned, but they're still a bit antiquated.'

'In what way?'

'By not insuring women drivers.' He smacked his good thigh with the palm of his hand. 'That's my point, Mr Taylor. They won't insure women drivers.'

'But you haven't any women drivers, have you?'

'I would have, if I could get her insured, Mr Taylor. There's one sitting right next to you.'

'This isn't my idea, Mr Taylor.' Mrs Noble now entered the fray. 'I've never considered myself a lorry driver. I run the office, look after the accounts, that sort of thing. I say that if Henry wants another driver, he should take one on, on a temporary basis. There's plenty of young fellers with HGV licences who'd be happy to do a few hours driving without being taken on full-time.'

'It all costs extra money, Mr Taylor, employing outside labour. It's my reasoning that if Brenda could drive that wagon we'd get it back on the road, we'd keep faith with the quarry managers and we'd get the job done and all that stone shifted. We'd earn money without spending on more wages. It all makes sense to me. Me and her would just swop jobs for a week or two.'

'I'm not a lorry driver, Mr Taylor,' whispered Brenda. 'And I don't think I could ever cope with a lorry loaded with tons of stone . . .'

'What about the family car?' I put to them. 'Are you insured to drive that?'

'No she's not, Mr Taylor, that's the problem. You've hit it right on the head. She's not insured to drive our car. When I asked about it, my insurance man said only men can drive motor vehicles. That's the policy of the Demetrius, he told me. In all their documents, it shows "he" and "him", so they reckon that doesn't allow women to drive. That's what my local agent, that chap Scott from Walton, told me years ago and I never questioned it at the time because it didn't matter then, but on thinking about it, since my leg got bust, I remembered Brenda had driven lorries in the ATS! It means she's capable of controlling summat as big and heavy as that. So she could drive our truck, Mr Taylor, she's quite capable if only she could get insurance cover.'

'Army trucks weren't as big as our lorries and they weren't loaded with stones,' Brenda said. 'It was different, most of the time we were transporting soldiers and light equipment about the camps. We didn't carry heavy goods and, besides, we didn't have to worry about insurance, the army saw to all that kind of thing.'

'Did you drive on public roads?' I asked her.

'Most of it was done on army bases, but if we did go on the roads the army insurance covered us. The emergency regulations allowed us to do quite a lot we couldn't do in civvy street.'

'So you can drive a motor vehicle?' I smiled. 'You're not an absolute beginner? Have you kept up your practice?'

'Only by moving lorries about here, in the yard. That's not very often, I might say. I'll shift one if it has to be moved quickly. Not outside, though, I don't go on the road. I wouldn't even take a car on the road, not with all this modern traffic and folks rushing about. Besides, I'm not the holder of a civilian driving licence let alone an HGV licence. We didn't need them when I was in the ATS, I was tested by the army and got one of their licences; it's lapsed now. It means I'm not licensed to drive on the roads.'

'It's not just that, Mr Taylor. It's the problem of Brenda being a woman and me wanting her to drive HGVs. She can soon get a licence and we can soon fix a bit of tuition and a test, but it's the insurance we've got to get sorted first and I don't want to delay things any more. That's why you're here, Mr Taylor. I want to get all this sorted out as soon as I can otherwise my business could be in trouble. And according to that chap Scott, Demetrius are adamant – they won't insure women drivers.'

I had no wish to become embroiled in what appeared to be some kind of domestic dispute between man and wife, so all I could do was to state the position of the Premier Assurance Association. Although I had no women motor vehicle policy-holders as my clients, some women did drive their husbands' private cars and they were fully covered. In fact, my own wife was one.

The Premier's policies stated that anyone could drive a motor vehicle with the policyholder's consent, provided they held the relevant current licence and were not disqualified. The term 'anyone' meant what it said – a driver could be male or female, and certainly I had never received any formal instructions to suggest women could not become policy-holders for drivers' insurance with the Premier. So far as I knew, there was no distinction between them and male policy-holders.

I began to wonder how common it was for some insurance companies to refuse to cover women drivers even if they were driving with the permission of a policyholder. I knew the army had allowed women to drive – indeed, HRH Princess Elizabeth, before she became Queen of England, was a driver and mechanic while she was in the ATS but I could not lose sight of the fact that those women drove military vehicles under the cover of military insurance and on military driving permits. Furthermore, most of their driving would have been on military property. The relevant emergency legislation dealt with the legalities of that period and in some instances those rules continued after the war. There was a brief time when holders of ordinary driving licences for Group A vehicles could also drive HGVs, but that period was now over. This meant that Mrs Noble would need an HGV licence before she could drive one of the firm's lorries, and she would need an ordinary driving licence to drive the family car. She would have to take a test for each category of licence.

'So.' I felt I must intervene in an attempt to clarify the matter from my own viewpoint. 'What you are asking, Mr Noble, is whether the Premier Assurance Association will insure females when they drive heavy goods vehicles? Your heavy goods vehicles in particular – and your wife in particular.'

'Got it in one, Mr Taylor.'

'And your present insurer refuses to issue that kind of cover?'

'That's right. According to Mr Scott, all they will say is that their rules always refer to motor vehicle drivers as "he" or "him".'

'But doesn't your certificate of insurance – the one relating to your car perhaps – say that the persons entitled to drive include the policyholder and anyone driving on his order or by his permission?'

'It does, and it doesn't mention the word "he". I mentioned that to Scott but he said his company wouldn't budge. "He" and "him" mean men, Mr Taylor, even if the word isn't used on my certificate of insurance. Scott said it was in the policy document and the same rules would apply to a heavy goods vehicle, so he couldn't insure Brenda as a driver even if she got a licence.'

'But the law is clear on that point,' I told him. 'Whenever the word "he" is used in legislation, it includes "she". There was a famous lawyer who said that so far as English law is concerned, he embraces she. A nice way of putting it!'

'I know that, Mr Taylor, but my insurance man said their policies are not part of English law, just as club rules are not. They're internal regulations. You get clubs who will not allow women to become members and they are not breaking the law. Demetrius Insurance has never allowed women to be insured as drivers and, it seems, never will. Which, as I said, is why you are here. You were recommended to me by a farmer friend – he said you and your company are wide awake to modern developments – so how about it? If you can get me comprehensive cover for Brenda, then I'll transfer all my insurance to your company. The lot. And that includes my private car and house, as well as the business. And transferring my no-claims bonuses I would hope! So how about that? I can't say fairer than that, can I?'

'Rather than give you an answer off the cuff, I'd like to check with my District Office, just to be absolutely sure,' I said. 'I know we do cover women drivers – my own wife is covered for driving our car – but I'm not sure whether any women are policyholders for vehicle insurance, nor am I sure whether that kind of cover would extend to a woman driving heavy lorries. I need to be completely certain about all this; there might be some wider rule on this or some agreement between insurance companies that I don't know about. I'll have to check.'

'Best be sure,' grunted Noble.

Brenda suddenly joined in. 'Well, I think it's all very stupid! In the ATS, women drivers were just as good as the men, if not better, and I see no reason why a woman can't drive a bus or a fire engine in civvy street, let alone a fully loaded lorry, whether it's articulated or not.'

'I'd agree with that,' I felt I had to say.

'Well, it stands to reason. If I want to drive a heavy goods vehicle, I should be allowed to do so, and I can't see why the insurance company won't cover me. It doesn't make sense in this modern age.'

'Does that mean you agree with me?' beamed Henry.

'It means there's a principle at stake here,' she said. 'I believe women should be allowed to drive and join clubs just like men. We've had women members of Parliament and I'll bet we'll have a woman prime minister before too long, and we've had women sovereigns, like the two Elizabeths and Victoria, so why can't women be insured to drive lorries?'

'But does that mean you'll drive for me?' persisted Henry.

'No it doesn't, we're talking about different things. I don't want to drive lorries, I'm happy running the office, although I wouldn't mind driving our private car if you'd let me. Then I could go shopping without having to ask you to drive me.'

'You could do that without any problem,' I said. 'My company will cover you immediately you get a licence.'

She smiled at me now. 'Right, well, if Mr Taylor can get me covered for that, I'll think about taking my test and getting a licence – for the car, I mean. Then you wouldn't have to run me into town for shopping, Henry. But when it comes to the lorries, I still think you should hire a driver, a man.'

'Suppose I can only recruit a woman?' he put to her.

'Well, that's up to her, I wouldn't object to that. If some woman wants to drive your lorries, I wouldn't stop her.'

'Right,' he said. 'Well, Mr Taylor, I still think the insurance for my lorries should cover women drivers, so if you could check that for me I'd be pleased, then if the Premier agrees we'll talk about full cover for the entire business – you know the sort of thing – fire, flooding, personal injury liability, the lot. All Risks Commercial I suppose they call it.'

'I'll get to work straight away,' I promised him.

'And don't forget there's my house and my private car, mebbe with Brenda as a driver, and some life insurance to think about. Or even summat to cope with broken legs!'

'I'll contact my District Office the minute I get home,' I told him. 'I'll get back to you as soon as I can, today if possible.'

15

'The sooner we get this settled, the better,' he said. 'Every hour off the road is costing me money.'

I left the Nobles to drive straight home so that I could get this matter settled with the minimum of delay. I did find it puzzling that Henry could not find insurance for women drivers. It was well established within my own company that women could be insured to drive their husbands' cars. In fact, the company had recently upgraded their policies specifically to cater for women, so I found it increasingly strange that Demetrius did not do likewise.

I made my call as soon as I got home, asking the telephone operator for the relevant number – Ryethorpe 47 – and then waiting while she dialled it. Eventually the receptionist in District Office answered. 'Premier Assurance Association, District Office, Ryethorpe,' she said. Although there was some crackling on the line, I could hear her quite clearly and so I gave my name and agency reference number, stated the reason for my call and was then put through to the District Manager, a man called Leonard Evans whom I had not yet met. He was far too important and elevated to visit mere rural agents such as myself – he delegated such tasks to his underlings – but I felt, for this kind of decision, I needed to speak to someone in authority. He listened as I explained the situation and said, 'Well, Mr Taylor, this looks like a good opportunity for you and the company if we clinch a deal with Mr Noble. Full cover for his business, eh? All risks? And his private house and car. Well, I can tell you that we have quite a growing number of lady drivers on our books and many of them are policyholders in their own right, although most are driving on another policyholder's insurance.'

'That's what I thought,' I felt I had to say.

'Right, but so far as I know we do not have any lady HGV drivers. Or bus drivers. Or fire-appliance drivers. I can't see why we can't cover that kind of business provided the ladies in question are properly licensed, but I'll have to ring Head Office for this one, just to be sure there is no hidden ruling on the matter. I'll call you back.'

He rang back within the hour.

'No problem, Mr Taylor.' He sounded pleased. 'Head Office recognize the fact that an increasing number of women are driving motor vehicles of every kind and they can see no reason why Mrs Noble cannot be insured to drive a heavy goods vehicle. They say they will cover any other woman for similar risks, provided she is over twenty-one, passes the cyesight test and qualifies for an HGV licence by taking the appropriate test. You have suitable proposal forms, have you? The All Risks Commercial policy? With comprehensive commercial vehicle cover? Private house? Fire cover, the lot. And Mr Noble's private car?'

'Yes, I have.'

'Good, well, you'll earn yourself a useful commission on this one, Mr Taylor. So there you are. You can tell Mr Noble we will be pleased to accept his proposals and that Mrs Noble, or any other woman, will be fully insured while driving his heavy goods vehicles. You can calculate the premiums from your literature. He might wish to pay annually or quarterly through his bank but it is no problem whatever he decides.'

And so it was that I returned to give Henry Noble the good news. I subsequently acquired all his insurance business including his house and private car. It was expensive but not much more than his previous company had been charging, and he was delighted. He said he would tell Brenda. I wondered if she would be as happy as her husband about this, but later I heard she had taken lessons in driving both private cars and heavy goods vehicles – but had failed the test for the latter.

When I called on Henry a month after I had finalized his policies, he was all smiles. 'She's done it,' he said. 'She was so upset when she failed her HGV test that she said no man was going to tell her she couldn't drive lorries, so she took more lessons and passed her test second time round. She'd taken her ordinary driving test for the car and passed that beforehand. She's now driving heavy lorries quite regularly – in fact, she's so keen we're going to invest in another lorry.

It'll mean getting a secretary in to run the office when I'm back on my feet but I think we'll be able to afford that, Mr Taylor, all this new business. So it's thanks to you.'

'I did nothing,' I said. 'I just made a few phone calls.'

'But you got things sorted out very fast, and that's what I like. So can you take a bit of business advice?'

'I can!'

'I hope you don't mind me prying, Mr Taylor, but a little bird told me you live in a rented cottage at Micklesfield.'

'I do, it's all I could afford.'

'Right, well, a friend of a friend told me that – a chap you recommended should use your company for his insurance, in fact. So I want to give you some good advice, as a thank-you. Buy yourself a house, Mr Taylor. By renting one, you're paying for summat that'll never be yours. Get your own house, the bigger the better, and if you think you can't afford it, get it anyway. It'll be the best investment you could make and buying one won't cost much more than renting it.'

'We are thinking about it but I've just bought a car, and I've still got my motorbike . . .'

'Be determined, Mr Taylor. Think positive. If you want to, you will. And you'll never regret it. I don't – this is all mine, all paid for and nothing rented.'

'You've done well.'

'Not without a lot of hard graft, I might tell you. So there you are then. One good turn deserves another. Buy yourself the biggest house you can afford. That's my way of thanking you.'

'I'll bear it in mind,' I said. 'I do need a bigger place, some-where with space I can use as an office, if possible, and a garage for the car.'

'If a suitable spot comes on the market, jump in with both feet, Mr Taylor. Oh, and by the way, I found out why that other agent, Scott, wouldn't insure women drivers. It turns out it was nowt to do with his company – it was him being stupid.'

'You mean it was his decision, not the Demetrius?'

'That's the way I see it, Mr Taylor. When I told him I'd

18

transferred to you, I had all his top brass come to see me. They wanted to find out what had gone wrong, why I had switched to the Premier, and they said if I'd gone above his head they would have covered me for having Brenda drive the lorries. They said they do insure women drivers, lots of 'em. They've nowt against women drivers, whether it's cars, lorries, buses or even fire engines, heavy cranes and aeroplanes!'

'So why wouldn't Scott agree to insure your wife?'

'Because he didn't want his own wife to drive his private car! He'd told her she couldn't be insured – that was how he managed to stop her from driving, and because he'd told her that he couldn't very well let any other client get cover for women drivers! She'd smell a rat!'

'What an idiot!' I said.

'Absolutely! It seems he thought his wife would see his clients' wives driving and want to do the same . . . Anyway, it all backfired on him, so serve him right, I say! I've no idea how many other people he spun that yarn to but word will get around, and they might come flocking to you! We might be awash with women drivers! Anyway, I just hope you're happy to have Noble's Haulage as one of your clients.'

'I am,' I assured him.

To clinch a deal of that magnitude, in a remote rural agency, was quite wonderful and it made me realize there were lots of similar small firms and companies within my agency's boundaries who were not on my books. Builders, plumbers, pubs, hotels, garages, surgeries, shops, a baker, several small manufacturers, agricultural dealers and contractors, farms, estates, private hospitals and schools, nursing homes, funeral directors, stonemasons, bus operators, taxi drivers – the list was almost endless. Some employed only one or two staff, others had considerably more.

I knew a builder who had about twenty men working for him . . . I sensed rich pickings! To capture one of those commercial enterprises would indeed be a bonus because the commission from just one large policy was often worth more than many smaller policies from private individuals. It made good commercial sense to please the business personnel within my agency but, in spite of the increased income it would provide, I knew I must not concentrate entirely on developing a greater income only from commission. I must generate new business of every kind while resisting the temptation to persuade people to take out policies they could ill afford. I considered that to be very important – I did not want anyone to overreach themselves financially but, at the same time, I honestly believed I was offering a valuable service to my clients. I knew that any good insurance policy could indeed be a lifesaver, otherwise I would not be doing this work.

There was another aspect which did not appeal to me, and which I would resist. That was to poach customers from other insurance companies by devious or unscrupulous means.

The example of Noble's Haulage was different – Henry Noble had been deliberately misled by a person he should have been able to trust implicitly. That was unforgivable. In that case, I had no qualms about accepting Henry as a client but I would not canvas potential customers with the sole intention of 'stealing' them from other insurance companies or agents. If such potential clients approached me to enquire about my services and the expertise of my company, then I would talk to them and explain things in a factual but fair manner, but I made a rule never deliberately to undermine any of my competitive colleagues by unfair means. I believed in fair competition and honesty in all my dealings. Any commission or new business I earned would be on merit, and not by deception.

There is no doubt the installation of my telephone made a huge difference, because I was now within easy reach of a wider range of customers. The telephone meant that potential customers could contact me personally instead of leaving messages or notes at the shops or post offices around my agency, and within weeks of having the phone installed I noticed a surge in the volume of business. As my earnings increased, I began to think more seriously about buying a house; during my rounds, I kept my ears and eyes open for a suitable opportunity even if it meant securing a mortgage to buy it; the Premier offered housing assistance to its staff in the form of a mortgage on very favourable terms – it would mean getting into debt but not the sort of debt that was considered degrading. Getting into debt was considered most antisocial but a mortgage an admirable way of borrowing money, so I had been led to believe!

My ambitions of house ownership were boosted when I received a telephone call from a gentleman called Patrick Truman, from Avensfield, a lofty moorland village on the southern edge of my agency. I had not previously encountered him, but he was well spoken with just a hint of Tyneside.

'My name is Truman from Avensfield. I've heard good reports about both you and your company, Mr Taylor,' he began. 'I would like to talk business with you.'

'That will be my pleasure. When shall I call?'

'I could come to you if it's easier,' he offered.

'No, thanks, I'm often in Avensfield and can pop in at any time. If it's important, I can make a special journey.'

'That's very kind of you, Mr Taylor, but it's not all that urgent. When you're next in the village would be fine.'

'Next Tuesday then?'

'Yes, that will be fine. Morning?'

'Ten thirty?' I suggested.

'Ten thirty it is,' he agreed. 'I live at Curlew House, the first on the left as you enter from Graindale Bridge.'

I knew the house and it was most certainly not any kind of commercial premises; it was a fine stone-built detached house with splendid views across the moors towards the coast. Probably dating from the Victorian era, it was solidly built, spacious and handsome. The sort of house I would love to own . . .

'Might I ask what kind of insurance you require? I want to be sure to bring the right documents and relevant information.'

21

'I'd like you to insure my buses,' he said.

'Buses? How many?'

'I think the last count was about a hundred, give or take a few.'

A hundred buses! 'Right, this sounds most interesting,' I said.

'Looking forward to seeing you, Mr Taylor,' and he replaced the handset.

I was buoyant at this possibility – another large piece of business could result, and I began to think even more about moving to a house of our own. When I told Evelyn about the call she was equally pleased, for we felt that I was now making an impact on the agency – and a good impact among the public, my potential customers.

Promptly at ten thirty that Tuesday, and with an extra polish of my shoes and brushing of my suit, I arrived at Curlew House with my briefcase full of documents and rang the front door bell. A small neat man with silver-grey hair and a fresh face responded; I estimated him to be in his late sixties or early seventies, but he was smartly dressed in casual trousers and a light shirt and moved with the grace and ease of a man half his age.

'Mr Truman?'

'Yes, you must be Mr Taylor. Bang on time, that's what I like, Mr Taylor, promptness in all things. Do come in. Can I tempt you to a coffee and perhaps a biscuit?'

'I can be easily tempted by both!' I smiled as I followed him into the depths of the house. He led me along a narrow passage whose walls were lined with watercolours of the North York Moors and coast and turned into a study. It was full of bookshelves rising to half the height of three of the walls and sported a wonderful old roll-top desk before a window with panoramic views. There was an extra chair beside the desk and he invited me to use it.

'What a wonderful view!' I exclaimed. 'You know, I'd love a house with a study or office like this . . . that's my ambition, Mr Truman.'

'Take my advice and buy the biggest house you can afford, Mr Taylor, don't be tempted to settle for something too small – space is a wonderful thing, especially if you have children in the house or need somewhere to be quiet from time to time. I spend a lot of time in here – I keep out of my wife's way. Anyway, let me organize the coffee and biscuits, then we can talk.'

I thought it significant that he echoed the advice earlier given by Henry Noble, and when he left me for a few minutes I took the opportunity to look around the office with its water-colours and books. One thing struck me immediately – this den or study did not appear to be one that was used by a bus operator.

There were no photographs of buses on the walls, no calendars from garages or petrol dealers, no timetables, nothing remotely suggesting that line of business. Perhaps this man totally separated his private life from his business life. In fact, the house was large enough to accommodate another office for there were extensive grounds and I could see some buildings from the study window. He returned, saying his wife would bring the coffee in a moment or two. Ground, he told me, not made from essence.

'A nice study,' I said. 'There's a cosy feeling in here.'

'My private little world.' He smiled. 'Now that I'm retired, I seem to spend more and more time in here; there's always something to interest me.'

'Have you been retired long?' I felt I should make an effort to show interest in him and his life.

'Three years. I worked in the confectionery industry in York; my role was to promote overseas sales of our chocolate products. Not the easiest of jobs over the war years, Mr Taylor, but I did manage to persuade both the Germans and Japanese to take some of our lines. I didn't do military service – much too old to be called up!'

'Oh, I see . . . I thought you were . . .'

And just before I could say I had thought he was a bus operator of some kind, Mrs Truman arrived with the coffee.

She was a pleasant woman with very tidy pure-white hair and rimless spectacles; she smiled, bade me good morning and left the tray on her husband's desk, asking him to be mother. 'I am house-trained,' he smiled and poured me a cup.

I did not press my questions as he organized a cup for himself, passed me a chocolate biscuit and then said, 'So, Mr Taylor, how is the insurance world suiting you?'

I told him how I had come into this business from my earlier trade as a butcher's assistant and how much I was enjoying the work with all its variety and interest. I mentioned my brief spell as a war-time motor mechanic in the army, specializing in motorcycles, and he smiled.

'You know,' he said, 'if I'd not spent my life working among chocolate and sweets, I'd have loved to have been a mechanic. It fascinates me, how things work, how engines manage to propel things like cars and buses and even ships, how the whole vehicle is assembled, brakes, steering, lights, electricals – it's wonderful stuff, Mr Taylor, a tremendous feat of engineering, making everything work in unison. You are very fortunate to have had that experience, very fortunate indeed. I think that's what got me interested in buses.'

'I shall need to have a look at your buses,' I said.

'Of course, and so you shall. I became fascinated by them because I needed something totally different from the confectionery industry, something to take my mind off Japanese shops selling our chocolate or whether the Americans would like sweets in different colours even if they had chocolate inside.'

He chattered for a while about his work and then said, 'Well, come along to have a look at my buses, Mr Taylor, then tell me whether they can be insured.'

'They're not insured now?' I must have sounded shocked.

'Not at the moment, no. There's never been the need. Now, follow me.'

Intrigued, I followed him through a rear door into the garden and across the lawn to a large stone-built shed. It had a pair of large barn-type doors painted in dark green and secured by a padlock and could be approached from along the side of the house, but it looked far too small to hold several buses – it might just accommodate one, a single-decker, with something of a squeeze. He pressed a key into the padlock, released the catch and swung open both doors to allow the light to flood inside. The walls were lined with shelves, all bearing model buses. Each model was about two feet long and eight or nine inches high – except the double-deckers.

There were dozens of them in all colours, double-deckers, trams and trolley buses, single-deck service buses, a United Service bus from a local company in its familiar red livery, long-distance tourers, even a double-decker London bus and a Greyhound from America. And many more, all shining and obviously cherished by their owner.

'Models!' I breathed. 'I thought, when you rang, we were talking about real buses! I thought you ran some kind of bus operating business.'

'Oh, good heavens, I hope this doesn't alter things, I do need to have them insured. Sorry about the misunderstanding, it wasn't intentional. My collection is quite well known, you see, and I just assumed you would have heard about it.'

'I'm afraid not,' I had to admit. 'So how did you acquire these? They all look to be of a uniform size.'

'They are; they're scale models. I made them over many years. These designs are known the world over and each of my models is faithfully reproduced from the original, down to the last inch, even the tyres and seats are precise scale copies. You might recognize other well-known styles if you care to go inside and have a look around.'

As I walked around in silence, I must admit I was staggered by the sheer professionalism of their execution and wondered if there was any other collection like this, anywhere in the country. Each was exquisite and beautifully kept in this dry building.

'They're wonderful,' I breathed. 'Absolutely wonderful. I had no idea they were here, that you did this sort of thing.

Surely people want to see them, Mr Truman? Your collection must be unique.'

'I believe it is, Mr Taylor, I know of no other. That is why I have been asked to display it at several venues in the south of England. It means I must obtain a suitable vehicle to carry the models, secure in the sense that they must not be allowed to fall about or roll off shelves, but also be secure from thieves and vandals. I am in touch with a gentleman who is looking into the possibility of converting a bread van, Mr Taylor; it seems the shelves in a bread van would be the most easily altered to accommodate my buses. I shall, of course, drive the van and, to disguise the real contents, I will keep the bread-maker's name and logo on the vehicle.'

'Not a bad idea. So doesn't your existing insurance cover you for transporting them for demonstration purposes?'

'Existing insurance? I have no insurance for them, Mr Taylor, which is why I rang you.'

'No insurance?' I almost shouted the words in disbelief. 'You mean this collection is not insured at all?'

'No, I've never seen the need. I mean, it was just a hobby for me, a way of pleasurably passing the time and a means of making me forget about making and selling chocolate. I've never considered them valuable.'

'But they are valuable, Mr Truman, they must be! They'll be worth a tidy sum individually but as a handmade collection of scale models of all these famous buses, all made by the same person, they must be worth a fortune. Suppose fire destroyed them, or thieves stole them or the building collapsed and flattened them all . . . They're irreplaceable, Mr Truman. If I'm to consider insuring them, I'll need a complete itinerary of your tour with dates, times and places, along with a valuation by someone who knows what they are really worth, say an auctioneer or antique dealer. The Premier might accept such a valuation, or they might send their own assessor to express a second opinion. We could be talking a lot of money, Mr Truman.'

'So this is the sort of thing you can do for me? Arrange

suitable insurance for them on tour, and during my exhibitions?'

'I'm sure I can, but first I need to speak to one of our specialists. This really is a most unusual proposal, not a common or garden insurance by any means. If these models prove highly valuable the premiums will be substantial and you might find the Premier insists on certain conditions so far as continuing security is concerned. If might not be as simple as you hoped. But, if you take my advice, you'll also get them insured while they are here, on your premises. Your existing house insurance probably doesn't cover them as a collection – if just one was stolen, perhaps your house insurance would cover it, but as a collection of this stature, you'll need a special clause written into your house insurance. It would be catastrophic if they were all stolen or destroyed.'

'What house insurance?' he asked.

My heart sank. 'You mean your house is not insured?'

'Well it was when we bought it, a mortgage-protection policy I think it was called, but once I had paid off the mortgage, that kind of thing became unnecessary. I was insured so that if anything happened to me the mortgage would be paid, that was important to my wife, for her peace of mind.'

'I'm talking of things like housebreaking, burglary, theft, damage, fire, water bursts, all the nasty sort of things that can happen to a private house. Surely you have an insurance policy for that kind of eventuality?'

'Oh, no, I've never bothered with that sort of thing, my wife and I are seldom away and we take good care of the house. I've never felt the need for insurance, Mr Taylor, but it was the exhibition organizers who suggested it for my buses. In fact, they won't allow me to display them without adequate insurance, which is why I contacted you.'

'Leave it with me,' I said. 'I'll contact one of our experts immediately. I'll go home now and do it, and I'll come back to you with his suggestions. He might want to talk to you himself: this is a most unusual request. So when does your tour start?'

'In a fortnight's time,' he said. 'It's billed as the Truman Collection. I'm well known away from here, or my models are. There's twenty venues over a three-week period. I'm expecting the advertising leaflets any day now, I can let you have one when they're printed.'

'Only a fortnight to go? Then I must move fast,' I said. 'Leave it with me, Mr Truman, I'll contact you the moment I have something to tell you.'

District Office reacted swiftly and arranged for an expert assessor to examine Mr Truman's models and to put a value upon them, and within five days I had a note from the District Manager's Office to announce that the Premier would cover the Truman Collection during its forthcoming tour. The assessor had placed a value of £50 on each model, and a total value of £7,500 on the entire collection, a huge amount. The assessor had also discussed the security measures to be taken by Mr Truman while on tour. A premium of £15 was proposed by the Premier to cover all risks, this low amount being due to the fact the tour was only of three weeks' duration – but there was a condition. The Premier also wanted the Trumans to take out a house and contents insurance for their home, with a modest excess to cater for the collection when it was on the premises and lodged in its usual secure shed. Mr Truman accepted the proposals, telling me that he expected the entrance fees during his tour would more than cover the insurance and travelling costs.

And so, with some help for me from District Office, the deal was done, and within a few days Patrick Truman was heading south with his converted bread van full of model buses. His wife did not wish to accompany him, smilingly telling me that she saw enough of his buses at home without wanting to spend her holidays either with them or in a bread van!

Four days later she rang me. It was just after nine in the morning, and she sounded upset.

'I thought you should know this, Mr Taylor. We had burglars last night. They broke into the shed where Patrick keeps his collection. I've told the police and they are coming to see me later this morning, although nothing was stolen. What a good job his collection wasn't there, eh? As things worked out, the only damage was a smashed padlock.'

'You're insured for that now!' I told her. 'You'll get a new padlock if nothing else! But I'll come and see you today and I'll need a confirmatory note from the police. Will you be telling your husband?'

'Not until he gets home. He'll worry himself sick about me if he finds out we've been raided in his absence. But yes, you could come and see me about the insurance. It was so fortunate, wasn't it, that the buses had all gone?'

'You could say the burglars had missed the bus,' was all I could think of saying.

# Two

*'Three women were talking to each other and
when one stepped forward and two stepped back,
I had to have an accident.'*
From a claim form

Not even the best or most expensive insurance will prevent
terrible things from happening; it merely eases the situation when they do. It might be said that insurance is unavoidably linked to the worst of human experiences such as death,
disaster and serious injury. I was constantly reminded of that
during my rounds in the remoteness of Delverdale and I think
the situation was made harder at times because I worked so
closely with my clients. In many instances, I was more of a
friend than a visiting businessman. I was trusted with family
secrets, sometimes financial and sometimes very personal, and
on occasions I was made acutely aware that suffering, in one
form of another, was very much a feature of daily life for
some people.

I had to deal with many instances where men had taken out
life assurances so that if they died naturally or in any kind of
accident their wives and families would receive financial
compensation. Exactly how they were compensated depended
upon the precise nature of the policy but such money, even if
it was a fairly modest sum, did go some way towards the alleviation of worry at that very worst of times. I was aware, of
course, that money did not solve every problem but, on occasions where poor people were involved, the arrival of a fairly
large sum of money could greatly ease their immediate worries.

## Rest Assured

Something that troubled me was that some of the most deserving cases involved people whose modest incomes and family circumstances would not allow them to benefit from the best of insurance policies; it was ironic that those with the highest incomes were best able to afford policies that would serve to enhance their lifestyle or the lifestyle of their dependants, while the poorest could not afford suitable insurance, even against personal injury or death. This meant, of course, that I had always to be on guard against trying to sell to the poorer people the kind of policies whose weekly or monthly premiums would be difficult to maintain from their low wages. Even if an endowment policy taken out for a period of perhaps ten, twenty or even thirty years was a means of saving and akin to winning a small fortune when it matured, I had to resist the temptation to oversell any of my products, in spite of pressure from District Office. District Office was constantly pressing for increases in the number of policies sold by its agents, however small those policies might be. I had to resist that pressure – after all, consideration for the personal situation of my clients was much more important than increased income for the company, or so I believed.

I had to confront this kind of problem when dealing with Eric Mowbray, a hard-working hill farmer with a few acres of rough land spread across the moors above Annistone. Hollins Farm comprised a beautiful and spacious stone house surrounded by sturdy outbuildings. They provided protection for the house against the savage weather that could sometimes afflict these exposed heights and included two barns, a suite of pigsties, a shippen and several implement sheds.

A flock of blackfaced sheep lived on the moors above the house, quite free of restrictions like fences and fields, while the more sheltered area of the farm, in the dale to the south of the buildings, had a range of fairly lush fields that were home to a herd of Red Poll dairy cows. Eric relied on his milk cheque for a regular income but was prepared to speculate on making money from other livestock. He had pigs, a donkey, a couple of goats, lots of geese, ducks and hens and even a pet peacock called Churchill, due to his pugnacious attitude. Much of his other income came from breeding lambs and pigs and selling them at the local markets; his wife also made a few pounds by selling eggs or dressing birds such as geese, ducks and hens. She was always busy at Christmas and was renowned for her speed in despatching a chicken, plucking it and dressing it for sale.

No one knew where the peacock had come from – it had just turned up one day looking for food and had quickly adopted the farm as its new home, making rather a lot of noise on occasions and sometimes terrifying the resident cockerels. Eric had asked around his friends and acquaintances when he went to market but no one admitted the loss of the peacock. Eric was happy for it to remain and so were his wife and sons. It became quite domesticated and even tame, coming to the door for food and displaying its magnificent tail feathers from time to time.

Approaching forty years of age, Eric and his wife, Anne, had two sons, Stanley (fifteen) and George (thirteen), both of whom would inherit the farm, as their father had done. In many ways the Mowbrays were typical hill farmers – decent, hard working and very pleasant people.

They never expected to make a lot of money, and did not expect luxuries like holidays nor flashy things like new clothes, a hot-water system, a bathroom, a new car or even a new wireless. They made do with what they had. Almost everything in the house had been handed down – even Eric's best dark suit had belonged to his father. Eric used it for funerals – he'd worn it at his father's funeral and would pass it on to one of his sons.

During a chat one day, Eric said to me, 'You know, Matthew, folks like us never expect to make money – you expect to work hard just to keep going, to pay your way. We do that, me and Anne, we pay our way, we've no debts but no savings either, we can't make enough to put anything away for savings. We've got to plough money back into the business when we can afford to, otherwise we get left behind when things change.

# Rest Assured

You've got to keep up with modern equipment and machinery. Our livestock reproduces itself, but machinery doesn't! Mind you, I wouldn't swap this life for any other, hard as it is. The lads will take over, they're showing signs of good husbandry already, it's in their blood. It's a good life even if it's very tough at times, there's plenty of good fresh air and I've always had a healthy appetite. And as for holidays, what good are they? A day out at market once in a week suits me.'

Like most of the hill farmers in the North York Moors, and Delverdale in particular, the Mowbrays did not own the property. The entire farm – house, buildings and land – belonged to Annistone Estates, but it was understood that when a farmer died, his eldest son would take over the tenancy and continue to farm the property. That had been the system for centuries.

Sometimes, several sons would take over, if that was the family wish, and although this continuation of the family farm was the traditional way of doing things, the war had brought about a distinct change of attitude. Some young men did not want to spend their lives working on a remote farm without a rest or a holiday, nor for wages that were lower than those of most other men of their age. In recent years, one or two had left the dale to find other work, and their accounts of life beyond the dale impressed those left behind. One outcome of the increasing shortage of willing young farmers was that some estates were amalgamating farms by merging land from one farm with its neighbour but selling the house and buildings as private dwellings. Hill farmers rarely retired, they could not afford to, so when a man reached the age where he was unable to work it was the custom for the son to take over the house and farm, with father and mother moving into a cottage on the estate while continuing to do light work on the farm or estate if and when required. Essentials like food would come from the farm, consequently living was cheap.

In Eric Mowbray's case, he had been grooming Stanley to take over the farm, but the school leaving age had recently been raised to fifteen, which meant his son could not yet work full time on the farm. Stanley was a well-built lad with a love of outdoor work and a very good knowledge of husbandry for one so young. His hobby was motorbike scrambling. Young George, at only thirteen and probably more academic than his brother, had at least two further years of schooling. As well as being enthusiastic young farmers, the lads were friends, and went almost everywhere together. This pleased Eric because he wanted them to operate as equal partners when the time came, rather than for Stanley to be sole inheritor. He felt sure the brothers would fully complement each other – as they were doing already.

It was against this background that I called at Hollins Farm once a month to collect the premiums for two small life policies that Anne had taken out for her sons. The premiums were half a crown per month for each policy, due to mature when each son reached the age of forty-five. The sum guaranteed upon maturity was £1,000 for each son, a massive amount, and if either died before maturity then their dependants would benefit by that amount. Anne was determined her lads would have 'something behind them', as she put it, some form of regular savings which would produce a nest egg. For people on a low income like this couple, the premiums were heavy but Anne paid them from her egg and poultry money and she was never late with her payments.

For all her prudence so far as her sons were concerned, Anne did not have a policy on her own life and neither did Eric. I found this surprising, but, as Anne told me during one of my visits, 'Matthew, why do I need insurance? If anything happens to Eric, there will be a home for me here with Stanley and George, they can work the farm and I can continue to earn my keep. Or I can go into one of the estate's cottages and the boys will look after me, they and their wives whenever they get married.'

'Things might change . . .' I tried to tell her.

'Change is always with us, Matthew, but we've never had things like insurance in the past, although I do think the lads need savings, for the future. We never had the chance to do that, so I want the best for them.'

'It's never too late for you, either,' I said. 'Times are changing, as you say; the war did that to us and people are thinking of pensions and an easier way of life in the future.'

'I don't know what an easy life is! We've never had it easy, nor our parents, but there is another thing to consider. We're starting to make a bit more money, but in spite of that we can't really afford to put away savings for ourselves, Matthew. Whatever we do put by is used by the farm, keeping up with new machinery or hiring tups and bulls, keeping the business going. Eric says money is like a fuel, it's needed to keep things moving on. Besides, Eric doesn't need a life assurance: if I go before him, the lads will care for him, like they'll care for me if he goes first. That's how it is with families. That's what families are for. And farms!'

I did not try to change her attitude but must admit I wondered whether this was a rather too rose-tinted view of the perfect life, because things can always go wrong, even with the best-laid plans and within the best-motivated families. During our chats, I began to wonder if Eric and Anne were placing too much responsibility – and too much hope – on Stanley's young shoulders, even if they claimed they had no wish to leave George out of things. The fact that George was considered equal pleased me even if the emphasis, perhaps unintentionally, appeared to rest upon Stanley. In spite of the family's assurances, I must admit I was rather concerned about their business because, as far as I knew, none of their livestock was insured and neither was their house contents. I assumed that the owners, Annistone Estates, had the house and farm buildings insured against risks such as fire and damage, but, even if that was the case, the Mowbrays had things of value inside the house. The estate's insurers would not cover those personal possessions. And then there was the livestock to consider . . . I wondered if their lack of comprehension about insurance resulted from the fact that all their belongings, including farm machinery and the origins of their stock of animals, had been passed down from father to son over many years? To have one's home furnished free of charge must be a huge bonus, even if some of the stuff inside was old fashioned. It wasn't just material things that were passed down, either. Fathers would pass on to their sons a huge wealth of knowledge and experience, including the result of generations of livestock breeding. For Eric Mowbray, this was represented in his herd of fine Red Polls and his Large White pigs. Those inestimable benefits were acquired in much the same way as the dining suite, chairs, beds and wardrobes. I knew that the government would compensate livestock owners if their herds were lost or slaughtered due to contagious disease, but no money could compensate for the loss of a herd whose ancestors went back through generations of the same family.

In spite of such history, I doubted if those ancestors had considered insuring their belongings. And if past generations had not worried about insurance, why should the current owners? That seemed to be the logic behind the way of life of many a hill farmer within my agency: even if a valuable beast died, they would regard it as quite a natural occurrence, without any thought of compensation or insurance payments. I began to think I should plant the idea of insurance in Eric's mind – life assurance, at least. Now that he was making more money and becoming more successful, I would present him with something to ponder.

An opportunity arose at the end of April when I was collecting the usual premiums for Stanley and George. As always, I was invited to sit at the kitchen table where Anne would produce a slice of apple pie or a chunk of fruit cake along with a mug of tea; this was one of the wonderful aspects of visiting farms in remote places. It was a long-established custom to feed any visitor, even if they arrived during the family's midday meal. It was no wonder my waist was beginning to expand as I made the most of this traditional but instinctive generosity! On this occasion, after I had dodged the waiting Churchill at the door and placed my heavy briefcase on the floor, Eric joined me because he chanced to arrive for his morning break, or 'lowance as it was known. Usually when I called he was down the fields or working somewhere in one of his many buildings.

He was an uncomplicated man, thin and wiry with a slight stoop from the neverending manual work. His weather-beaten face, usually with a day's growth of beard, was almost mouse-like, with a sharp nose and chin and darting grey eyes, which never seemed to miss anything. He was a very pleasant and popular person. Anne, equally popular, was rather more stout, with a cheerful round rosy face and an engaging smile; whenever I saw her she was wearing a flowery apron, which seemed to envelop her figure, and, indoors or out, she wore stout shoes.

On this occasion, Eric broached the subject of insurance, which pleased me. 'I wanted a word with you, Matthew, about life insurance. When I saw your car outside just now, I thought I'd pop in to say hello.'

I had been rather reluctant to mention the matter when I was a guest at their table, even if I did believe it was to their mutual benefit, and so he had saved me that embarrassment. Having pondered the matter, I wasn't quite sure how their animals could be insured. I'd never known hens and ducks, or even a peacock, to be the subjects of insurance policies – although it was possible to insure something very valuable such as a prize stallion or a bull, or a tup used for breeding. Some specialist companies would insure farm animals against lightning strikes or causing damage to motorists and gardens when ramblers left field gates open, but in general herds of cows and pigs or flocks of sheep were not insured, as the cost was prohibitive.

Nonetheless, there were lots of possible insurances even if the Premier did not insure individual hens, cows, sheep or pigs. But all that could wait; if he wanted to break the ice, as it were, by discussing life insurance for himself, then I was more than happy to listen.

'Times are changing, Matthew, and changing fast,' he said, sipping from a huge mug. 'I remember my dad and granddad both saying they'd never pay for summat they could not see – they couldn't understand insurance and reckoned it was akin to gambling. Their thinking was you spent it without getting it back as a rule, but if you did get it back it was worth more than you'd spent on getting it – that was gambling in their books and they weren't gamblers, Matthew. That's generations of Methodism for you! They'd rather prevent fire by hanging a hot-cross bun in the rafters than take out an insurance to cope with it if it happened.'

'I agree there is an element of risk with insurance of any kind.' I felt I had to say that. 'I can see the logic of some people thinking it is a form of gambling. After all, it could be said the insurance company is gambling when it accepts you as a risk.'

'All life's a risk, Matthew, any farmer knows that. Anyhow, as for life insurance, well, my forebears thought if they took it out they would die, just as they never made wills for the same reason. They allus said that if you made preparations to die, then you would. As for wills, well, they weren't really needed, stuff just got passed down in the family and we never were rich enough to own a farm. Allus rented property, we have, like this farm. It's been in our family for generations even if we don't own it.'

'Like most other farms in the dale?'

'Right, few of us ever owned our own spread, no matter how hard we worked. Anyway, mebbe it was those policies our Anne's taken out for the lads that made me start thinking about it or summat you said to her one day, but it does seem to make sense. Put a bit by, let it make a bit of interest, money for nowt in other words – it's a good way of saving, Matthew. I reckon I should have one of your policies, and Anne as well.'

'If that's what you want, I'm sure I can find something suitable.'

'We can just about afford it now, things are steadily getting better and Stanley will soon be leaving school to work here. That should increase our turnover and profit, he wants to go into pigs in a big way. Breeding, he reckons. And he's talking about a beef herd as well as our dairy cows. He's got his head screwed on, has that lad, he can spot trends, see the way forward. You have to speculate to accumulate, haven't you?'

'You're absolutely right, Eric. Well, let me explain the various options open to you, such as a straight whole life insurance for you both or perhaps an endowment policy either in joint names or for you both individually, say until you're sixty or sixty-five. I can give you some idea of the premiums and the anticipated profits if you decide to go for the endowment with profits option . . .'

And so, as I opened my briefcase to find some relevant literature, I launched into my well-rehearsed sales patter, but always mindful of what would best suit this couple. I had to take into account their work, their age, their state of health, their growing family and what they could afford by way of premiums for the duration of any policy – and that duration could be ten years, or twenty or even more. I spent more than an hour with several refills of my mug of tea and more cake, answering questions, putting doubts at rest, making recommendations and calculating premiums for a range of different proposals. As we chatted, I gained more respect for the couple – they were far from stupid and I realized they must be very skilled business people, probably more than others gave them credit for.

I could see they were specialists within their own field of activity and obviously making plans for the distant future. Clearly, they expected the same level of professionalism and commitment from me and I think I provided that. The outcome was that each decided on an endowment policy in their own names, Anne's to mature when she was sixty and Eric's when he was sixty-five, each being a policy for £1,000 with profits. That was a huge amount of money by their standards and, due to their ages, the premiums would be quite high – around £4 a month between them. I learned they drew less than £5 a week from the business for their housekeeping but Eric convinced me they could afford the premiums. As he pointed out, their housekeeping money was higher than the wages of many people living locally.

Eric's policy would be over a 27-year period and Anne's over 24 years. In the event of the death of either, a guaranteed £1,000 would be paid to the estate of the deceased; we were all convince that these would be wonderful investments for the future.

I completed the necessary proposal forms, confirmed in writing the details of the cost of premiums, the likely profits that would accrue over the years and our requirement of their doctor's assessment of their health. In addition to the doctor's certificate form, I left a pile of documents with them both for reference and to study at their leisure before the deal was finalized.

As I left Hollins Farm, I felt a glow of satisfaction, firstly because it seemed Eric and Anne were forging a highly successful farming enterprise, secondly because they were making firm plans for the future and thirdly because they now appeared to appreciate the importance and value of good insurance. And, I must admit, I was pleased I had secured these policies, because they would provide me with some useful commission!

A few days later, the Premier accepted their proposals and the Mowbrays agreed to their terms, which meant the couple were immediately covered by a combined life insurance and endowment policy. I hadn't insured any of their livestock, household contents or farm machinery, but realized their lives were more valuable than a threshing machine, scruffler or even a bull! I could see the Mowbrays were heading for success and happiness. I could keep further policies in mind for a future chat.

Then the first disaster struck.

Stanley was killed in a freak accident.

It was a Sunday afternoon in June and he had been riding his scrambles motorbike over a local course. He had been with friends, all riding their own bikes, and they had been hurtling around an oval course high on the edge of the moor, over the rough ground, through a stream, over rocks and across boggy marshland. Local lads had been doing this sort of thing for years without a problem; motorbike scrambling was a very popular local sport and young boys could participate because it took place off the roads where no driving licence, tax or insurance was needed, neither was there a lower age limit.

Subject to parental permission, children of almost any age could ride scrambles bikes on private land – occasionally, one heard of eight-year-olds learning to handle them. A scrambles bike was smaller and lighter than one used on a road, with a lower range of gears and no mudguards, but it sported very thick, knobbly tyres, which enabled it to cope with the rough landscape. Riders were usually well equipped with suitably protective boots, leggings, gauntlets and crash helmets and, inevitably, both rider and bike were covered with mud. If a rider did have a mishap, the chances were that he escaped with only a few cuts and bruises.

But Stanley Mowbray had not escaped this time. I learned that he had been riding quite carefully along a narrow path with a steep gradient dropping away to his right, which led into a gully with a beck (the local name for a stream) at the bottom. His front wheel had struck a slippery rock concealed among the heather and he had been catapulted down the slope with no chance to save himself. He had landed heavily on the rocks in the beck and the bike had crashed on top of him, causing severe head injuries. No one else had been involved in the accident, although his friends had witnessed the terrible chain of events. I went to the farm to express my condolences to the family, and attended Stanley's funeral (I tried to attend the funeral of any of my clients), but it was sometime afterwards that I rang Eric and Anne to remind them that Stanley had been insured, and that in the case of his death, whether premature, accidental or due to murder or manslaughter, the sum of £1,000 was due for payment.

The fact he had been riding a motorbike at the time of his accident was not a problem because it had been off road. His life insurance, not a motorcycle insurance, covered him. I was acutely aware that his parents had far more than money to concern them at that stage, but I had to fulfil my obligations.

I told them I would require a certified copy of the death certificate and an abstract from the police report about the fatality, along with details of the coroner's inquest when it was concluded. Those documents would be sent to my Head Office, after which payment would be made to Stanley's dependants.

It was sometime later when I drove to Hollins Farm with the cheque for £1,000, although I had been making my regular month-end visits to collect George's premium and those of Eric and Anne. Even then there was an air of gloominess about the place, with just a hint of neglect, and, although Anne had apparently regained some of her earlier enthusiasm for life, I got the impression that Eric was finding things difficult. He did not say a lot – Yorkshire moorland farmers are not noted for their volubility anyway – but from what Anne told me, I knew that all their future plans had suffered a terrible blow. Eric had had such great hopes for Stanley working alongside him: they would have been a wonderful team; there had even been a hint they might consider buying their own farm as Stanley became more experienced and worldly, and their enterprise expanded. Some of the local estates were disposing of farms and houses as costs and staff wages began to increase and as farmers' sons left the area; there was a distinct likelihood that some very good farms would come on the market over the next few years.

But now all those plans had been shattered.

I could not involve myself in the family's unhappiness, it was no concern of mine even though I did feel a huge amount of sorrow for them in their plight, but, as I continued to call for their monthly premiums, I could see matters had not returned to normal. Eric was increasingly withdrawn even if Anne and young George were struggling in their attempts to further the family plans while continuing to run the farm. Most of the times I called, Eric was nowhere to be seen. Anne would say either that he was in the fields, working in the outbuildings or, sometimes, at one of the cattle or pig markets in the vicinity. For reasons I could not fathom, I felt she was covering for him, that he was not working as he had in the past, that he was out somewhere doing little or nothing. Certainly the farm continued to look neglected. Stanley was missed – but so was Eric.

Then a much worse tragedy occurred.

Eric was found dead in one of his fields. He had a massive wound to his head and his shotgun was beside him. Like almost everyone else in the dale, I heard rumours that he had committed suicide, having been unable to cope with Stanley's death, but other, more malicious rumours also began to circulate. Sadly, there were stories that he was in debt, that he was meeting another woman on his outings to market and that he had long been prone to bouts of depression, but I knew that none of those rumours had any substance. I began to wonder if Eric's death was a tragic accident even if it did have the appearance of suicide.

When I reported this by telephone to District Office, however, I was told that if Eric had committed suicide the Premier would not pay the insurance due on his death. Suicide was a form of homicide of one of His Majesty's subjects, and was classed as a felony, the most serious of crimes. A person who committed suicide was known as a *felo de se*, a felon of himself. Even though the victim had killed himself, and so placed himself beyond the reach of human justice, it was still considered wrong and illegal. Rather like in the past when a suicide forfeited his property and received an ignominious burial away from a churchyard, it seemed Eric had forfeited his right to the proceeds of his life insurance.

Because the reason for his death had not been ascertained, I could not promise any money to his dependants at this stage. Payment, if any, would depend upon the verdict of the coroner's inquest. That was several weeks away and the police had many enquiries to complete in the meantime. I telephoned Anne to explain the delay and she said she understood.

A few days after Eric's death, I received a visit from PC Clifford, the village constable of Micklesfield, in whose area the death had occurred. He called one evening when he knew I would be at home. Evelyn provided us with a cup of tea and a biscuit each and we went into the sitting room while she bathed Paul in his tin bath on the kitchen table.

'It's about Eric Mowbray,' PC Clifford began. 'You've heard he died rather tragically?'

'I had heard, yes,' I told him. 'It's so sad, he had such plans for the farm, he was one of my clients, as I'm sure you know.'

'Right, yes I did know. I call there regularly, checking his stock records once a quarter and so on. Anyway, I'm dealing with the sudden-death investigation, and it's my job to compile a report for the coroner. I have to fill in this form, it's called Form 48.' And he produced one from his briefcase. 'I have to ask questions about insurance on the life of the deceased, which is why I am here.'

'I understand.' I nodded.

'It is not unknown for people to get rid of spouses or family members in the hope of gaining benefit from big life insurances,' he said. 'They try to make murder look like an accident. I am sure you – and your company – are aware of that.'

'Yes, that was explained on my induction course.'

'So, Mr Taylor, I would like details of any insurance on Eric Mowbray's life.'

'There was just the one,' I said with confidence, adding, 'Well, what I suppose I should say is there was only one life policy with my company, that's the Premier Assurance Association. It was an endowment policy, with profits, and with a life insurance element, taken out over a period of 27 years. On death before maturity, it will pay £1,000, but if it went to maturity it would pay £1,000 with any profits that might have accrued. He took it out only very recently, I can give you the exact date in a second.' And I found the necessary information in my records, which I showed him.

'Would you know if he had any other life insurance with another company?'

'I don't know,' I had to admit, 'but I doubt it. I think ours was his only life insurance. I ought to add, PC Clifford, that, as you are probably aware, our company does not pay life insurance if the policyholder commits suicide.'

'Yes, I know that. I've never come across an insurance company that does pay out in cases of suicide. But, for your information, this does not look like suicide. That's my opinion and, I might add, the opinion of my superiors. It's almost certainly a very tragic accident.'

'Really? I heard he'd shot himself . . .'

'That rumour was circulating, and I can tell you he was shot with his own shotgun, that is a certainty. However, the position of the wound was such that he could not have shot himself. It was in the back of the neck. There is no way anyone could deliberately shoot himself there with a shotgun. He would need to have been a remarkable contortionist to achieve that.'

'You're not saying he was murdered, are you?'

'No, he was alone at the time, we are confident of that. We've had expert advice on this, from the pathologist and senior police officers, and it is a ninety-nine per cent certainty that it was a dreadful accident. The ground was wet and slippery, he was on a slope, we found marks to show he had lost his footing and we think he took a heavy tumble, which caused him to lose his grip on the gun so that it dropped to the ground and discharged itself into the back of his neck. It must have flown into the air as he lost his footing and landed behind him with enough force to make it discharge. It's highly unlikely an experienced man like Eric Mowbray would take risks with a loaded shotgun, but it's obvious that something went very suddenly and drastically wrong.'

'He was a regular user of shotguns, I knew that,' was all I could think of saying.

'He was, he was highly experienced. I don't think there's any doubt he lost his footing in slippery conditions, lost control of the gun and somehow shot himself accidentally. A freak accident. There is no reason to think he committed suicide, Mr Taylor, none at all. I know he was upset at the loss of his son, but according to Mrs Mowbray he had come to terms with that and was almost back to his normal self. From what I have learned, he was not the sort of man to commit suicide, whatever the circumstances; he was too strong for that.'

A few weeks later, the coroner's inquest returned a verdict of 'accidental death' and the far-reaching evidence confirmed that Eric was not in debt, that he had not been seeing any other woman and that his state of mind was positive and he had been planning a secure future for himself, Anne and George. The coroner, in delivering his verdict, stressed that all the evidence, in particular the location of the fatal wound, meant that Eric could not have killed himself.

When I took the cheque to Anne, she told me how relieved she was that Eric had taken out his life insurance, for it was to prove an enormous help in providing her with a new focus in life. She knew she could not run the farm even with the willing help of young George, and she could not afford to take on a labourer, so she had decided to sell up – everything would go: livestock, poultry, implements and machines, even dear old Churchill the peacock. And, in due course, everything was indeed sold.

George decided he wanted to join the Royal Air Force when he was old enough, and, with the help of a mortgage, Eric's insurance and the proceeds of the sale of the machinery and livestock, Anne bought the village shop in Walstone. It had a nice cottage attached and it was all hers; she asked me to insure her new premises and all the contents. After all, no one knew what the future held.

In my dealings with the folk of the moors, I realized there remained a considerable element of superstition among them, particularly where death was concerned. For example, if a carrion crow flew three times over a roof, it was a sign that someone in the house would soon die. On one occasion, when I visited a house shortly after the death of the lady owner, I found both doors and all the windows standing open in spite of the cold weather. That had been done, I was told, to ensure her departing soul had an easy exit from the premises. There was also a belief that if a person lay upon a pillow containing feathers from a wood pigeon, a domestic dove or game bird, his or her death would be slow and perhaps difficult.

The secret of a swift and easy death was to withdraw that pillow, but if death was to be prolonged, perhaps to cater for the late arrival of a much-loved relative, then the pillow should be left in position.

Against this kind of background, it is not surprising there was a good deal of superstition attached to the making of wills and to the logic of taking out a life insurance. I was already aware of this, but was reminded of the depth of these beliefs when I was asked to call on Cissy Hurd, who lived at Adderstone Cottage in Little Freyerthorpe. Not having a telephone, she had left me a message at the shop. It was in a sealed envelope to shield her words from prying eyes, and when I opened it in the privacy of my little car, Betsy, I saw it was signed by Mrs Frances Hurd, the wife of Joseph. She asked if I would visit her between two and six one Wednesday afternoon, when she knew her husband would be away from the house.

Joseph Hurd was a self-employed wheelwright and blacksmith, a highly skilled craftsman who could combine those two disciplines with apparent ease. He had two adjoining workshops behind Adderstone Cottage, one for his wheelwright business and the other for his blacksmith's work. Horseshoes were prominently nailed to the doors of both premises – for good luck.

On the day in question, and after satisfying myself that Joseph was not on the premises (his bicycle was missing), I tapped on the door of the cottage and Cissy opened it. She was a plump, pretty woman in her late fifties with iron-grey hair, blue eyes and a round, smiling face that always seemed to sport ruddy cheeks and a glow of happiness. She was one of those women who managed to cope with a huge amount of voluntary work, helping with the church flowers, organizing the cleaning, being secretary to the WI, a member of the parish council, correspondent for the local paper and more besides. I knew her quite well, for she could often be seen walking from home to the village shop and I would stop and offer her a lift whenever I saw her.

'Come in, Mr Taylor, I've got the kettle on, you'll have a cup of tea and a bun?'

'Thanks, Mrs Hurd, yes.'

'Cissy, everybody calls me Cissy.'

'I'm Matthew, and everybody's starting to call me Matthew's Insurance!'

'That's how I got to know about you, somebody in the shop was talking about Matthew's Insurance so I thought it was time you and me had a chat.'

She led me into the tiny but exquisitely neat sitting room with its fire blazing in a black-leaded grate, rows of shining brass ornaments standing on the mantelpiece and horse brasses nailed to the beams of the ceiling. A large black kettle was already boiling on the hob and teacups were arranged on the round table in the corner, a table covered with a large dark green velvet cloth. It was dark inside, because moorland houses only had tiny windows, being built for cosiness in winter rather than the wonderful views.

'Sit yourself down, Matthew, tea'll be ready in a minute.'

I selected a chair at the table so that I could open my briefcase and spread out any necessary papers for her to see. As Cissy busied herself with the tea and cakes, I found leaflets about life insurance, business premises insurance, home and contents insurance, even motor vehicle insurance and endowment policies, in the hope I could find something that suited her.

'So how can I help you?' was my opening question once she was sitting opposite me pouring tea.

'Well, now, Matthew, you must be wondering why I've asked you to call, and at a time when our Joseph's out.'

'Does he go out every Wednesday afternoon?'

'It's market day at Micklesfield, as you know,' she said. 'He goes there every Wednesday to drum up new business. Takes orders for cartwheels, arranges delivery of new ones, takes orders if folks want him to make a tool or implement of some kind. He gets all sorts of jobs from there – these Wednesday trips to market have always brought him a regular flow of orders.'

48

'So you don't want him to know about our meeting?'
'Not just yet.' She smiled secretively. 'Mebbe later. Now,
this is the situation. He's a lot older than me, I'm fifty next
birthday but he's sixty-five. He can't retire because he can't
afford to, so he says, but I do know he's got a bit put by in
the Post Office. When he started out on his own, he allus put
a bit by in the Post Office, every Saturday morning. Whatever
was left over at the end of the week was put by for us, a nest
egg so to speak, for us to retire on.'
'A very sensible thing.'
'Aye, up to a point, Matthew, up to a point. He's never
increased what he puts by. He's putting the same into his
account as he did when he was twenty, which isn't much, and
now he goes off to market on a Wednesday and spends a lot
there, drumming up business, as he calls it. I reckon he should
be putting more by.'
'I see. So you're wanting some kind of savings scheme?'
'That's how I was looking at things, Matthew. As I said,
I'm fifteen years younger than him and his work carries no
pension. It would be nice if he could retire with some sort
of an income without working for it, but if he dies, well,
I'll have nothing, will I? Except this house. It is ours, by
the way, it was his family's before he took it on. At least
I'll always have a roof over my head, I can manage without new clothes and I can bake and grow my own vegetables, so I'll not starve.'
'You will need some money, though – you can't exist with
none! So you want me to suggest some kind of policy based
on his life? So that if he dies, you're not left destitute?'
'Summat like that, yes. Is such a thing possible?'
'His age is a problem, I must be honest. Even if the Premier
accept his proposal for life insurance, the premiums will be
high and it will necessarily be over a short term – ten years,
perhaps. I feel sure my bosses will demand a medical as well,
but nothing's impossible, there are some very fit men of his
age. I must tell you, though, that you can't expect a large sum
at his death. And, of course, he would have to agree to be

insured! You couldn't do it behind his back; you could insure your own life without him knowing, but not his.'

'He'll never agree, Matthew, he's frightened.'

'Frightened?'

'Aye, he thinks if he takes out a life insurance it's a sure way of making him die. He says he's fit enough to keep working until he drops dead, and he wants to do that – he can't think what he would do with himself if he didn't have his work. He'll never settle for sitting down and doing nothing.'

'So what about you? Have you considered insuring your life?'

'Me? What good would that do? I'm younger than him. It's me who needs to think of the future without him, not him thinking of a future without me. He couldn't cope without me anyway, he might be able to hoop a cartwheel better than any man around here, and make a metal tool for any kind of purpose, but he can't boil an egg or make a Yorkshire pudding. He'd be no good without me.'

'So if you died first, he'd need help?'

'He would and he'd have to either find another wife or get somebody in to do his cooking and washing. And that would cost more than he gives me for housekeeping, I can tell you that!'

'So there's a valid reason for having your life insured as well as his.' I smiled. 'I'm suggesting that because it might provide the solution. If my company refuses to accept a proposal based solely on his life, they might consider a joint life, on both of you. Because of your age, that spreads the risk over more years, which makes the idea more acceptable. I am sure I could find a policy which is based on both your lives – and if we linked it to an endowment policy with profits, even over a short period, say ten years, then similar rules would apply. That way, you'd both build up a nest egg at the same time as being insured. A very good plan. I think you should consider that – it's a good way of getting him insured at his age. And there is the business to consider – I know you're not insured through me, but another way of persuading the Premier to look favourably upon you both would be to insure the business for all risks, with an endowment policy for both of you, life based. I am sure that could be done at very little extra cost.'

'It's all very complicated, Matthew, far too complicated for me. You see, there's the question of paying for this as well. Joseph gives me enough for running the house and getting food and so on, I'm never kept short, but there's nothing extra that would pay for insurance. He knows what I spend and is dead set against insurance, as I've told you.'

'Has he ever considered what he would do if anything happened to you? I don't necessarily mean if you died. Suppose you were ill and put into hospital for a few weeks or months. How would he cope? I think that is the way I need to approach him, to get him thinking in terms of having to pay someone to care for him, wash and cook, if you weren't there.'

'He'd just say he could afford to pay someone out of his own pocket.'

'Yes, but for how long?' I asked. 'Could he do that if he was incapable of working himself? Due to his increasing age? Or if he was injured. There's a lot to consider, Cissy. Do you think he would listen to me if I called in when he's at home?'

'There's only one way to find out!' She smiled ruefully.

'The alternative is for me to track him down when he's at the market in Micklesfield. I live there, the market's almost on my doorstep.'

'That might be best, I wouldn't want him to think I was going behind his back, doing something sneaky.'

'It's not sneaky, it shows concern for the future. Right, leave it with me. I'll make sure I bump into him next time he's in Micklesfield, I'll make it look unplanned, too, but meanwhile I'll do some research to find out just what kind of policy I can offer for both of you, bearing in mind his age.'

When I rang District Office, I was put through to my boss, Montgomery Wilkins, the District Ordinary Branch Sales Manager – Life, who had accompanied me on some of my early canvassing rounds. A familiar figure, with his black beret, which he wore in honour of his wartime hero, he considered himself an expert on his subject.

When I explained the situation about the Hurds, he said, 'Well fancy that, Mr Taylor, fancy that indeed! Do you know, I was just thinking of insuring older people and have recently concluded some important research into the topic. Now listen to this. In the mid-nineteenth century, the average life expectancy for a man was only forty years, and only slightly more for a woman. Certainly some lived longer but others, many others, died earlier. We are talking averages here.'

'I follow, Mr Wilkins.'

'Good. Well, by the end of that century, only fifty years later, life expectancy in men had risen to fifty, and women to fifty-five. An increase of ten years in male life expectancy in only half a century, and an encouraging increase in women. Now, I have examined statistics from our own archives as well as obtaining figures from government sources, and now, in the middle of this century, where we are right now, the average life expectancy in men is sixty-seven and seventy-one for women.'

'So we're living longer?'

'We are indeed. And that is taking into account our war losses. Where will things be in the year 2000, I wonder? Will most men be living to the ripe old age of seventy-five, and remaining active? And women? Their life expectancy could be as high as eighty by the year 2000. The graph I have drawn up does suggest that, Mr Taylor.'

'What you are saying, then, is that older people can be considered an increasingly good risk, Mr Wilkins?'

'Absolutely. And I have conveyed that message to Head Office, who have done similar research, with our actuaries calculating risks attached to older people who remain active and, of course, pass the required medical examination. In short, Mr Taylor, I can say that Head Office is prepared to consider life assurance proposals from older people. I suggest you persuade your Mr and Mrs Hurd to apply without delay. Get them to complete a proposal form – they could be breaking new ground so far as your agency is concerned.'

'I will,' I assured him.

My next task was to find Joe Hurd while he was attending the market at Micklesfield, there to convince him of the merits of life insurance. Micklesfield was one of the largest villages in Delverdale, boasting perhaps six hundred residents, two pubs, a village shop, a post office, a butcher's shop, a plumber's shop and a reading room, along with an undertaker and several small businesses.

The largest and busiest of its pubs was the Unicorn Inn, owned and run by my in-laws, the Meads. Derek and Virginia were Evelyn's father and mother. The pub was a working farm as well as an inn, and it was also the venue of the huge annual Delverdale sheep sale. As well as being the focus of many rural activities, including the game of quoits, whose players used a clay pitch behind the pub, the inn was popular with visitors who came for the salmon and trout fishing on the River Delver. A dozen guests could be accommodated in its bedrooms and its food was renowned throughout the dale, thanks to the skills of Evelyn's mum. Her Yorkshire puddings were famous well beyond the limits of our dale, due in part to her ability to produce the most tasty of onion gravy.

My father-in-law, Derek Mead, was the landlord, a very large gentleman in his late fifties with a round red face, a mop of thick grey hair, a splendid handlebar moustache and a voice like a foghorn. No one caused any trouble when Derek was on the premises, but he was a jolly, laughing character whose voice could always be heard above the buzz of general conversation. Nothing was too much trouble for Big Deck, as he was known, and he was a gentle and sympathetic man – although he wasn't above physically ejecting an unwelcome guest from his bar if need be. Sometimes, visiting youths who were strangers to the area attempted to make nuisances of themselves, but Big Deck saw them off with a loud roar and a demonstration of his remarkable strength. There is more than one story of youths literally flying through the air as they were expelled with the tip of his boot.

Some landlords in the dale had jobs other than their licensee's duties, often relying on their wives to run the pub during daytime opening, and Derek ran a thriving farm based at the Unicorn; it had a milk round, a dairy herd, sheep, pigs and poultry. As if that was not enough work for a married couple, the weekly fruit, vegetable and domestic utensils market was held on Wednesdays outside the inn. This had been a feature of Micklesfield for centuries. Outside the Unicorn was a large cobbled area known as the Market Square, even though it was really a footpath past the inn, albeit slightly wider than average, which curled around the end of the building into the farmyard. In the past, it had probably been a much larger market with livestock, but now it comprised mainly fruit, vegetable and produce stalls. These included a cheese stall, a cake stall, a fish stall and various regular stalls selling handicrafts and art works and Big Deck earned an income from renting space to the stallholders.

On market day the Unicorn also benefited from a special provision in the liquor licensing laws. It was known as a General Order of Exemption or, as some described it, a market-day extension. Although the Licensing Act of 1921 had reduced licensing hours, the law continued to permit local magistrates to grant this kind of order where they were satisfied that persons attending public markets required refreshment throughout the day; this meant that the Unicorn could open at 10 a.m. and remain open until 10.30 p.m. rather than closing during the afternoon. The result was that the Unicorn was always busy on market day, inevitably with gentlemen 'doing business'.

It was here that Joe Hurd came each Wednesday afternoon along with many others, and there is no doubt some deals were done and promises made, but the original function of the market had altered. The livestock element of the market had certainly gone; even if deals were done between livestock dealers, none of their animals were brought here for display or sale. Instead, housewives came to buy from the stalls, although they did not venture into the inn – a woman alone in a pub was considered to be of loose character – so the bar area was the province of the men, all enjoying the long opening hours.

I must admit I had seldom ventured into the Unicorn on market day, usually because I was completing my banking returns and paying my takings into the post office in the morning and being too busy elsewhere in the afternoon. Now, though, I found myself having to accept the challenge of speaking to Joe on what was surely his day off with friends. If Cissy thought he was working hard, I would not wish to disillusion her, but I could understand why he was spending money here instead of paying it into his post office savings account.

When I arrived at the Unicorn that Wednesday just after dinner time I spotted Joe's bike in the car park and walked around to the front, where the market was in full flow. It was a fine and dry day. It was half past one and all the stalls were busy, mainly with housewives; the local bus service made sure it got them there, left them for an hour or two or longer if they wished, then took them back home again. Evelyn's mum, Virginia, always set aside a dining room in the pub for the sale of sandwiches, cakes and tea. This meant the ladies did not have to venture into the bar area for refreshments during their day out at market – it kept them 'respectable'.

As I walked between the stalls, bidding hello to traders and their customers, I recognized lots of familiar faces from the villages within my agency, mainly women, although there were a few men, those retired, perhaps, or not in work. There was a vibrant buzz of activity and I gained an instant impression of a busy and happy occasion, even if the market was far smaller than those in the local towns.

When I went into the saloon bar of the inn, however, there was a complete change of atmosphere. For one thing, the entire place was dark and thick with tobacco smoke, which rose from a host of pipes, cigars and cigarettes. I caught my breath, doing my best not to cough as I paused momentarily in the doorway before ploughing through the mass of male bodies. There were men everywhere, standing in groups, playing darts, massing around the bar counter, sitting at tables with pints of ale while playing dominoes or cribbage, or just talking. Shouting might be a better word because the level of noise was extremely high, and for a moment I thought about leaving because everyone was so engrossed that I felt I would never get to the bar let alone gain anyone's attention.

But Big Deck, towering above the heads of his customers, spotted my arrival and boomed, 'Matthew, come and let me get you a drink, on the house. You're a stranger in these parts – well, in here at any rate! It's not often you pay us a call like this!'

I nodded and smiled as I pushed my way through the crowd, some of whom I recognized as clients; one or two acknowledged me. I noticed Crocky Morris, too, without the familiar basket of pots on his head. I wondered where he had left his distinctive basket, for he went nowhere without it. Finally, I found myself at the bar.

'So, what can I get you?' asked Big Deck.

'I'll have a pint of bitter please.'

'First time anyone comes in here they get their first pint free, Matthew. That means I hope you'll come again. Evelyn kicked you out, has she?'

He pulled a rich golden pint with a wonderfully white frothy head and passed it to me. I accepted with a smile, raised it and said, 'Cheers, Deck. Thanks for this one!'

'So what are you doing here? Wanting to hire a stall? You could sell a bit of insurance among this lot – that's if they've any money left over for luxuries like food, clothes and insurance!'

'That might be a good idea!' I laughed. 'A market stall; that would mean I wouldn't have to drive round all these villages canvassing from house to house!'

'And you'd catch 'em when they had money to spend! And when they've had a noggin or two they can be quite generous with their money. That's important – it's no good trying to sell things to folks who don't have money to spend or who don't want to spend it. See how it works in here? All these fellows come prepared to spend some hard-earned cash today, just on enjoying themselves, and so they do! The rest of the week they're probably as miserable as sin without a penny in their pockets. Mark my words, take my advice and get among them, Matthew. They'll all know who you are, Matthew, word gets around in places like this.'

'I don't mind them knowing, I'm always willing to talk business . . .'

'Right, well, if it's a market stall you're after, I can't let you have one just now but opportunities keep coming up as folks move on . . . Tell you what, though, I could let you have the bottle and jug.'

I had not even considered using the Unicorn as a kind of base for my activities. I had never discussed this with Evelyn's parents, not out of any desire for secrecy but because we seldom saw them. Even though they lived in the same village, they were such busy people that normal socializing was almost impossible. But Big Deck had produced a very valid suggestion and I was very short of space at home. I needed an office of some kind, some type of focal point, and if I could use an established location in a busy area, it might just help to expand my activities. But the bottle and jug in a village pub? Was that feasible?

The idea did have merit. Instead of wasting precious time visiting people on speculative and unproductive visits, they could see me here and discuss things with me. My mind switched into overdrive as I recognized the potential of this unexpected idea. I'd be selling a product at market, just like other people.

'Bottle and jug?' I asked.

'Aye, there, at the end of the bar. You might not have used one, they're going out of fashion now, but we've still got ours and it's used sometimes, by older folks more often than not. See, it's still got Bottle and Jug written on the glass.'

I was aware of the purpose of the bottle and jug, and I could see the small square glass window at the end of the bar counter. The stone walls of the old inn were about three feet thick and this window looked through that thickness into the market place beyond. It was like peering through a short oblong tunnel. In days gone by, purchasers of drinks for consumption away from the inn would come to the window. The beer would be supplied either in corked bottles or pumped into a jug brought by the buyer. Men sometimes sent their children to this hole in the wall to buy a jug of ale, but changes in the law meant that it could be sold only to people aged eighteen or over, and that the container had to be sealed. The window known as the bottle and jug was now largely redundant but still used on occasions by buyers of bottles to take out.

'How do you see me using that?' I puzzled.

'From the outside. You could use the base to spread your leaflets out, a spot of advertising, and you could stand there and discuss things with customers – all day if you wanted, or for just an hour or so. Up to you. You could even come in here to keep an eye on things, looking out like we're doing now. Your papers would be out of the weather, and you could stand under the eaves, they're wide enough to keep you dry . . . Winter time you might not want that, but, as I said, you could stay in here and keep an eye on things out there. It would be a bit like the doctor in his surgery, eh? Folks would know where to find you every Wednesday, and let's face it, Matthew, they do come here from most parts of Delverdale. It should save you a lot of pointless journeys up and down the dale.'

'Most of my leaflets are designed to be taken away and read before people commit themselves so there's no real need for me to be present all the time. Folks could simply help themselves. I could spread out my leaflets and leave them, then come back to spend a few minutes talking to people . . .'

'Well, whatever you decide. That space is yours if you want it, Matthew. It's no good for anything else.'

'What's the cost? I know you charge for each pitch out there.'

'For you, nothing. Family and all that.'

'No, I should pay you something. Well, the Premier will pay, really, I'll put it down to expenses.'

'I'm not asking for anything, Matthew.'

'A shilling a day,' I said on the spur of the moment. 'I would come here when you open, put my leaflets out and pay the shilling rent. Then I could come and go as I please. We're talking about market days, aren't we? Only market days?'

'We are, but if it works you might want to leave your stuff there on other days, say Saturdays, when we're quite busy, and in summer with tourists starting to increase in numbers. Think of the potential, Matthew. Bottle and Jug insurance!'

I went outside to look at the space and found a large square inlet through the stone; it was about two feet high, two feet wide, and three feet long, with just the one window at the internal end, and already I could envisage it accommodating small shelves, which I could make to fit or even display stands for my leaflets. I decided to rent it, at least for a trial period.

I went back and told Big Deck, who said I could begin immediately, but he waived the fee for that first day, then said he would send me a bill for a shilling. I suspected such a bill would never arrive! And so it was that, there and then, I spread a selection of my publicity leaflets in the bottle and jug window. Several of the men from inside saw me at work and could not contain their curiosity, so they came out to find out what I was doing – and one of them was Joseph Hurd. I told them of my plans and gave each of them a few leaflets to take home. I did manage to catch Joseph for a few moments alone, to try to persuade him that a life insurance for his wife was advisable. But he was not convinced.

'I'm not in favour of insurance, Matthew. Besides, she's younger than me. I do know I should be pretty desperate if owt happened to her, but she'll outlive me, she's as fit as a fiddle and she's capable of fending for herself when I go . . .'

'But suppose she did die before you, Joseph, or have a tragic accident that made her unable to work in the house . . .'

'If she died, I'd probably find somebody else to marry, to

cook and wash for me. There's plenty of widows about who'd welcome a good home and a reliable chap like me, and if she got crippled with summat, well, I might have to get somebody in or she could tell me what to do, but we don't know what's in store for us, do we?'

I knew that Joseph could not understand the need to pay out good money for something he might never get, and I was equally aware of his superstitious fear of life insurance, but he did slide some of my leaflets into his jacket pocket. I felt sure he would read them at home, perhaps without Cissy seeing them, and he would be here next Wednesday, and the Wednesday after that and the following Wednesday . . . I was certain I would be discussing things with him in the future.

I attended my special hole in the wall each Wednesday and talked to Joseph on regular occasions, but he never changed his mind. He did not believe in insurance either for him or Cissy.

Then eighteen months later there was a tragedy. Cissy was walking along the lane near her home after doing some shopping in the village when she collapsed. She was alone and lay undiscovered for a while. No one knew how long she'd been lying there, probably about half an hour according to her daily routine, but a passing motorist found her and drove her to the surgery in Micklesfield; Doctor Bailey said she must go straight to hospital. The helpful motorist took her immediately, the doctor telephoning ahead to warn the hospital to be ready to receive her as an emergency, but it was too late. She died that evening; she'd suffered a massive heart attack.

Six months later, Joseph married a widow from Gaitingsby and she moved into his cottage to cook and wash for him. She wasn't insured either, but he continued to attend the Unicorn every Wednesday. On occasions we did talk about insurance, but in spite of what had happened to Cissy he would not insure his new wife or himself. He said his new woman had been left quite a useful sum by her former husband so she was comfortable, as he put it.

I did not try to persuade Big Deck to insure himself, his

wife, his premises or his business with the Premier because he let it be known that he had specialist cover taken out years ago through the insurance department of the Licensed Victuallers' Central Protection Society.

His idea that I should use his bottle and jug then began to pay dividends. I wrote the letter U for Unicorn on every leaflet I left there and soon I began to receive completed forms through the post, usually to ask for further information but sometimes to make a positive proposal. The letter U told me they had been taken from that hole in the wall, and I generated some good business.

I became determined to spend more time there and thought my shilling rental for the bottle and jug window ledge was value for money – especially since I never received a bill for it!

# Three

*'To avoid a collision, I ran into the other car'*
From a claim form

I must confess that while concentrating on teaching Evelyn to drive any thoughts of finding a house of our own were relegated, albeit temporarily, to the back of my mind. Although I did not actively hunt for a house just then, however, I did keep my eyes and ears open, particularly when travelling around my agency. The problem was that village houses rarely came up for sale. In many cases, they passed from one family member to another, although builders and speculators were now beginning to consider villages as possible sites for new properties.

The idea of living in a village and using a car to travel to work was becoming a reality and many villagers were now seeking work beyond their own parish boundaries while continuing to live in the community, which meant that houses rarely came on to the market. Another factor was that petrol rationing was rumoured to be nearing its end, which made village life even more appealing. Living in a village was cheaper than living in a town, too, chiefly because the rates for rural properties were much lower than those in the towns. The difference would help pay the cost of travelling to work. In addition, food was cheaper, with much of it being produced by householders. Many kept pigs and hens and grew their own vegetables.

As this vigorous new interest in living in villages began to manifest itself, and with new houses likely to be built in our dale, I wondered if we might consider a brand new house. One built to our own specification, with an office, outbuilding or two, and a garage. Or would we make do with an older property? One we could convert to our own needs?

The possibilities were intriguing but my immediate priority was to get Evelyn through her driving test. By now she had developed her roadcraft to the extent that I felt she was almost ready. She was very capable and had no problems with things like changing gear on hills, clutch control, three-point turns, hill starts, reversing into confined spaces or emergency braking. There was the added question of the theory of driving, which involved a study of the Highway Code and answering hypothetical questions about what to do in certain circumstances, but I did not feel she'd have problems with those aspects of the test. Thanks to her upbringing on the farm, she could cope with changing a wheel, cleaning the plugs, topping up the oil and radiator water, adjusting a fan belt or even fitting a new exhaust.

I spent hours at home, quizzing her when she was washing the pots or doing the ironing. I'd ask, 'What are your legal obligations if you are involved in a traffic accident?' or 'What does a red triangle on top of a road sign mean, and how does its meaning differ from a red circle?' or 'What is the sequence of traffic lights?' or 'What is the overall stopping distance when travelling at forty miles an hour?' When she was able to respond quickly with the right answers I knew she was ready for her test.

'I think you should apply,' I suggested to her one day over tea. 'You're ready, you've got the skills and the necessary theoretical knowledge. Once you get a firm date, we can arrange for you to have your final lessons with a professional instructor – he'll know the sort of things the examiner will be looking for.'

'I'd like a bit more practice,' she said. 'I know I can drive, and I know I am safe but it's different when taking a test . . . On the day itself I might be too nervous to do things properly.'

'It's up to you.' I was quite happy for her to get more road

63

miles to her credit if that increased her confidence. 'But I think you're just about ready. Just imagine throwing those L-plates away!'

A couple of days later, I decided to take her along some of the more difficult roads in the dale, especially those with sharp bends and very steep inclines, and then we would venture into town at a busy time so she'd have to cope with pedestrians walking in the road, traffic lights, children, dogs, roundabouts, other motorists and all manner of unexpected hazards. I wanted her to realize she was capable of coping with any of the conditions she might encounter on the road.

But I hadn't bargained for Crocky Morris.

Crocky, a stocky man in his late sixties or perhaps early seventies, with several days' growth of whiskers, was a pedlar, which meant he travelled on foot from house to house carrying for sale goods which could be delivered immediately. Although Crocky walked around each village selling his wares and sometimes walked from one village to another, he was a great user of the railway that ran the length of Delverdale. He used the local train service to start his day's activities, travelling to the village of his choice by the first train in the morning and catching the last one home – at around 6 p.m. – at the conclusion of his daily toil. However, quite a lot of his time in the villages was spent in the pubs. He'd often call at an inn first thing in the morning, long before opening time, where the landlord would treat him as a friend and supply him with a quick pint to get him on the road. Beer for Crocky was rather like petrol in a car – it was his fuel, except, of course, it wasn't rationed.

Pedlars differed from hawkers, the latter also travelling around selling goods by horse or other beast of burden, or using some kind of transport bearing the legend 'Licensed Hawker'. The merchandise sold by hawkers could be delivered later, whereas in the case of pedlars it had to be available immediately. To legally carry out their work, pedlars required a certificate granted by the local police, and hawkers needed a licence from their local council.

# Rest Assured

Unfortunately, these laws made no mention of insurance, and other people, known in the insurance world as 'third parties', who might be affected.

Several of my clients had been startled by the sudden appearance of Crocky and his basket as both rose from behind a hedge or wall where he'd been having a nap or popped out from behind a tree after attending to the needs of nature. Horses had been startled, motorists had run into ditches or into one another and flocks of sheep had fled. I often thought Crocky should be insured against the injuries to others that might result from his mere presence, even if he never had an ounce of ill-will in his mind.

Crocky was renowned throughout Delverdale for his unusual method of carrying his wares – usually crockery, hence his name, and sometimes other items such as pans and cutlery. He used a huge circular basket with high sides, which he carried on his head. Even when people bought his goods and the basket's contents were reduced or shifted he could always maintain its balance. Not only that, he could keep the basket skilfully balanced on his head after he'd had a few pints of beer and it was said that the more he drank the less likely he was to drop it. In fact, I had never known him do so.

Late one afternoon, while Paul was attending a birthday party for his cousin Jamie, I took Evelyn for a long run into town, where she coped admirably with shoppers and school-children, and, later, with workers as they left their offices, shops and small factories. I think she found the experience exhilarating as well as being a confidence booster. Then we returned to Micklesfield via the lower route along Delverdale – through Crossrigg and Graindale rather than across the moors. She had no problems with the steep gradients, narrow roads, sharp corners and large puddles, but on the final mile of our return to Micklesfield she had to descend the notorious Hollowood Hill. This is about half a mile long with a gradient of 1-in-3 and a sharp left-hand bend at the bottom, where the River Delver flows alongside the road. At that point, exactly on the bend, another road enters the carriageway from a thick patch of riverside woodland.

Evelyn was doing very well. She had stopped at the summit, put Betsy into bottom gear and was descending with her left hand on the gear lever to prevent it jumping into neutral. If that happened, the car could run away downhill because the brakes alone were not strong enough to hold it. Her other hand gripped the steering wheel and her right foot was on the brake pedal. Everything was just right.

Then, as we reached the corner that turned sharply to the left on the final short descent down to river level, two things happened. It is difficult to say which happened first, as they were both so sudden and unexpected. Like an apparition, Crocky Morris materialized out of some trees immediately to our left; with his basket on his head, he wobbled into the road just as Evelyn considered herself to be almost safely down the hill and, acting instinctively, she swung the steering wheel to the right with both hands in her efforts to avoid him, removing her hand from the gear lever. At that very instant, another car, a sporty red MG tourer, appeared from the opposite direction; it was gathering speed to help it climb Hollowood Hill and its driver was suddenly confronted by Betsy on the wrong side of the road and a man with a basket on his head wobbling around among it all. And at that moment, Betsy jumped out of gear and began to gather speed.

I was helpless because I could not reach the controls, but the oncoming car driver's reaction was amazingly fast. He swung to his left and accelerated along the grass verge, wary of the river on his nearside. He missed Betsy and Crocky but instead of climbing Hollowood Hill he disappeared into the minor road which led into woodland. And there he stopped.

Before I had time to think, Evelyn had regained control of Betsy by slamming the gear lever into third to cope with the increasing speed, then braking to a gradual halt as she returned to the left of the carriageway. She had behaved with remarkable coolness and skill. From that moment, I would never doubt her abilities even if she failed her test.

And Crocky just wobbled away as if nothing had happened.
'Oy!' shouted the other driver, a man who had emerged
from the woodland and was heading towards us. 'Oy, you with
the basket on your head . . .'

But Crocky was not going to hang around. With his amaz-
ing agility and energy, he switched himself into top galloping
gear and began to run down the final length of Hollowood
Hill. In spite of his age, Crocky was extremely fit and he could
run. As he had several hundred yards start on the irate driver
he could maintain his lead, and as we climbed out of our car
we were in time to see Crocky disappearing into the distance
with his basket bouncing and shaking but never falling off. I
think he was heading for the railway station; the down train
was due about now and I guessed he would be making for his
home at Crossrigg. The man, whom I did not recognize, now
drew level with us and stopped. He had given up the chase.

'Are you all right?' he asked Evelyn with evident concern.

'A bit shaky,' she said. 'But thanks, you reacted very fast . . .'

'No problem, I don't drive in rallies for nothing! But you
don't expect to see old men with baskets on their heads leap-
ing out in front of you like that . . . You did well, young lady,
very well. Are you the learner then?' He indicated the L-plates.

Evelyn nodded, still shaken.

'If I was an examiner, I'd pass you on the spot!' He smiled.
'You ought to drive in rallies, you've got quick reactions. I
saw everything. Well, no harm done, but who is that batty old
chap?'

I told the man about Crocky, and he shrugged his shoulders, saying that if Crocky drove cars like he walked he'd
have been disqualified years ago.

We had a long chat and decided we could not take any
further action; no one had been hurt and Evelyn had survived
a real emergency. I promised the man I would speak to Crocky
about his behaviour when the opportunity arose. The man
shook our hands and departed, reversing out of the wood and
roaring up Hollowood Hill as if it were a racing track or rally
route, but Evelyn wanted me to drive the rest of the way home.

I refused. The best way to regain confidence after being shaken in that way was to immediately resume driving. And so she did – very well indeed.

I was not surprised that Crocky disappeared so quickly from the scene of the mayhem, and, although I was furious at the danger he had presented to Evelyn, my anger had subsided long before I saw him again. I knew our paths would cross in the near future and, equally, I knew I could never ignore him. He was always at large in Delverdale, and one of his weaknesses was that he could never resist a challenge. There were many stories of him rising to the occasion by performing some kind balancing feat or display of strength, often to win a bet of some kind. One I remembered from childhood was when he accepted the challenge to walk from Lexingthorpe to Micklesfield, a distance of about six miles, with a mangle balanced on his head. These were heavy iron-framed constructions with two wooden rollers, a large hand-turned wheel with gears and a wooden handle and wooden trays to hold the clothing both before and after being mangled. It required four men to lift the mangle on to his head and, once he'd found the point of balance, he set off at his usual fast pace accompanied by men on horses and bicycles. He won his bet – I think it was for one pound – by walking from the parish church in Lexingthorpe to the one in Micklesfield without once halting for a rest and without removing the mangle from his head. He had plenty of witnesses to prove his claim, but someone else had the problem of returning the mangle to its owner in Lexingthorpe. That required a horse and cart or a small lorry – Crocky had no intention of carrying it all the way back again.

On another occasion he went to Guisborough to attend its Saturday market, this time without his basket of crockery. It was a day off and he went along with some friends in their car, but when they arrived they saw a man carrying three baskets of plums on his head. The round, high-sided baskets were smaller than that used by Crocky and they were made for stacking, but one of Crocky's pals loudly said, 'I bet you could do that, Crocky, a tour of the market place, weaving among the stalls, with three baskets on your head!'

'He could not!' snapped the man with the baskets. 'This takes years of practice . . .'

'Well, that might be but my pal here could do it, and he's no fruit and vegetable man!'

'Ten bob says he can't!'

Never one to resist a challenge, Crocky had said, 'A pound says I can do it with six baskets! Full baskets that is. With plums. Round the market, full length of the high street and back again.'

At this, the man with the baskets roared with laughter and shouted to some mates on a huge fruit and vegetable stall, 'Hey, you lot, there's an old chap here says he can do the full length of the street and back again, through the market and all these people, with six baskets on his head.'

In less time than it takes for a cat to shake its whiskers, Crocky found himself surrounded by disbelieving market traders. Two other men offered a further £1 each. Word of this challenge swept through the regular traders like wildfire and reached some of the customers, and so it was that Crocky, whose appearance was that of a frail old man, was told to start at the market cross at the top of the town, walk along the road through the stalls on the right as he faced them from the cross, continue to the very last of the stalls, cross the road and return via the other side of the street, finishing back at the market cross. I was not there to witness this event but it became a piece of local folklore, the story probably being enhanced with every telling.

According to the tale, Crocky stood at the market cross as two men built a small tower of six full plum baskets, reaching a height of about six feet, and then raised the complete tower on to Crocky's head. He set off to the cheers of the crowd, walking at his usual very fast pace and passing along the sides of the stalls as he headed for the distant end of the high street. As with his mangle-carrying exhibition, he appeared to have no difficulty, because he reached the far end of the market, crossed the road and returned along the other side. Men were waiting at the cross to lift the baskets from his head and by this time a considerable crowd had gathered to witness this display. Crocky won rousing cheers from everyone, was paid his bet and thus became a legend not only in Delverdale, but also in Guisborough.

Those who knew Crocky were wise enough never to issue him with that kind of challenge, but from time to time visitors arrived in the district and, upon first seeing Crocky, did not believe he could carry that basket of pots all day on his head, and without ever dropping it. It was almost inevitable they would issue challenges of some kind. And Crocky would respond.

One such man was a Londoner called Ernie Stewart, who had come to Crossrigg with a pal from the city for a week's fishing in the River Delver. A couple of men in their forties, they had obtained lodgings in the village and happened to be in the White Hart Inn early one evening when Crocky arrived after his day's work in the dale.

As always, he entered the bar through the swing doors while carrying his basket on his head. He could time his entry to perfection, always getting clear of the doors by the time they swung shut. By this stage of the day, Crocky's basket was usually only half full, and he would swing it from his head with a practised sweep of his arms and place it on the floor in a small recess at the end of the bar. Then he would order a pint and sit on a bar stool to enjoy it. This regular after-work visit by Crocky to the White Hart was part of the village routine and the locals never considered it at all unusual. For Ernie and his pal, however, the sight of an old man successfully pushing through the swing doors while balancing a basket of crockery on his head was unforgettable.

I was not present during the conversation that followed, but understand that Ernie Stewart spoke to Dave Brown, the landlord, and quizzed him about Crocky. Dave, being rather proud of Crocky's remarkable skill, painted a glowing picture of the old man's prowess while relating some noteworthy moments.

Stories of the mangle-carrying, his ability to slide on icy patches without dropping his basket, the tale of his circuit of Guisborough market and several more accounts were all told with relish and probably some embellishment as Ernie and his pal listened in awe. Then Ernie's pal said, 'But the old feller only carries one basket at a time. Ernie here can carry five.'

'Really?' said Dave, recognizing the beginnings of yet another challenge to Crocky.

'He's from Covent Garden, the fruit market, a porter there. He can carry five or even six full baskets on his head, one on top of the other. More if he has to.'

'Is that right?' Dave asked the silent Ernie.

'Yes, mate, it's all part of the job, we all do it,' muttered Ernie.

'Crocky just has the one,' said Dave with false modesty. 'He carries cups and saucers in it, plates and jugs as well. Up and down the dale. All day. And he's never dropped it once.'

'You don't drop 'em when you know how to keep 'em balanced – instinct, it is, years of practice,' said Ernie's pal, whose name was Stan. 'I reckon Ernie and the old guy should have a race. Mebbe we could run a book on it.'

'A race?' asked Dave with apparent shock on his face.

'Well, a demonstration, Ernie here showing how he can carry five baskets to your old man's one. Mebbe a bet or two on which of them gets back first without dropping anything. A bit of fun.'

'You'd have to ask Crocky about that,' said Dave. 'He's out working every day except Saturday and Sunday, and on Saturdays he likes to go off to market to get in his new stocks. He hasn't much spare time and he is getting on a bit, he's in his late sixties, they reckon. At least. Seventies, even.'

'Well, we're only here for the week, fishing. It would have to be one evening.'

'Crocky will be tired, he'll have been out all day – he does about twelve miles every day on foot, carrying that basket . . .'

'Well, we'll have been out fishing all day and Ernie could give him a few yards start . . .'

'Look, lads, it's nothing to do with me,' Dave said. 'If you want to take Crocky on, talk to him about it. And you might have to buy him a drink or two to get him talking to you. He doesn't take kindly to strangers.'

Waiting until Crocky had almost finished his pint, Stan sidled along the bar counter towards him and asked, 'Fancy another, mate?'

'Who's buying?' Crocky's whiskery face turned towards his benefactor.

'The name's Stan, from London, visiting. Fishing holiday.'

'So what's the catch?' asked Crocky.

'Catch?'

'You said you were a fisherman,' grinned Crocky. 'Catch. Fishing. Get it?'

'Oh, you're too fast for me. Look, there's no catch, I'll be honest, me and my mate want to talk to you, about basket carrying.'

'So where's my pint then?'

By this stage, most of the regulars were listening to their conversation, fully aware of how it would end. Stan dipped into his pocket and passed the money over to Dave, who pulled a pint for Crocky. Crocky accepted it with a curt nod.

'Ernie's a porter from Covent Garden. He carries baskets on his head, you know. Fruit and veg. All day, every day. Five baskets most of the time, more sometimes.'

'Gerraway!' Crocky beamed.

'No, it's right, he does. You can ask him. I was wondering whether you and him could give a demo, a sort of race, with a book on it . . .'

'I don't carry fruit baskets, I have crockery, in just one basket.'

'Well, that's just fine, just fine. He could do his stuff with, say, three to your one. We could stage a race with money on it, bets, mebbe, or winner takes all.'

'I'm an old man, I get tired after a full day out.'

'We'd give you a bit of a start.'

'And where would you get your baskets round here, mister porter.'

'I've got three in the car, Ernie uses them on holiday instead of suitcases. Borrows 'em from work. He can carry 'em on his head with his things in, clothes and that. Even fish if we catch any.'

'Do you do this often? Take people on like this?'

'At work we do, we all do, just for a bit of fun. Races around the market with full baskets. Apples, carrots, potatoes, whatever. See who can carry the most. We had one chap carried seven and they say, years ago, a chap actually got up to twelve. Full an' all, but I can't believe that. I don't think Ernie could get up to twelve and they reckon he's the best.'

'Well, I don't know.' Crocky was pretending not to be interested but his pals in the bar knew what was now expected of them.

'You can't let us down, Crocky,' called one of them. 'You can beat this southerner with his three baskets even if you are old enough to be his dad. Say yes, Crocky, we'll all put a half a crown in the hat. Winner takes all. We can't be fairer than that.'

'And free pints all round!' chipped in Dave.

'Sounds good to me,' said Stan. 'How about it, Ernie?'

'I don't want to take advantage of an older man, Stan, especially after he's been out at work all day . . .'

'I could mebbe manage if it was a short run,' said Crocky. 'A mile or so. I know a good route, starting right here, outside the front door. Turn left along the village, then left again up that slight slope up to the Rigg, then on to the main road and it's downhill all the way back here. A mile, mebbe a bit more. Fifteen minutes it would take at the most, less mebbe. We'd be back here before dark.'

'Ernie?'

'Well, if the old feller thinks he can do it, then yes, let's have a go.'

'What about the book?'

'These lads here will pay half a crown into the kitty and I'll stick five bob in, it's all good for business,' said Dave. 'There'll be a kitty of three or four quid, more if I know this

73

village. We should get a good turnout once words gets around. Winner takes all and I'll give a free pint to all who put up their money.'

And so the grand race was settled. It would be run on Thursday evening at seven o'clock, allowing Crocky time to get home after his day's peddling. Crocky would carry a full basket of crockery and Ernie three baskets full of apples. The contest would start and finish at the front door of the White Hart, with both men leaving at the same time – a concession granted by Crocky. With apparent sporting generosity, he had said, 'I know my way round that course and, besides, I'm as fit as any southerner no matter how young he is.'

A couple of the regulars would act as guides around the course; they would use bikes if they wished but their task was to ensure that Ernie did not get lost and that no cheating occurred, such as one of the contestants taking a short cut.

On a fine autumn evening at the appointed time and place, therefore, Crocky and Ernie arrived at the White Hart. Crocky had already had a couple of pints of bitter but Ernie said he did not drink before a race. Dave acted as starter and a group of about twenty local men and lads had assembled to watch. Each had put half a crown into a pint pot borne by Dave, who had also sponsored the runners with his own five shillings. There'd be at least five pounds in the kitty. 'Get ready,' said Dave.

With a swift movement, Crocky raised his basket on to his head; Ernie did likewise with his three, and they awaited the call to start.

'Go,' shouted Dave, and off they set to the cheers of the assembled drinkers.

The first part of the triangular course, probably two fifths of the entire circuit (700 yards or so), was on the level and then it took a sharp left turn, almost back on itself, as it rose gently through a wooded area for about the same distance again. It emerged on a hilltop known as the Rigg; part of the village was on one side of the Rigg, part on the other, hence

Crossrigg. The final descent was a deep incline via the main road back into the village.

All I know is that Crocky set off at his familiar cracking pace and by the time they reached the incline he was well in the lead, but on the shallow climb youth began to gain over age and experience; neither had lost their baskets, and the observers on their bikes reported no sharp practices by either man. By the time they emerged on to the steep road that took them back into the village, Ernie leading, a small crowd had gathered in gardens, gates and front doorways as word of the race reached those whose homes lined the route.

The hill down from the Rigg was known as the Mount, and it was a very steep downward incline into the foot of the village. That is where Crocky scored over his challenger. He was accustomed to the steep hills of the region; Ernie was not. And Ernie had three baskets on his head, not the easiest of things to cope with when descending a very steep hill. Although he had walked the route prior to the race, he had not done so with baskets on his head and there is no doubt he was finding great difficulty in maintaining their balance while descending so steeply.

Crocky, on the other hand, was highly skilled and well accustomed to coping with this kind of predicament, and he had no trouble managing with just a single basket on his head. Not even the steepest of local hills could defeat him. Sadly, the same could not be said of Ernie. I am told by one of the observers that he lost his balance, or rather his baskets became unbalanced. As he struggled to maintain his momentum and keep them upright, he tried to move his legs faster so that he remained beneath the wobbling baskets, and, although he reached up with his hands to steady them, he could not prevent the top one toppling off. And when it went, the second one followed. Within seconds, two baskets and lots of spilled apples were bouncing down the hill and disappearing into the gardens of the hillside houses to the cheers of the villagers as Crocky moved steadily onwards and downwards to his reward at the pub.

Eventually Ernie arrived with just one full basket on his head. Nonetheless, there was a big cheer for him along with plenty of free drinks because he had given some wonderful entertainment to the village. Ernie had the grace to congratulate Crocky upon his achievement, and Crocky pocketed his winnings.

I knew nothing of this race until it was all over. The first hint of a problem arose when I took a telephone call from one of my clients, a Mr Grant of Crossrigg.

'Ah, Matthew. Tell me this, am I insured against a large round basket and several pounds of apples crashing through the roof of my greenhouse?'

One of Crocky's most disturbing traits was his habit of falling asleep under a hedge or behind a wall after a lunchtime drink in a local pub. He was not particular where he took those naps – it was not unknown for him to fall asleep in someone's front garden, although the most usual places were under walls and hedges along the boundaries of fields and woods near the outskirts of a village. He would sleep unnoticed for about an hour, curled up around his precious basket as if protecting it from the world, and then he would rouse himself, rise to his knees, place his basket on his head and stand up to continue his mission of the day. It was that act of standing up, sometimes with a rather loud groan or two and always with his basket on his head, which frightened horses and terrified old ladies who were not accustomed to such a vision arising as if from the very bowels of the earth. It was not a normal or pretty sight by anyone's standards.

Even during my first few months of working for the Premier, I had dealt with several claims involving drivers who had run off the road whilst trying to avoid Crocky as he rose from a ditch or simply through being startled by his sudden and unexpected appearance from an unlikely place. Evelyn's experience was just another in a long series of such scares. Whereas many drivers throughout the country claimed to have been frightened by ghosts or black dogs if they ran off the road without explanation, those driving through Delverdale usually blamed Crocky. Unlike their counterparts who blamed ghosts, however, those who blamed Crocky were usually telling the truth.

Although many road users could claim to have been surprised by this kind of activity, Crocky did present me with another curious problem. A retired military officer, Major Berkeley Carruthers, who lived at the Old Hall at Graindale Bridge, decided to buy a new horse. He paid one hundred and fifty guineas for a splendid thoroughbred hunter, which was sound of body, wind and limb and had a superb temperament as well as being tireless and courageous. It was ideal for riding across country, not necessarily to hounds, but there was no doubt it would be a wonderful mount in the fox-hunting season. The dark and beautiful animal, almost black in colour, was a fine complement to the major, himself a handsome man of renown and charm. In his hunting pink or with his bowler hat, hacking jacket and jodhpurs he cut a fine figure on a horse and he knew it.

Shortly after buying his new horse, which he called Savoy in honour of the famous black horse of Charles VIII of France, the major decided to ride across country to spend the afternoon with an old friend, Sir Ralph Cross at Lexingthorpe. Although the villages were about ten miles apart by road, they were only some six miles as the proverbial crow flies, and about seven by the old drovers' road that crossed the moors. Major Carruthers intended to use that old drovers' road; it would be a good test for his new mount. On a fine, sunny morning in May, therefore, he and Savoy sallied forth, and the major was soon enjoying the scent of heather and feeling the wind on his cheeks and the turf beneath his horse's hooves as he sped across the moors like a dashing hero from a Gothic novel.

On the approach to Gaitingsby, he galloped along the bridleway that skirted the riverbank; in Gaitingsby, that bridleway led into the road that passed through the village, and it was the major's intention to take that route for almost a mile before heading back up to the moors for the final leg via the old drovers' road. Where the bridleway joined the village road there was a five-bar gate complete with hunting sneck, but the major wanted to test Savoy's jumping capabilities. Instead of opening the gate by using his crop to slide back the specially constructed sneck, the major decided to leap the hawthorn hedge that adjoined the gate – rather than the gate itself, in case Savoy hit his legs.

It was perhaps unfortunate that in the split second before Savoy began his leap, Crocky was at the other side of the hedge and in the very act of rising to his feet with his basket on his head. The horse, unable to halt its run, did attempt the leap but was completely disorientated in mid-flight and slewed to its right in its frantic attempt to avoid the apparition rising just ahead.

The major was momentarily uncertain how to cope, and he allowed the horse its head, but it landed awkwardly and fell. The major, well practised in the art of falling off horses, curled himself into a ball and rolled clear of the hooves of the floundering animal, which took a heavy tumble. Miraculously, both of them missed Crocky, who simply stood and observed the scene around him. As the major, heavily winded, struggled to rise to his feet Crocky went forward to help him, with the basket wobbling worryingly on his head, and he was able to assist with a firm hand – but it was too late to catch the frightened horse. It staggered to its feet then took off at a fast gallop with its reins dangling and its stirrups hanging free, and although Major Carruthers bawled its name the horse galloped away. In seconds, it had disappeared around a corner behind a copse of conifers as the major bellowed at Crocky, 'Don't just stand there, man, get after it!'

Trotting as fast as he was able with a basket of crockery on his head, Crocky set off in pursuit, but it was no good. By the time he reached the edge of the patch of conifers, the horse had vanished. Major Carruthers came to a panting halt at his side, too out of breath to curse either Crocky or his vanished Savoy; he stood for a few minutes, stooping almost double as he fought to get some breath into his lungs. His heart was pounding and the unfortunate major was too shocked to do anything, at least for the next few moments. Crocky stood at his side, also saying nothing and doing nothing. What could he do?

'That was a bloody stupid thing to do!' snapped Carruthers when he had regained enough breath to speak.

'What was?' asked Crocky.

'You, standing up like that, frightening my horse . . .'

'I thought you meant it was stupid jumping that hedge when there's a perfectly good sneck on the gate – that gate opens easily, not like some round here,' said Crocky, not in the least overawed by this man. To his credit, the major knew there was little point in blaming the old man.

'I was testing my new horse . . . now where the devil has it gone? Savoy!' he shouted, but there was no sign of the animal; this was a village, not the open moors with endless vistas, and there were houses, gardens, copses, woods, the riverside, the railway, barns and shelters of all kinds; roads led out in four different directions. In fact, there were lots of places for a terrified horse to hide and many directions in which to take flight.

'I'll keep a lookout for him,' promised Crocky as he turned to leave the major.

'And how am I going to get home if I don't have a horse, and how can I let Sir Ralph know, he'll be expecting me.'

'You should make your way to the railway station,' suggested Crocky. 'There could be a train due any time now, depending where you want to go, and there's a telephone kiosk near the post office. Well, good day to you, sir, and I hope you find that horse. He looked like a good animal to me, from what I saw of him.'

'A fat lot of help you are! You realize my horse has never been here before, it doesn't know its way around, it could be anywhere!'

'If it is, somebody will see it and let you know.'

'My name is Carruthers, I'm from Graindale Bridge, if

anybody asks . . . Oh my God, this is dreadful, humiliating, I feel such an idiot dressed like this without a mount . . . So where is the post office? I'll tell them in there and ring the police.'

'Down there,' said Crocky pointing towards the riverside. 'Well, I must be off, I've a few calls to make before I call it a day. I'll keep a lookout for your horse while I'm out and about. It can't have gone far, can it?'

'A riderless horse can go miles, in any direction, and if it's frightened it might go into hiding, into a barn somewhere, into the woods...God knows where it could be. It doesn't know this area, it might get panic-stricken. Where do I begin looking? Where, for God's sake . . .' And, shaking his head, the major headed for the post office to organize a search.

It was the major's account of the event both in the post office and on the telephone which eventually led to my hearing of this yarn, with a little tale-telling by Crocky in most of the pubs he visited. The major was one of my clients; he had his Bentley insured with the Premier, and also his house and contents, and I would visit him annually to collect his premiums. It was a couple of evenings after this event that he rang me.

'Can you call and see me, Mr Taylor,' he asked. 'As soon as possible. I have a matter to discuss.'

'Yes, of course. Tomorrow?'

'Tomorrow would be ideal. Shall we say eleven?'

At eleven, I presented myself at the front door of the Old Hall and was admitted by a housekeeper, who showed me into the library. She indicated a chair, asked if I liked my coffee black or white, and said she would inform the major that his guest had arrived. The major arrived before the coffee, shook hands and made light conversation about the weather until his maid left the room.

'Good of you to come so quickly, Mr Taylor.' He never called me Matthew, although it would not have surprised me if he'd referred to me simply as Taylor.

'My pleasure.' I sipped from the small bone china cup. 'So how can I help?'

'A matter of insurance, Mr Taylor. My house and contents policy. Perhaps I should remind you of its provisions, you must have a lot of clients with differing policies. Mine is all risks, a really comprehensive policy, I am given to understand. Or was given to understand by one of your predecessors.'

'I believe so; that's what we recommend to persons of stature with houses of this size, Major Carruthers.'

'And I believe such policies cover lost property, even when it is lost by the owners when they are away from the house. If my wife lost, say, her necklace while visiting her sister in London, then we would be covered? Am I right?'

'Yes, you are covered with that kind of policy. All risks means exactly that, Major Carruthers. You would, of course, have to report the loss to the police and we would need an abstract of their report, to confirm the loss and the value of the missing property, as I am sure you understand.'

'Good, it is just as I thought, so I wish to make a claim for lost property, Mr Taylor. I have informed the police and done all in my power to trace the missing property, but, to date, there is no sign of it.'

'And what have you lost?'

'My horse, Mr Taylor. A valuable animal worth at least a hundred and fifty guineas.'

'A horse? I'm not sure a horse is covered, Major Carruthers. I don't think a horse is considered to be property, it is livestock.'

'Not considered to be property? Why not? I bought the damned thing, it cost me money, I own it, and now it's lost. What is the difference between losing a horse and losing a piece of jewellery?'

'There are special policies for the insurance of livestock such as stallions, bulls, race horses, prize-winning dogs and so forth. You have no insurance which specifically covers your horse? For veterinary fees, injuries and so forth?'

'No, dammit, I haven't. I've only had the thing a few days.

I think my house and contents policy should cover the loss, Mr Taylor, so if you would care to provide me with a claim form I shall formally present my case to you.'

It was then that I gleaned the full details of how he had come to lose his precious horse. I listened as his tale unfolded, with due reference to the part played by Crocky Morris, and offered my sympathies. I said I would keep my ears and eyes open for signs of the horse as I went upon my daily rounds, and handed him a claim form.

'I will contact my District Office for their opinion,' I told the major. 'And I hope you are successful, but I can't guarantee the company will pay out for the loss of a horse. It is not dead, is it? Or stolen? Merely escaped?'

'Dead? No. Stolen? No. Escaped? Debatable. Lost, yes. It ran away like a frightened dog might do. And if my knowledge of law is anything to go by, I do believe a dog is regarded as property. Any animal can be property except those wild by nature. Pheasants are not property, nor are rabbits, which is why the poaching laws were created: one cannot be guilty of stealing a creature which is wild by nature. Even so, a person is guilty of poaching if he takes an animal without authority by trespassing on land in pursuit of it. It's the trespass that makes it illegal. But one can own domestic animals, and so they become one's property. Like my horse.'

My knowledge of such intricacies of law was almost nil and, without reading in depth the precise wording of the major's insurance policy, I was not sure whether or not his claim for a lost horse was legitimate. The answer was for him to present his proposal on a completed claim form and then let our experts make the decision. But then I thought of another important factor.

'One point, Major Carruthers. If valuables are kept in a house, anything in excess of a hundred guineas must be declared and listed separately. As you would for an item of jewellery. I know you have just got the horse and it is not listed on your policy – I have not been asked to amend it to that effect.'

'So I am not covered? Is that what you're saying?'

'Yes.'

'In that case my horse is valued at ninety-nine guineas. How about that?'

And so it was that Major Berkeley Carruthers completed a claim form for the loss of a horse worth ninety-nine guineas. I told him it would be despatched to my District Office without delay and they would contact the local police for the necessary abstract of the formal report of the loss.

'So there we are, Mr Taylor, job done. It's a case of nothing ventured, nothing gained. You'll keep me informed?'

'As soon as I have a reaction from my District Office, I will contact you.'

'Good man.'

And then, as if by magic, or through a timely cue of some kind, his telephone rang. He had an extension in the library and his housemaid put the call through. I was about to take my leave but after a moment's careful listening he waved at me to sit down a little longer.

I heard him say, 'Really? Good God, where? Are you sure it's him? Yes, the family crest is on the saddle, there's some gold lettering. Right, I will arrange to collect him later today, thank you most kindly, most kindly.'

He replaced the handset and said, 'Well, well, well, Mr Taylor, you've probably gathered what that was all about. It seems Savoy has been found. That was the police. He is on a farm at Gaitingsby with no apparent injuries and so I shall make immediate plans to collect him. My petrol ration will permit the trip. It seems you may now scrap that claim form.'

'I'll keep it just in case it is not your horse,' I said with just a modicum of caution. 'You'll let me know if it is him, will you? Then I can scrap this.'

He was clearly most happy and relieved at this outcome and almost forgot to bid me goodbye; now his only thoughts were of getting Savoy safely back home, and he hurried off to hitch his horsebox to his car. He rang that evening to confirm that the horse was definitely Savoy and that he was not injured, neither had any of his tack been lost or stolen. He told me to tear up the claim form, which I did.

It was my intention, when next I was chatting to someone from District Office, to determine whether or not a horse could be considered as lost property in claims on domestic household insurance. I have to admit I kept forgetting to ask and, over the weeks, the problem faded from my mind, but I did wonder what other problems Crocky was storing up for me.

With the war having been over for several years, people were becoming more accustomed to their new freedoms. More money was being earned and spent, daring new fashions were featuring in the shops, brighter colours were being used in clothing and house furnishings and decoration, women were wearing trousers, known as slacks, and tights instead of stockings and suspenders, gardens were producing flowers in addition to vegetable crops and there seemed to be more leisure time for people to enjoy. It was possible to take cheap holidays overseas by flying from England, more roads were being built and existing ones straightened or widened and cars were improving, with some even boasting internal heaters.

And among all this fast-moving change, a man called Edwin Coverdale decided to build a large architect-designed detached house on land overlooking the River Delver in Micklesfield. It would have every conceivable luxury, including central heating and shower baths. Edwin was a young and highly successful businessman based on Teesside. Among his various business interests which included a brewery and an hotel, he owned a large garage that specialized in Rover cars. A man of vision, he forecast that larger and more modern cars would become popular because he felt sure that the government would soon bring an end to petrol rationing.

Edwin decided that he and his wife, Ruth, should enjoy life in the wonderful countryside of the North York Moors. In particular, he wanted any children to grow up in the countryside (even though he had no children at that time) and so he had bought several acres of beautiful riverside land and built upon it his fine detached house, high enough above the water to avoid any flood risk, but with wonderful river views. He could commute to work, by train if necessary, and spend all his spare time in the countryside.

His pride and joy, however, was his nine-hole golf course. He would frequently rise early from his bed and play several holes before heading for Teesside, believing that some gentle exercise and fresh air enabled him to produce his best efforts when at work. And so it was that just after twenty-past seven one fine and dry Thursday morning, Edwin was enjoying a few holes before setting off to work. The train to Middlesbrough was at that point leaving Micklesfield to head further up the dale.

This meant that Crocky Morris was walking from the station, complete with basket on his head, and making for the Unicorn Inn, where he might be allowed a pint or even two before opening time prior to heading into the village to peddle his wares. Licensing hours meant little to Crocky, and if he had no cash at that time of the morning then he would pay with one of his pots.

As he was walking along the road past Edwin's fine new spread, Edwin was not far away over the recently planted hedge, swinging his iron at the little white ball. Edwin, a powerful man, connected with the ball, but instead of producing a very healthy thwack he sliced it and it sped away like a bullet, but not in the intended direction.

At that very instant, Crocky happened to be walking past a henhouse built of wood and upright corrugated iron sheets that stood on land on the side of the road opposite Edwin's fine home. Simultaneously, Roy Jenkinson, the manager of Crossrigg CWS (the Co-op shop), was driving his Austin 10 towards the railway station on the way to Crossrigg to begin his day's work. He spotted Crocky walking on the opposite side of the road but, in a blur of events, Crocky suddenly spun on his heels and buckled at the knees; Roy slammed on his brakes and swerved to avoid Crocky, who appeared to be stag-gering towards the centre of the narrow road. Suddenly the windscreen of Roy's car shattered, scattering a few small shards of glass on his lap and leaving a large hole.

Crocky came to a halt almost in the middle of the road, the basket still in position on his head. Roy veered to his left, ran off the road and ended his short journey in the hedge surround-ing Edwin's grounds. Luckily he was not hurt, even if he was rather surprised at this unexpected turn of events.

It is claimed that Edwin's face appeared above the hedge as he asked, 'Has anyone seen my ball?' but that is probably not a very accurate account. The car embedded in his hedge might have caused him to think of something else at that precise moment.

I became involved some time later because Roy was one of my clients and, after listening to his account and talking to Edwin, it appeared that when Edwin had sliced the ball with a very powerful stroke, it had flown over his hedge to narrowly miss Crocky. Crocky had been walking past in bliss-ful anticipation of the first pint of his day as the ball passed very closely behind him to strike one of the corrugated sheets of the henhouse. This had made a tremendously loud noise, startling Crocky, who, not knowing what was happening, had instinctively buckled his knees to avoid whatever was being thrown at him or exploding nearby. So instead of hitting Crocky on the rebound, the golf ball had been deflected by the troughs and peaks of the corrugated iron, setting it on course to smash Roy's windscreen. In swerving to avoid Crocky and then, at the same instant, having his windscreen shattered by an unknown flying object, it is not surprising that Roy's journey ended in Edwin's hedge. Later, Roy discovered a golf ball was the culprit because he found it in his car.

Fortunately, his car was not badly damaged. Other than a smashed sidelight on the nearside and a few scratches, there was no damage other than the mighty hole in the windscreen. It was almost as if a huge bullet had passed through; the screen had not broken up into lots of tiny pieces because those screens were designed not to. They were designed to be opened however: by turning a handle inside the car, the screen could be opened upwards and outwards to provide a flow of comforting cool air on hot days, and that mechanism had not been damaged by the errant golf ball. Lack of serious damage meant that Roy could continue to drive to work to relate his experiences to his staff; as there was no other vehicle involved, no one was injured and Roy had given his name and address to Edwin, he was not obliged to report the accident to the police.

Roy came to see me that evening about claiming from his insurance and I assured him he was covered for such damage because he had fully comprehensive cover, so we completed a claim form. The company paid without a quibble and without questioning how a golf ball from a private house had come to shatter a car windscreen on a public road. Perhaps it was a fairly regular occurrence . . . Later, I was to learn that Edwin had replaced Roy's windscreen free of charge, fitted some new sidelight glass and touched up the scratch marks on his paintwork, so Roy made a small profit from the experience. I understand he also bought a few celebratory pints for Crocky on the proceeds.

In pondering things later, I did not think Crocky could be blamed in any way for that series of events, although I did wonder what would have happened if that golf ball had struck his basket of crockery. Crocky would never pay to have his crockery insured but there were times I thought it necessary – I wondered if I would ever be able to persuade him!

# Four

*'Will you please come to look at my garden path,*
*it's got a hole in it, my wife tripped and fell and*
*now she's pregnant.'*
From a letter to an insurance agent

For some residents in the villages of the North York Moors, the idea of having a toilet inside the house was abhorrent. After years of regarding the necessities of nature as something one accomplished as far from the house as possible, no decent or right-minded person would ever agree to such a distasteful thing being done within the home. Indeed, why would anyone *want* to do that kind of thing indoors? Toilets were extremely unpleasant and very smelly places, and it is not surprising they were erected as far as possible from the living quarters.

Those toilets were, of course, without water. The tiny buildings, usually of brick or stone, were invariably very small. There might be a window or small open space in one of the walls so that unpleasant smells could be wafted away (although this allowed flies to come in) but there was usually no means of lighting, washing or heating. The usual design of the sitting area comprised little more than a strong wooden board about three feet long and two feet wide supported by the walls at the rear and by the two side walls. Wooden or brick panels might support the front of the seat. In the centre was a large round hole with a lid and shaped edges to provide some degree of comfort, while beneath was a large metal bucket-like container.

## Rest Assured

At the base of the rear wall there was usually a small door through which the container could be pulled out and taken away to be emptied. Children, of course, would often sneak up to the little house while it was in use, for they could be entertained by the sight of a large bare adult bottom if they opened that trapdoor whilst the toilet was in use, which they often did for a laugh. Emptying the container at regular intervals was very important, particularly if there were a lot of people in the household, and to minimize the ever present stench cans of disinfectant powder or bottles of disinfectant liquid were placed at one side of the seat for immediate use. If disinfectant was not available, ordinary garden earth was usually sprinkled upon the deposit, hence the term earth closet, and in some cases fire ashes were used in an attempt to smother smells and ward off flies.

Rolls of soft and gentle toilet paper were a rarity in rural toilets; instead, sheets of newspaper were cut into convenient squares and hung from a nail. Some of the more enlightened and perhaps wealthier people used lighter and more gentle tissue paper, and I believe some families made good use of the papers normally used by women for curling their hair. Reading matter comprising old magazines and books was often available in a pile on the seat and sometimes cheerful pictures adorned the walls, all of which meant that some people spent quite a lot of leisure time in what was often called the smallest room.

Regular removal of the contents of the toilet was usually undertaken by the man of the house, who emptied it on to his vegetable patch, which could produce surprisingly good results; or, if there was no garden, the stuff might be thrown down a drain or into a nearby stream or river. No one seemed to worry about its effect upon fish and other creatures of the river and no one questioned the use of drains for that purpose. After all, what were drains for? In some cities and towns, this product, known as nightsoil, was collected for a fee and removed for commercial use as manure.

In towns, of course, and even in some villages, there was

always the likelihood that spillages would occur, and so the Highways Act of 1835 and the Town Police Clauses Act of 1847, both still in force during my time as a Premier agent, made it an offence for any dirt, filth or offensive matter to be allowed to run or flow on any street or highway. The message was simple – if you spilled something while cleaning out the toilet or let your toilet overflow then you were responsible for cleaning up your own mess.

There is no doubt that the human deposits left in these little rooms were highly regarded as a form of garden manure, being particularly valued among men who had to grow their own produce to feed their families. In addition, human urine, once collected in huge quantities for use in the processing of alum, was very good for whitening the stems of celery. This skilled use of human waste was an important and valuable form of recycling, and there is a lovely story of an elderly moorsman, whom I shall call Sep, who put his house up for sale upon the death of his wife.

The house had been in the family for generations, but, with his own health failing, Sep felt he must sell it and go to live with one of his daughters. When a potential buyer came to look around, Sep showed him the old earth toilet at the foot of the garden. The buyer opened the door and looked inside, then said, 'But there's no lock on the door!'

'There's no need,' said Sep. 'We've never had any of it stolen.'

The Victorians, whose legacy lived on within the moors even into the 1950s, did not like to call such intimate things as toilets by their real name, so when a person went to perform their natural functions they might say they were going to shoot a lion, to powder their nose, to see a man about a dog, to go to the woods, to visit the rest room, to call at the doodah, to send a message, to visit the little boy's room or to call at the smallest room in the house. I am sure there were other simi- larly coded messages within clubs, societies and families.

Likewise, the toilet itself had nicknames: it was called the nessie – a shortened version of necessary room – or the privy, closet, petty, khazi, donnakin, among other names including, of course, the thunderbox. When modernization converted earth closets into water-operated flush toilets, the facility acquired a great deal of respectability encapsulated by its new name – the WC, which meant water closet. Once one could refer to it as the WC, rather than the toilet, it became a symbol of status within the community because not everyone could boast of possessing a WC. Lots of people and institutions cheerfully placed those initials on their toilet doors.

WCs began to appear in all manner of places, even within the interior of some houses – but always on the ground floor – and with great pride the initials were emblazoned upon many doors. In spite of this development, a large number of earth closets remained, but, likewise, lots of new water closets remained stubbornly at some distance from the dwelling house. This meant it was important to pay a visit before going to bed, otherwise one might have to cope with snow and storms when making that important journey during the cold night hours. Placing near the back door a pair of wellingtons, a heavy coat and some means of lighting the way was always regarded by visitors as a most thoughtful gesture.

Most of the cottages in my agency, particularly those that were rented, continued to have earth closets at the bottom of the garden. Quite a large number of privately owned houses had been modernized, albeit with their new WCs remaining in outside buildings, some of which had been converted from former earth closets. As I moved around, I discovered that one or two of the more adventurous householders had actually installed their WCs indoors – and one or two *extremely* brave ones had placed them upstairs near the bathrooms!

That kind of daring behaviour had been compared with keeping one's manure heap in the living room or hens in the bedroom, but I think the change in attitude had something to do with the fact that Queen Victoria had had a WC installed in her house at Sandringham. Word of this strong leadership was now permeating the more remote parts of the moors – although the common man's familiarity with royal behaviour

91

might also have been due to the fact that the Royal Family was becoming more amenable to public scrutiny and interest.

As a rural insurance agent, I never really expected to be concerned about other people's outside toilets, but as more and more people installed these newfangled water closets at the bottom of their gardens, in their backyards or even inside their homes, the question of suitable insurance began to arise. I was never quite sure why anyone would want to insure an outside water closet, because theft of its contents was most unlikely, although I was aware that people did store a variety of objects in those useful dry outbuildings. Garden tools and lawnmowers were often stored there, the family tin bath sometimes hung from the wall, household utensils like brushes and shovels could be usefully kept there, too, and even unwanted furniture like cots and children's high chairs and outdated family portraits or books could be kept there. At times, it was most difficult to enter an outside toilet to achieve the purpose for which it was intended, so full was it of assorted domestic items. And there were rarely any locks on the doors. From time to time, I had to alert my clients to the necessity of locking such doors against thieves if they wanted to claim from their household policy should anything be stolen, and, as time went by, locking the toilet became commonplace, even if it was not done for reasons of personal privacy.

One curious tale arose from this type of modernization. It concerned Josh Fowler of Baldby, a large, stout fellow who described himself as a daytal man. During the nineteenth century and into the twentieth, daytal men hired themselves out for agricultural work, or work on local estates. Originally they were paid by the day, hence their name, but later it became the practice to hire them by the week. Even so, they retained their well-known name. Most daytal men were able to tackle any kind of work, ranging from hedging to ditching by way of sheep dipping, haymaking, harvesting, thatching, stone walling, mole catching, milking and ploughing, although a few would be specialists in one of these. It was always said

of a good daytal man that 'he could ton 'is 'and ti owt' –
which meant he could turn his hand to anything. In addition
to this rather insecure work, most daytal men rented a smallholding and earned extra money by rearing livestock such as
pigs or sheep, or perhaps keeping geese or other poultry and
selling them or their eggs. Some grew vegetables and flowers, and others made agricultural implements or tools. As a
group, daytal men were very versatile and hard-working, even
if their efforts resulted in rather small incomes.

Josh, now in his sixties, was perhaps luckier than most of
his contemporaries because he owned his small spread at
Clough Head, Baldby, having inherited it from his father, who,
in turn, had inherited it from his father. About ten acres in all,
with lots of useful outbuildings, it was too small to be a viable
farm, but there was enough land for Josh to keep pigs and
poultry, and to grow vegetables, which he sold in the local
markets and to local shops. In addition to his daytal work, he
had a steady supplementary income from his modest smallholding, but, like all such men, knew he would never be rich.
His wife, Nancy, looked after the poultry and would sometimes do extra work such as cleaning, and it is fair to say that
Josh and Nancy were very content people, happy with their
lot in life.

They never took holidays because they never had the time
or inclination, and certainly they would not want to fritter
away their money on such an unnecessary expense; there
would be no pension from their work and they were quite
resigned to the fact they would have to keep working until
they died. However, both had managed to take out small insurances on their lives, which included clauses that would enable
payments to be made if either was unable to work, through
injury or long-term illness.

Then Nancy died very suddenly and unexpectedly from a
heart attack.

Not only was Josh devastated emotionally, but his once-
thriving smallholding began to appear neglected. Necessary
repairs were left undone, the vegetable plot became overgrown

with weeds, pigs were sold but not replaced and he did not have Nancy's skills in preparing poultry for sale.

Very soon Josh appeared to lack the energy or desire to work for other people. I do know there was genuine concern for him; I had kept in touch because Nancy, a sensible, forward-looking woman, had insisted on their taking out the life insurance, and upon her early death Josh received £500. That was a lot of money for someone like him at the time, and I wondered if it had contributed to his loss of sharpness. Perhaps, I thought, with such a considerable sum of money at his disposal, he had no need to work, at least for a few more months.

Then another family tragedy happened. Josh's son-in-law, the husband of his daughter, Jean, died in a traffic accident in the West Riding of Yorkshire where he was employed as a factory worker in the woollen industry. It seemed as if fate was dealing a very bad hand to the Fowler family, and it was not helped by the fact that Jean, a young widow with two young children, found herself without a home. While her husband worked for the woollen mill near Halifax, the family had lived rent-free in a terraced house that belonged to the mill owner, but that was now required for the family of another employee. With the customary note of sympathy, Jean was given three months' notice to quit.

With no job and two children, aged eight and ten, Jean had a bleak future – and then she realized she *did* have somewhere to go. She could return to Baldby. Even though, as a teenager, it had always been her ambition to leave the isolation of that remote village to experience the bright lights, excitement and opportunities of the city, she now realized her future lay back in her former home. And, from what she had learned in letters from friends back home, it seemed her dad needed help too . . .

And so it was that Jean, along with eight-year-old Michael and ten-year-old Emma, returned to Clough Head. Jean could earn her keep by doing all those things her mother used to do; the children could attend the local school and she knew her father had an old car, which meant she could learn to drive so she could take trips out to Guisborough or Whitby if she wanted anything special in the way of clothes or household goods.

And, of course, as Josh's only child, Clough Head would be hers one day. There was a huge incentive to make her presence felt and to improve everything at her former home. Whereas she'd often thought she would have to sell it when her parents were gone, now she knew she would keep it. Although she missed her husband dreadfully, Jean knew she had a wonderful start to a new life – even if it was a mirror image of the old! Suddenly, her future looked extremely bright, on top of which she was still young enough to attract another man . . .

I met Jean for the first time as I made one of my regular monthly calls to collect the premiums for Josh's life insurance and, even after the short time she had been living at Clough Head, I could see the transformation. It was May and Josh was working in his vegetable plot, which was now clear of weeds; the house looked smart, too, with a tidy yard, clean paint and shining windows. As I walked through the gate, I called across to him and he raised his hand in greeting, saying, 'Jean's round the back, Matthew. I'll knock off in a minute – tell her to get the kettle on.'

Jean was a younger version of her mother, with dark hair instead of grey, but with the same smiling face, rosy cheeks and slender figure. A short woman, only about five foot tall, she was wearing a pair of man's overalls, which were far too big but very practical because she was swilling down the woodwork at the back of the house, washing down doors and windows of the house and outbuildings with a brush at the end of a hosepipe. I bet they hadn't been washed for years – her mum would have been far too busy and perhaps a little old to tackle that kind of robust work.

'Hello.' She turned off the tap on the wall of one of the outbuildings. 'Can I help?'

'Matthew Taylor, Premier Insurance,' I introduced myself. 'This is one of my regular calls. I've just seen Mr Fowler, he said to come round to the back.'

95

'And I bet he said I had to put the kettle on! He always does that with callers. But I'm ready for a break. I'm his daughter, Jean, I live here now. But come in and tell me about yourself.'

'And people round here call me Matthew.'

And so it was that I met Jean and learned of her sad background, although it was quickly evident that she was transforming the family enterprise and making the house more comfortable, with modern furnishing and colours. Flushed with the vigour of youth and able to plan ahead, she was also redeveloping the smallholding with considerable success – that was evident the moment anyone walked through the gate.

Josh joined us in the kitchen and told me he was still working as a daytal man, but Jean explained to me that she was anxious to modernize the entire business and improve the house. She even suggested that when Josh was out at work elsewhere he should hire his own daytal man for jobs around the smallholding. Josh objected most violently to that, saying that nobody could do his work as well as he could do it himself, but Jean pointed out that if Josh earned more per day than the man he hired then it was a profitable exercise. Josh took a lot of convincing but I must admit I took Jean's side during that good-humoured discussion over tea and cakes in their kitchen.

'He still hasn't spent that insurance money he got for Mum,' she told me eventually, with Josh listening. 'He says he doesn't feel like spending it on himself – it was for her, so he reckons . . . I've tried to tell him she'd want him to make good use of it.'

'Well, she organized those policies, Matthew, persuaded me it was a good idea. Nancy was good at that sort of thing, good with money, it's rightly hers . . .'

'Well, she can't use it, Josh, and I know she wanted you to benefit from it,' I said. 'That's why Nancy struggled to pay the premiums in the early days. She knew you would need it if anything happened to her. It's your money, Josh.'

'I think you should spend it on the house,' said Jean. 'We need to get it up to date, make it more comfortable. Mum would have loved central heating and a nice bathroom with hot water on tap, and an indoor toilet – two in fact. One upstairs and one down, WCs both of them. There's plenty of room for that sort of thing.'

'Well, I agree there's a lot we could do, but as for indoor toilets, no chance! You don't have toilets in the house, Jean. Who in their right mind would want such a mucky thing in the house? Cows might do it in cowhouses, but that doesn't mean we should copy them! I don't mind the earth closet out there being made into a WC, but as for putting one inside the house, well, I can't imagine that! You'd never get me using it, that's for sure!'

'You get indoor toilets everywhere these days, Dad! In hotels, smart houses, schools, cafés, even inside big shops and Buckingham Palace . . .'

'That might be but we have to live and eat beside it—'

'Do you have an inside toilet, Mr Taylor?' Jean interrupted him.

'No, I must admit we don't. Ours is downstairs in an outbuilding, but it's a WC now. It was converted some time ago by my landlord. We are hoping to have a house of our own one day, and I know my wife would like an indoor toilet, upstairs preferably. And another downstairs.'

'There you are, Dad, Matthew's up to date – it's the way things are going.'

'My grandparents, who are still alive and living near Whitby, still have an earth closet.' I felt I hadn't to take sides during this discussion, and added, 'Mind, they've no running water and no electricity in the house.'

'Just like us not so long since!' Josh grinned. 'Nancy managed to get quite a bit done to the house, you know.'

'No thanks to you, Dad!' snapped Jean, albeit with good humour.

'I must be off,' I said to them. 'I'll let you sort out your domestic matters without me listening in!'

And so I collected the money due from Josh, signed his premium receipt book and left. In the weeks that followed,

Jean's impact was clear for all to see. Not only was the small-holding running more efficiently, with Josh responding by working away from home on more occasions and a labourer coming in to do the routine work, but builders and plumbers moved into the house. Central heating, a hot water system, a new bathroom with a shower bath and two indoor toilets, one upstairs and one on the ground floor, were being installed. I reckoned Jean must have been extremely persuasive to win Josh's approval for such a dramatic change – although later I heard that she had received some insurance money of her own following her husband's death, which had partially financed those alterations. Josh mentioned it one day when I called as usual for his premium. Jean was in the village doing some shopping for groceries. 'Well, Matthew, it was mostly her money even if I did chip in with a bit of Nancy's insurance, so there's nowt much I could do to stop her, but I must admit I like having hot water on tap and a bath's a real treat now, especially as t'bathroom's as warm as t'water. You never got warm bathrooms when I was a lad. You bathed in front of the kitchen fire if it was cold or you never got bathed at all. There's no wonder we only got bathed once or twice a year.'

'So you've got modern WCs now, two of them? Both indoors?'

'Aye, so we have, Matthew, but I never use 'em. I'll tell you what, I'm right glad I sleep at the far end of the house, well away from them things. You'll never catch me using an indoor toilet. I still go to my old one outside, down the end of the garden. It's still an earth closet, and by gum it does produce good manure. You should see how my beans are coming on . . .'

A week or so later when I met Jean in the post office at Baldby she smiled as she told the tale of her dad never wanting to use the indoor toilets. She said it was something to do with the fact that while working in the fields as a daytal man toilets were never within easy reach, so he was accustomed to finding somewhere quiet and secluded behind a hedge or haystack. I now knew what 'going behind the hedge' really meant – years earlier, it was illegal for the driver of any carriage to leave his vehicle unattended while he went behind a hedge. It seemed that was regarded as the perfectly normal way of doing things, at least for men. In spite of Jean's pleas, however, she said Josh could never come to terms with using indoor toilets.

'But he's going to have to face the problem next week.' She smiled. 'I'm having that old earth closet converted to water, so it will be out of use for a day or two. He'll have to use the ones indoors or keep his legs crossed all day.'

'He could go behind the hedge!' I laughed.

When the men came to begin work on the conversion, Josh was at home. He had no work that day, and although he had made sure to patronize the isolated toilet at the bottom of his garden before they actually declared it out of bounds, he could not last for ever without a repeat visit. But a repeat visit was out of the question – the toilet would be out of commission for at least two days and probably three. The big question facing Jean – and no doubt worrying Josh – was whether he would admit defeat and accept modernization by making use of one of the indoor water closets.

In the end, what happened was this: Josh was working on his vegetable patch when he was, as they say, taken short in a mighty serious way. There was no suitable cover in his garden or indeed around his plot; he did not want the work-men to watch him or Jean to see him rushing into the house as a form of salvation, so he adopted the strategy of his working days. He decided to find a good thick hedge with plenty of supporting cover, somewhere no prying eyes would see him – and, as a lifetime resident of Baldby, who, as a young lad, had explored every corner of the village and its surrounds, he knew precisely where to go. His intended destination was only a couple of minutes away across the fields, well away from public view. Indeed, he had often used it for this very purpose as a child. Now occupying the corner of a field next to a copse of silver birch and sycamores, the remains of what had once been part of Baldby Abbey were well off the beaten track.

Overgrown with briars and weeds, two surviving partially complete walls of stone, each about ten feet high, formed an open corner. This had once been a far outreach of the abbey, but in the 1950s it was ignored by everyone. Even though tourists walked around the main part of the ruin, which was some distance away and closer to the village centre, nobody appeared to own it. People wandered around without payment or restriction, but they did not venture to this remote point because it meant crossing private land. That, however, did not deter Josh.

With massive relief on his mind, therefore, he rushed into the shelter of the two walls, scrambled through the vegetation, advanced backwards towards the deep recesses of the corner and lowered his trousers.

Then the ground gave way beneath him. He fell about eight feet into a stone-lined ditch full of shallow running water, and, partly owing to his age and weight, he landed awkwardly and broke his left ankle.

Now something of a mess for all sorts of reasons, he tried to hoist himself out of the deep ditch but could not get a grip on the upper edge, nor would his leg support him. Terrified, dirty and alone, Josh resorted to shouting, and it was fortunate that, aided by the amplification qualities of the hollow in which he found himself, he was heard by a visiting historian, who was attempting to identify the outer limits of Dalby Abbey. He came to Josh's rescue and, to cut short a long story, Josh was rescued and taken to hospital, where his ankle was put into plaster. Later he returned home and for a while was confined to his bedroom – which meant that, as he could not descend the staircase on crutches, he had to visit the new toilet upstairs. And so it was that Josh Fowler found himself compelled to accept modern ways.

When he was more mobile, I paid him a visit to help him register a claim, as his insurance policy would pay him £5 per week while he was incapable of working, starting three weeks after his injury. There was no difficulty getting his claim processed and a week later I received confirmation that he would receive £5 by post each week, commencing on a given date and continuing until he returned to work.

Off I went in Betsy, my trusty little Austin 10, to pass this news to Josh, and I arrived at Clough Head on a fine warm day just as a man was walking up the lane towards the house. We arrived together at the gate, which the man held open for me, and I drove through to find Josh sitting on a seat in his garden with his foot in plaster, issuing instructions to a young man who was clearly his labourer for the day.

Upon our arrival, Jean emerged from the house to ask if we'd like a cup of tea and some biscuits. Josh was clearly in the mood for receiving visitors! As we organized some chairs outdoors under Josh's direction, I discovered that the third visitor was a Mr Geoffrey Todd, the historian who had so fortunately found Josh in the ditch. Jean arrived with the refreshments and we sat around in the warm sunshine rather like old friends at a garden party. Josh was clearly in a most affable mood, probably because I had brought news of a steady income during his incapacity, and he made us very welcome. Mr Todd, a hearty individual, told us that Josh had done a wonderful service to his research by falling into the ditch – beyond doubt, he said, those two surviving parts of wall marked the outer extremities of the old abbey.

When Josh said he'd often gone there as a child without mishap, Mr Todd explained that Josh was now much larger and much heavier, which could explain why the stone had collapsed beneath him. He said the stone that had given way under Josh had been supported only by a few tree roots and some bits of rotting timber. Enough to support a child, but not a large gentleman.

'But most important from my point of view,' said Mr Todd, 'was that ditch. We had no idea there was water underground, and of great interest is the fact it was still flowing. We were able to put some dye in a pond in the abbey grounds, and it came through the point where you fell and eventually into the stream that flows to the south of Baldby.'

'So what was the purpose of that ditch?' I asked.

'It was a toilet.' Mr Todd smiled. 'It was called the reredorter or necessarium. It was set away from the main buildings, but the essential thing is that it was kept clean by flowing water. Reredorters, usually with roofs and individual cubicles, were built over running water, which makes it a very early water closet, I suppose. Sometimes they could make use of natural running water, and sometimes they had to build channels, as was the case here. The monks stood where you stood with their backs to the wall, and did their business into the ditch below, or they sat on seats, which were separated by screens. The important thing was that reredorters were built directly above running water so that their waste could be washed away.'

Josh said nothing but I saw the gleam in Jean's eyes. 'So our modern water closets are not such a new idea after all?'

'No, the monks were ahead of us by several centuries; this abbey was built more than eight hundred years ago.'

'Aye,' said Josh after a long silence. 'But those toilets were away from the living areas, not built indoors. Even they knew better than to put toilets indoors!'

And we all smiled.

One feature of the moorland was the tracts of wasteland that lay around the villages that occupied the higher parts of the hills. Although it had the appearance of being uncultivated and not owned by anyone, most of it did have an owner, usually an estate or large farm. Much of it was covered with heather and bracken, while the lower slopes might bear conifers, mountain ash trees, gorse bushes, briars, rough vegetation, marshy areas and even just grass. In the latter case, this was usually shorn smooth by sheep. Even if some of the big landowners possessed these spacious spreads of apparent wilderness with no physical signs of boundaries or walls, the extent of their limits was known to and respected by the local people.

By contrast, as a result of the Enclosure Acts, many smaller farms had clearly defined boundaries, which were often marked by dry stone walls or hedges, but even so some of their land had the appearance of being uncultivated.

Much of the land had once been common land, but over the centuries it had been claimed by estate owners and farmers and enclosed to become private property. The outcome was that by the middle of the twentieth century very little genuine common land remained. Nonetheless, some had survived in isolated places. Such small parcels were widely respected by the local community as belonging to no particular person but available for use by all, and many farmers let their flocks of poultry or geese run free upon them. However, the fact that such pieces remained free of personal ownership was usually an indication that the land was worthless for cultivation of crops and probably valueless as a grazing area for cattle or sheep. Indeed, much of it survived in small plots as village greens or verges alongside rural lanes, where sheep grazed, but beyond the villages the land was usually left to its own devices.

Such a parcel existed beside a rough track that descended from the moor to join the lane linking the villages of Baysthorpe and Gaitingsby. The descent from the moor was very steep and the track was unsurfaced, being riddled with huge potholes that had been excavated by torrents of water to expose large rocks. A motor car would have great difficulty coping with such a rough surface and so the track was used only by tractors, horse-drawn vehicles or pedestrians. No one claimed ownership; the County Council Highways Authority said it was not theirs, which was why it did not have a smooth tarmac surface, and none of the local farmers or estates claimed ownership. It was not known whether it was an official bridleway, a public right of way or a private road and so it was left to its own devices, being relentlessly attacked and damaged by the severe weather of the higher moors. Lots of fast-moving water flowed from those heights, although much of it was channelled into narrow streams, or ghylls, as they were known, which flowed like miniature waterfalls down the hillside; in flood conditions, however, they frequently overflowed, but this surplus water rarely did any harm, other than scouring the surface of the hill.

Local people called it Beacon Bank, but this name did not appear on any maps. Centuries earlier there had been a beacon on the hill above, and close to the top of the track were the derelict remains of High Beacon House, a former farm. At the foot of the track, however, not far from the road between Baysthorpe and Gaitingsby, was Low Beacon Farm. It possessed land along the bottom of the dale and some steeply sloping fields that rose up the hillside. As the land rose towards the moors, it became steadily more rough and unusable, much of it consigned to heather, bracken and gorse with lots of ghylls flowing even in the summer months. While cattle enjoyed the pastures along the bottom of the dale, the rough land above was fit only for sheep.

Low Beacon Farm was owned by Baysthorpe Estate, and the tenant farmer was Henry Whitehead. Baysthorpe Estate had stated in writing that they did not own Beacon Bank; that statement had been made when Henry's father had asked them to repair the lane following some flood damage. The letter added that it appeared no one owned the lane, and Henry now accepted that. From time to time and for his own convenience, he would make running repairs such as filling in a hole or clearing a route for rainwater, but in spite of his attention the state of the surface grew steadily worse.

Henry was a hard-working man in his late forties, a strong man both physically and mentally, if a little dour. A well-built man almost six feet tall, he had very dark skin, a mop of jet black hair and dark eyes, which gave him an almost Mediterranean appearance. He was a good farmer with a superb dairy herd of Friesians and in his spare time he liked, as he put it, to 'mess about' in his shed; there he made things of metal, stone or wood, or a combination of them all; but everything he made was, so he reckoned, useful to have around the house and farm. Typical of his inventions was a long pole with a V-shaped fitting to the top, below which was a stout ring with a small net slung beneath it. It was, he said, for picking apples from high branches, the idea being you hooked the V around the stem, gave a quick tug and lo! The apple fell into the little net. It didn't always work and it took a long time to pick an entire tree full of apples. Sadly, not many of his inventions actually worked, such as his automatic egg cleaner, his triple-bladed turnip slicer or his mechanical coal shovel for kitchen fires. But he kept trying!

With two teenage sons, he was married to Gladys. She was a busy countrywoman who seemed to be involved in almost everything in the village – she was secretary of the parish council, secretary of St Hilda's Anglican Parochial Church Council, secretary of Baysthorpe Women's Institute, Chairman of Baysthorpe Agricultural Show Committee, President of the Baysthorpe and District Pony Club and more besides. She even ran a rota of volunteers, local village ladies who would visit lonely old people in the locality. If the old folks were unable to feed themselves or do their own shopping, for example, then Gladys's ladies would help. How on earth Gladys managed to fit everything into her day was one of those great mysteries of rural life, and it is not surprising that on most of the occasions I called at the farm to collect the insurance premiums she was out. Usually she left my money on the windowsill of the wash-house, but if Henry was working near the house he would be left in charge of the premiums.

Although the farm buildings were insured through the estate, Henry had some life and sickness insurances for Gladys and himself, a house contents policy, his private car insurance, insurance for his tractor and other implements, and selected insurance for his livestock. Like most farmers, his herd was not insured as a whole – few farmers could afford the cost and indeed few insurance companies, other than specialists or mutuals, accepted that kind of broad risk to groups of live animals.

On a fine spring afternoon in April, I called as usual to collect Henry's premiums, fully expecting the cash or perhaps a cheque to be waiting for me on the wash-house window-ledge. I was rather surprised to see Henry washing his hands in the kitchen. Dressed in muddy overalls, he beckoned me inside, saying Gladys had gone into the village to see somebody about the annual vegetable and produce show. It was about three o'clock, teatime in his world, so he asked if I'd fancy a cup of tea and some cake. I accepted with pleasure, and so, after sitting down with him in the kitchen to enjoy some pleasurable and entertaining incidental chatter about his daily routine, I pocketed the cheque and prepared to leave.

'Have you time to look at summat?' he asked as he accompanied me to the door.

'I can always make time.'

'Right, come with me.'

He led me across the vegetable garden, through his orchard of apple and pear trees and across a deserted paddock of long grass as he headed for the foot of Beacon Bank. During the short walk, he chattered about his work, how well his lambs had done that year and how his milk yield had increased. I could see that he was very happy with himself, but he didn't tell me what I was going to inspect. Then, when we reached the dry stone wall at the far end of the paddock, he halted and pointed.

'There, Matthew. What do you think of that?'

Ahead of us was a small stone structure of some kind. It was about as high as a telephone kiosk but three times as wide and twice as deep. From my vantage point, I could see that it had a frosted window on the side nearest us, currently standing open on its latch, and there was a door at the front, gleaming with fresh green paint. There were white letters on the door, but at that distance I couldn't read them. Everything looked very new and clean; even the cement in the stonework was very recent. It was not standing in Henry's grounds but was about twenty yards away from his boundary on a patch of land near the side of the lane that led up to Beacon Bank. There was a gate leading from Henry's paddock on to that lane, and he opened it and led me through.

'It looks very strong and new, but what is it?' I asked.

'Just you wait and see!'

As he led me towards it, I could read two letters in white on the door: WC. A toilet? Out here?

'It's a toilet!' I cried. 'So what's it doing here?'

'I put it here.' He beamed with obvious pride. 'Built it with my own fair hands. Just finished it this morning. Now you look at this, Matthew!'

By now we had reached the door, still smelling of fresh new paint, and he pulled it open. Inside, it looked exactly like an old earth closet except that the paint was new. There was a wooden box-type seat, painted in fresh dark green paint, and the hole was covered with a round wooden lid with a handle.

I wondered if this interior had come from an old earth closet, to be resurrected and given a new role in Henry's loo. I noticed pictures on the walls, some reading matter at the side of the seat and a proper toilet-roll holder complete with a new roll. And there was even a bolt on the inside of the door. But one thing was missing if this was indeed a WC. There was no water supply.

I must admit that for a moment I didn't know how to react, but I said, 'This looks like a work of art, Henry. A super loo, fresh smelling, too . . .' and I praised his workmanship before asking, 'But where's the water? It says WC on the door.'

'Ah, I'll show you. Come in.'

Inside he lifted the lid in the seat and said, 'Look down there.'

Directly below was a small gully, a stream of water that was in fact one of the ghylls from the moors.

'Well, blow me!' I laughed. 'Your own water supply!'

'I knew one of those ghylls ran underground somewhere about here so I did a bit of exploring and found it. Now, we get ramblers up and down this lane. Some use the hedgebacks but some come to my house asking to use the toilet, so I reckoned I could build one out here. I reckoned if I built over this running water, it would never need maintenance and the pipes won't freeze up in the winter. I reckon this is my best invention yet! And I can use it if I'm working on this part of the farm.'

I didn't like to tell him about the monks' latrines in the old abbey just over the hill, and congratulated him on his inventiveness and enterprise.

'I think it will be very popular,' I said, meaning every word. 'I'll pass the word around – it's not often you find a WC in the middle of the countryside like this. A wonderful idea, Henry.'

'I'm happy to keep an eye on it,' he said. 'Keep it stocked with paper and reading materials, make sure the water's always running, although it's never dried up all the time we've been living here . . .'

And so it was that Henry's toilet became a part of the landscape of Delverdale. It was a handsome stone building, quite suitable for the countryside in which it stood, and I later learned that it was well patronized by ramblers, some of whom took to scribbling messages of thanks and appreciation on the door and walls. I had no idea whether Henry required any kind of permission to build it at that location, nor was there any question of ownership of the land it occupied. Everyone accepted and admired Henry's toilet as a most useful addition to the local scenery.

Then disaster. Two youths from Middlesbrough stole a car from a pub car park in the town and managed to dodge the police as they set about a frantic and undoubtedly dangerous drive around the moors one Sunday afternoon. Somewhat inexplicably, they found themselves at the top of Beacon Bank and stepped out to admire the scenery, or perhaps to attend to the needs of nature, the latter being the more likely explanation if they had been drinking beer. Unfortunately, the driver did not set the handbrake and did not engage reverse gear to provide extra holding power while parked on the steep slope. While they were both out of the car, a Morris 10, it set off and started to career out of control down Beacon Bank.

Guided by the ruts in the lane, it gathered speed, and when it reached the more level part it hurtled on to the verge – and rammed Henry's smart new toilet. Fortunately, it was not occupied at the time. The two youths ran away but were seen by a sheep farmer as they tried to distance themselves from the event – sadly, they were never caught. Henry was left with a battered Morris 10 firmly embedded in the debris of his flattened toilet. He rang the police but it later emerged the Morris had not been insured; it had been parked on the pub car park bearing a 'For Sale' sign, so the rightful owner had not insured it because he had had no intention of taking it on the road. The thieves were not insured either, and I had to tell Henry that his toilet was not covered by his house insurance. He knew it was not covered by the estate's insurance either, because it was not built on his land, which of course meant that it was on the estate's land, and so was not 'within the curtilage of Low Beacon Farm'. There was also no way it could be covered by Baysthorpe Estate's policy. During these discussions, the owner of the wrecked car came to remove it and later I went to have a look at the remains of Henry's construction.

'It's the principle,' he said with some dejection in his voice. 'There was I, doing a service for the community, and along come some uncaring clowns from the town to wreck it all. And there's nothing anyone can do about it. Mind you, Matthew, it didn't cost much to build – the stones were lying about on the moors, I got the seat from an old earth closet that's been replaced by a WC and I had the cement and paint anyway. It cost nowt but a bit of my time. But it's the principle of the thing. But like Bruce and his spider, I might get round to rebuilding it if I can find the time.'

But he did not have to rebuild his toilet. Ramblers who had used it over the years learned of its demise and several local clubs joined together to raise funds to restore it. And so, within a few months, a brand new replica of Henry's toilet appeared and he was asked to formally open it. He did so by cutting a piece of toilet paper strung across the door.

It is still there on its piece of common land below the summit of Beacon Bank, still catering in fine style for passing ramblers and still served by fresh running water from the moors.

But I have no idea whether it was ever insured.

\*     \*     \*

It was inevitable that these experiences would lead to a discussion between Evelyn and me about the sort of toilets we would want in our next house, if and when we bought one. I made the point that if we bought an old house it would probably be equipped with an earth closet or perhaps an outdoor WC but it may not be blessed with an indoor water closet, either upstairs or downstairs. What did emerge, however, was that we should make sure we had a WC – that was the starting point.

Even if the house was old and in need of some restoration, a flush toilet was essential even if it was out of doors and even if it meant spending money on the conversion of an existing earth closet or some other outbuilding. I made the point that if we continued to use my house as an office, with clients arriving at any time of day or evening to discuss business, then it would be important to have for their use some proper downstairs toilet facilities, perhaps with a handbasin and towel. We did not want strangers wandering upstairs to use the toilet and, of course, a downstairs WC would be a huge asset for all our own domestic needs. We decided we could usefully have a WC downstairs and another outdoors, the latter being handy when gardening or doing any kind of outdoor work.

'So what about one upstairs?' I put to Evelyn.

'Oh, I'm not sure about that. It doesn't seem right, having a toilet upstairs near the bedrooms.'

I was quite surprised to hear her rather old-fashioned reaction to this, so I pointed out the benefits so far as night-time was concerned, or with children and visitors in the house, and that a WC did not smell like an earth closet – everything was flushed away down modern drains Such a toilet could be part of the bathroom, I added, saying I thought it a good idea to have an upstairs bathroom with a toilet nearby or even within it.

'So you're saying we should have three toilets?' She sounded alarmed. 'All water closets. One outdoors, one downstairs indoors and another upstairs indoors?'

'That sounds a good idea to me.'

'Isn't that a bit posh?'

'Posh? It's practical, I'd say.'

'We won't be buying something like Graindale Manor or Highfield Hall,' she said. 'And even my parents' place at the Unicorn doesn't have all that many toilets. There's just the one upstairs for guests and family, and one outside. People have to queue on a morning if they're full of guests.'

'Well, all I can suggest is that we wait to see what's on offer whenever we look at possible houses to buy. But we have made one decision – whatever we buy must have at least one water closet even if we have to fit it ourselves.'

'Don't you dare try and do that!' She laughed.

After our discussion, I felt my experience of other people's toilets had been of great benefit. And to have *three* water closets in one house must surely be an indication of one's social standing.

Or was I too flushed with enthusiasm?

# Five

*'I ran into a gate post and suffered
injuries to my dog.'*
From a claim form

One Wednesday while I was attending my 'surgery' at the bottle and jug of the Unicorn, a woman came to me and said, 'Ah, Mr Taylor, I'm glad I caught you.'

She was middle-aged with ruddy cheeks and iron grey hair, quite thickset, with sturdy low-heeled shoes on her feet and a headscarf round her hair. She was carrying one empty basket and another full of eggs – a countrywoman beyond doubt.

'Yes? Can I help?'

'My neighbour asked me to have a word with you if I saw you on your rounds.' She smiled. 'He'd like you to pop in for a chat when you're passing.'

'No problem. So who is this neighbour?'

She told me his name was Leopold Ripley, and he lived alone in a rented cottage next door to her farm. She was Libby Rutherford from Wether Hill Farm, which was on the southern edge of the moors midway between Gaitingsby and Baysthorpe; Mr Ripley occupied Wether Hill Farm Cottage, half a mile down a lane that ran alongside the farm's boundaries. Ripley's place was the only habitation down that lane – it was next door to the farm but by no means a close neighbour, and not the sort of place one would happen to be passing, because the lane, a private route, ran into the hills beyond it and eventually disappeared among the heather. It would mean a special journey, but I didn't mind that and promised I would visit him.

Mrs Rutherford had no idea why he wanted to speak to me, so I would go prepared with a wide range of leaflets and proposal forms. I was on the point of asking her a little more about Mr Ripley, whom I had never met, when another woman arrived and said, 'There you are, Libby! I thought you must have gone home. I was just going for a cup of tea and a bun and thought you'd like to join me.'

And so Libby was whisked away before I had time to learn anything about Mr Ripley, but as the pair departed I assured her I would call on him very soon. I was due to visit both Gaitingsby and Baysthorpe within the next few days as several clients in those villages had policies that were almost due for renewal. I'd try to deal with them all together to prevent unnecessary journeys and felt sure I could find time to visit Mr Ripley, particularly if it meant more business.

On the Friday following, therefore, I eased my way down the lane towards his cottage. It was rough and full of massive potholes, some containing water from a recent rainfall. There had been no attempt to surface the track, the only repairs being effected by depositing stones and ashes in some of the deeper holes in an attempt to make them more level. I was concerned for the springs of my car but Betsy seemed to cope without too much jarring, rattling and groaning, and at least half a mile after leaving the surfaced road I noticed a small stone house on my right. Smoke was rising from one of the chimneys, so it appeared that it was occupied.

As I approached it was almost hidden behind a hawthorn hedge, which had not been trimmed for years, but it looked comfortable and pretty, if a little neglected. Certainly some of the paintwork could have used a fresh coat, but the dark grey stonework was clean and its blue-tiled roof looked in good order. There was a gate through the high hedge and so I parked on the lane, collected my briefcase and made for the front door, which bore a heavy brass knocker. As I approached I could hear piano music coming from somewhere inside. At first I thought it must be the wireless, but I did not recognize the tune; then I realized that the pianist kept stopping and starting, rather like a child being taught how to play a piece. Not really wishing to interrupt, I waited until one of the short silences broke the spell, then rattled the knocker and waited.

Moments later, the door was opened by a rather short, bespectacled man in his seventies, who was wearing a cardigan, brown corduroy trousers and carpet slippers. He had a huge mop of unruly grey hair, an equally large grey beard and moustache, and a pipe with a glowing bowl poking through it all. I wondered how on earth he never set himself on fire, and whether any kind of fire insurance catered for people accidentally setting their beards alight. He peered at me over his little round spectacles and said, 'Yes?'

'Mr Ripley? Leopold Ripley?'

'Yes, that's me. And you are?'

'Taylor, Matthew Taylor from the Premier Assurance Association. I was asked to come and see you.'

'Were you?'

'Er, yes. That is why I am here. I couldn't ring in advance to make an appointment, as you don't have a telephone.'

'Noisy damned things, I'm told, always going off in the middle of the night or not going off at all, and you have to shout your head off to make yourself understood . . . I can manage without a telephone, thank you.'

And then he paused as if expecting me to leave. I wondered if he thought I was a telephone salesman. It was clear that I had to explain my presence.

'Mrs Rutherford from the farm along the road said you wanted to talk to me about something. Insurance, I expect.'

'You're not trying to sell me insurance, are you?'

'No, I'm just responding to a call. I was asked to pay you a visit. If there's some mistake, then I apologize for interrupting you and I'll leave . . .'

'Who did you say told you to call?'

'Mrs Rutherford from the farm. Libby Rutherford.'

'Oh, Libby, yes. A good friend. She brings me apple pies

and Yorkshire puddings, a very nice lady. Always makes sure I'm looked after. Makes damned good onion gravy, you know, wonderful with Yorkshire puddings. So why did she ask you to call?'

'She said you wanted to discuss something with me.'

'Did I?'

'Because I'm the insurance man for this agency I thought it was something to do with that. Life insurance, house insurance, fire insurance, car insurance, an endowment policy, perhaps?'

'Ah, no, I have no insurance, never thought it was necessary, and I don't have a car . . . so is that all?'

'Well, if you don't want any insurance there is no point in my wasting your time. I'll get back to my rounds, I'm on my way to Gaitingsby.'

'Ah, Gaitingsby! Nice little place. Libby collects my shopping from there, you know. She looks after me very well indeed. Takes me into Guisborough sometimes for an outing. I buy her lunch as a thank-you. Now, why did she want you to come and see me? Can you tell me that?'

'I was hoping you might tell me.' I laughed.

'Well, don't just stand there, Mr Taylor, you'd better come in if Libby has sent you. I do believe the kettle was boiling just as you rang, and perhaps if we have a nice cup of tea we might be able to work something out. Come in, that's if you're not in a desperate rush to get anywhere.'

'I'm not in a desperate rush.' I found myself growing rather curious about this character. 'I'm renewing a few policies in the area, but my work can hardly be described as urgent or desperate, so if you did want to see me about something in particular, we might be able to jog our memories if we give it a little more time and talk it through.'

'Well spoken. What was your name again?'

'Taylor, Matthew Taylor, from the Premier.'

'Ah, good, well, follow me.'

He led me into a rather dark room, which faced south. Apparently smothered in papers of various kinds, it had a window overlooking a hay meadow, but most of the glass was obscured by masses of ivy, which had been allowed to rampage across the building. A beautiful grand piano filled a corner near the window while a coal fire burned in the grate; a blackened kettle was sitting on a hob and singing gently as it puffed small clouds of steam into the room.

'Sit down, Mr Taylor, do sit down, if you can find a chair without any paper on it . . . There, at the other side of the window. Move that stuff on to the floor. I always think the floor is the best place to keep sheets of paper and music – at least it can't fall off the floor. Now, tea. I think I may have a mug somewhere, so how do you like your tea?'

'Milk please, no sugar.'

'A man after my own heart. Now, where did I put the teapot?'

And, as I sat in that room, my eyes became accustomed to the darkness and I could see that every possible surface was littered with music and blank sheets of paper; lots of books lined an inner wall and I could see they were all concerned with music, composers and composition, some containing scores from classical composers like Mozart, Beethoven and Chopin, along with famous stage shows, while other books were little more than collections of various pieces of lesser known piano music.

Eventually, Mr Ripley returned with a tray bearing mugs, a milk bottle, a teapot and a few biscuits. I realized he lived alone – a widower perhaps? Or a bachelor who had never married?

'My mother said I should never present guests with a milk bottle, but when you can't find the jug I find it is very useful to hold the milk.' He grinned. 'You don't mind?'

'Our jug at home is just like your bottle!' I joked.

Having discarded his pipe somewhere, he fussed over me for a few moments, making sure I was comfortably seated, had somewhere to put my mug and plate of biscuits and that my tea was to my liking, then he settled down on his piano stool and placed his mug and plate on a side table nearby.

'There we are! Mr Taylor, isn't it? Well, here we are, all nicely done. So, tell me, why did you want to see me?'

I began to wonder how long this sequence of peculiar exchanges was going to continue and, not wishing to repeat myself indefinitely, said, 'Was it something to do with your music? I'm an insurance agent – Mrs Rutherford asked me to call, so you must have talked to her about it, whatever it was.'

'Ah! Music! You mentioned Gaitingsby, did you not? A few moments ago?'

'Yes, I'm going there next.'

'That rings a bell, yes indeed it does. Gaitingsby. And music. Now, what do you know about maypoles, Mr Taylor?'

'Maypoles? Not a lot, although we danced around one at school, years ago.'

'It's all coming back to me now. You mentioned music and Gaitingsby. Yes, I've got it! I am a composer, Mr Taylor, as you might know. You may know the name if you are of a musical disposition. Leopold Ripley. I specialize in folk music but can turn my hand to most other kinds. Always the piano, though. I compose only for the piano, and if people want to use my music as the basis, say, for a violin piece, guitar or whatever, then I have no objections provided I receive due credit for my work. After all, many composers have made great use of the work of the greats.'

'I see you have lots of music in the house, books and so forth. Did you want me to advise you on some suitable insurance?'

'No, it wasn't that. It was to do with the maypole . . . Ah, I remember. A friend of mine has a maypole he wishes to donate to a suitable village and he asked if I knew of a likely recipient, Mr Taylor. Yes indeed. I had words with the parish council of Gaitingsby, who spoke to Lord Gaitingsby, who has a suitable patch of land.'

'There is a patch of grass in the village near the river,' I said. 'It's flat and easily accessible, not used for anything in particular.'

'The Green. It's a sort of an unofficial village green. I know

117

it, Mr Taylor. It is owned by His Lordship's estate, but he is quite happy for a maypole to be erected there. I shall get my friend to donate the pole. In fact, I think I have already set things in motion.'

'It will be nice to have a maypole in Gaitingsby,' I said.

'My sentiments exactly, Mr Taylor. Which is why I am composing some special music for the children and young people to dance to. Around the maypole. Gaitingsby's very own maypole music, which a friend will transcribe for the violin and which we shall use for the opening ceremony. On May Day next, of course.'

'It sounds very interesting and exciting, so how can I help?'

'You are an insurance agent, you say?'

'Yes.'

'So how can you help with a project of this kind, Mr Taylor? Is that why you are here?'

'I was asked to call in to see you about something,' I tried again.

'Ah, yes. Libby sent you, you say? I must have mentioned something to her . . . Ah yes, got it! Insurance. The pole will need to be insured, Mr Taylor, in case it falls down and kills someone or tumbles through someone's roof, or people get injured. Lord Gaitingsby insists on having it insured against all risks before he will give his approval for it to be erected on his land. He doesn't want anyone claiming damages from him. That was it. Thank you for reminding me.'

'Will it be a permanent fixture?' I put to him.

'Yes and no. I think we shall leave it standing throughout the summer months, but perhaps in winter we shall lower it and put it in storage, although I can't imagine what sort of shed will be long enough to cope with a maypole and, of course, while it is down, we shall have it repainted and maintained in whatever way a maypole is maintained.'

'I am sure the Premier will be happy to insure it, Mr Ripley. I will need to know a few facts about it, like its value, the sort of risks you need to be insured against, the owner's name and who will be responsible for paying the premium. I think the company would agree to an annual payment but you might find there are conditions attached, almost certainly from the safety aspect.'

'Absolutely, Mr Taylor. I believe that is precisely what Lord Gaitingsby has in mind. He is very keen to ensure the utmost safety for the maypole, and those who make use of it.'

'I ought to add that there is also the matter of public liability to consider especially if children are to dance around it and play around it while it is *not* fulfilling its May Day functions as well as when it is. So who is the owner, Mr Ripley?'

'Do you know, Mr Taylor, I can't remember the damned fellow's name.'

'You are talking of the present owner. I mean, who will own it when he donates it to the village? The parish council? A special committee? The Women's Institute? Lord Gaitingsby's estate?'

'Oh, that will be me. My friend is giving it to me because he has no use for a maypole right now, but because I have nowhere to put it I am giving it to the village.'

'Ah, I see. So you are really the donor . . .'

'But he wants it to go to a good home, Mr Taylor. I discussed the village idea with him.'

'Then if you are giving it to the village, the village will be the owner.'

'Ah, of course. You're absolutely right. So at the moment my friend is the owner, but he is giving it to me so I will become the owner for a while, until I donate it to the village, who will then be the real owners. It is all very complicated, Mr Taylor.'

'I need to know precisely who will be the owner during the time it is established on the Green, Mr Ripley. For my proposal form. I can't just say 'Gaitingsby village'.'

'Very true, Mr Taylor.' He now seemed to remember my name even if he managed to forget most other things. I thought, however, that once I disappeared from his sight he'd forget all about me. 'There is a committee, you see, the Gaitingsby Maypole Committee.'

119

'And is there a chairman of that committee, or a secretary?'

'Talk to Alastair Dowling about that, Mr Taylor, he's Lord What-do-you-call-him's estate agent.'

'Yes, I know him.'

'Well, he will become responsible for the maypole once it arrives in the village, but at the moment it belongs to my friend and I can't remember the fellow's name . . . I've got it jotted down somewhere, Mr Taylor. I think perhaps I should write all this down then when you come again, you can fill your forms in and we shall be insured to His Lordship's liking.'

'I think the best thing for me to do is to leave a selection of proposal forms with you, then the moment things start happening you can contact me and we can finalize all this. If you talk to Libby, she can contact me at the Unicorn, or telephone me, and I'll come straight away.'

'An admirable arrangement, Mr Taylor.'

'Meanwhile, I shall contact my District Office to try and get some idea of the cost of the premiums. I am sure we already insure other maypoles, but it's rather a specialized type of cover and I am not sure of the premiums.'

'Well, I must say I am pleased we have got all that sorted out, Mr Taylor. Now, did you say you would teach the children how to dance around the maypole?'

'Me? No, I never said that!' I said, somewhat shocked that he regarded me as a maypole dancing expert.

'I thought you had danced around one as a child, and that you would know the routine with all those coloured ribbons. We will need an experienced person to guide the children through those intricacies, Mr Taylor, and I think you might be just the fellow. I will write some special music for the opening ceremony and a dance or two, and you could train the children . . . I think we will make a good team, Mr Taylor. I am so pleased Libby sent you to see me.'

It was clear that, whatever the real story of the maypole, Leopold Ripley was rather confused about the whole affair, so I decided the wisest action on my part was to leave before things became even more complicated, and then to have words with Alastair Dowling, Lord Gaitingsby's estate agent. As I was heading for Gaitingsby next, that was not a problem. I bade farewell to Leopold, promising him I would return very soon with details of the insurance proposals for the maypole, and he saw me to the door with a smile of happiness somewhere deep within his whiskers. His pipe was still missing; I guessed he'd left it in the kitchen while making our tea and hoped it was not likely to set something on fire.

Leaving him to puzzle over my purpose for calling, I made for Gaitingsby and decided my first call should be Alastair Dowling. I needed to get the matter of the maypole sorted out.

'You wouldn't get much sense out of Leopold,' he told me when I was settled in his office, 'but he writes very good music. It's his living and he is well known in certain spheres. And, yes, he is writing some special music for the inauguration of the Gaitingsby maypole.'

From Alastair I learned that a gentleman called Eugene Talbot, a wealthy philanthropist who had been born in Gaitingsby sixty years earlier and was now living in Kent, had decided he wanted to leave something to the village for posterity and had decided upon a maypole. He wanted to have one specially made for the occasion, and due to Leopold's strong association with folk music, and the fact that he lived so close to the village, Mr Talbot had contacted him for advice about the height, colours and general design of the proposed pole, including the most suitable type of base.

Mr Talbot had never offered to give the pole to Leopold – once the edifice was complete, it would be transported direct to the site in Gaitingsby and erected with due ceremony. Alastair told me that Lord Gaitingsby was very enthusiastic about the whole idea and was very happy to allow the pole to stand on his land, the Green, and for the public to make full use of it on May Day.

'So who is the legal owner of the pole?' I asked.

'Well, it will belong to the village,' said Alastair. 'It won't be ours, we will have no responsibility for it; all the estate

121

has done is allow it to stand on its land, which is why His Lordship insisted on suitable insurance. We don't want to be landed with a claim of any kind if something goes wrong.'

'But surely someone is responsible for it?' I put to him.

'If I were you, I'd speak to Jean Sampson.'

'Thanks, I'll call on her next.'

Jean Sampson, a retired shorthand typist who had worked in local government, was secretary of Gaitingsby parish council. She was in the garden of her neat bungalow when I found her, and over the gate, I explained the reason for my call and she smiled understandingly.

'Leopold does get rather confused about things, but yes, the parish council is taking responsibility for the maypole. We can meet costs for maintenance and insurance from our precept, and one of our members with a large barn has offered storage space during the winter months. Everything is in hand, Mr Taylor, all we are waiting for is the maypole itself, and we have been promised it will arrive in good time for its inauguration on May Day.'

'So what about its insurance?' I pressed. 'I was asked to approach Leopold because His Lordship insists on proper insurance.'

'I'm not quite sure how Leopold got himself involved in this at all, but our insurance is done through the county council at County Hall; if, for example, we install a new street light, we inform the county council, who add it to their policy.'

I knew how the system worked. All the county council vehicles, for example, were held on a huge single policy, which was issued to the county council by a very large insurance company; that comprehensive policy included all other areas of insurance from buildings to roads via personal liability to fire risks.

'The maypole will be included on that policy.' Jean smiled.

And so all my running around came to nought, although I did learn a little about maypole insurance and something about a composer called Leopold.

On 29 April, a splendid maypole in bright new colours, one

122

of the tallest in the north of England, was erected on the Green at Gaitingsby. Meanwhile, careful plans had been made for the opening ceremony, which would take place two days later, on May Day. It would include maypole dancing by the village schoolchildren (not tutored by me), along with a picnic and other games, sports, music and entertainment.

Music for the maypole dance had been specially composed by Leopold Ripley and the formal cutting of the ribbon, which would mark the beginning of the celebrations, was to be undertaken by Lord Gaitingsby.

Evelyn, Paul and I all went along on the day and it was a splendid occasion that evoked warm memories of the calmness of life in rural England. As we moved among the crowds, I spotted Leopold; he came across to me and said, 'Mr Taylor, how well those children danced. You must be very proud of them – clearly you are a natural and highly talented teacher of maypole dancing. Do call again whenever you are passing. I'd love to have another chat with you. We might work together on some other project.'

'I'd be delighted,' I said, hoping he never asked me to sing.

If my attempts to secure insurance on a maypole came to nothing, it was a different story with Arnold Thacker's farm. It was called Baysthorpe Castle and occupied a lofty site beside a narrow road that skirted the lower slopes of the moors between Baysthorpe and Freyerthorpe. The sturdy grey stone farm buildings were visible at a considerable distance, yet close up it was virtually hidden by the deciduous trees that flourished on the lower slopes of the dale. From a distance, the farm looked like a ruined castle – which is precisely what it was. In the past, it had been a thriving and historic castle with links to national affairs and, although a lot of it was now derelict part of it was occupied by Arnold and his wife and part served as farm buildings.

Arnold telephoned me one evening and asked if I would call 'Ti hev a chat aboot some hinsurance for t'farm buildings.'

123

'I thought your farm was owned by Gaitingsby Estate,' was my immediate response. 'They insure their own properties, Arnold, all you need worry about is insurance of your personal belongings, machinery, valuable livestock and so forth.'

I had met Arnold on several previous occasions, one of his main haunts being the market at the Unicorn, where he sold sides of ham, bacon, brawn and other products.

'Aye, but ah've just bowt t'castle,' he said. 'T'estate's selling up and me being t'sitting tenant gat hodden it for a good price. Noo it's mine, thoo sees, seea ah'll hetti hev it hinsured.'

'You've bought the castle?'

'Aye, has a hedge against hinflation, seea my haccountant said. He thowt it was a reet good hidea, mak it me own, thoo sees, Mr Taylor. Hall mine for keeps . . . A good hinvestment, ti be sure on't.'

'I'd agree with that, Arnold. I'm thinking of buying a house for the same reason, so well done. And, yes, I can come along to talk to you about insurance.'

And so it was that a few days later when I was in Baysthorpe village during one of my canvassing rounds I called to have a chat with Arnold. I had telephoned in advance to make sure he would be on the premises and was fully armed with all the information I thought he would require.

I'd researched various types of farm insurance for him and was confident I could produce something to suit his requirements – after all, this was nothing more than a fairly routine farm proposal, which should cater for things like fire, damage, theft, personal belongings, machinery, certain livestock, growing crops and milk insurance, breaches of the boundary fences and animals straying through gates left open by ramblers, accidental injuries, lightning strikes to cattle, and so forth. There was a lot to consider but much of it was routinely incorporated into farm insurance policies and the final outcome would depend on precisely what Arnold wished to insure and how much he could afford.

Although I had seen Arnold's farm from a distance and known of it since I was a child I had never visited the former castle. During my lifetime, it had never been accessible to the general public because it had always been occupied and used as a working farm, consequently there had never been a reason for making a visit. Whereas many former castles and pele towers were ruined and unoccupied, allowing centuries of weather and vandals to destroy them, Baysthorpe Castle had been lucky. It had always had people living within its ancient walls, even if the outer shell was now beyond repair, and I wondered what I would find within those walls. As I drove Betsy over the narrow thirteenth-century packhorse bridge that spanned the River Delver just below the farm, I could see the distinctive shape of the castle with its four square towers and high stone walls. Even if the tops of the towers were missing and the upper portion of the walls absent through the passage of time and weather – and probably people removing stones for their own building work – the place had the appearance of an ancient but once-powerful stronghold. Long ago, another high wall, also fortified, had completely enclosed the central towers and courtyard but that had long gone, although a few remnants could be seen among the dry stone walls and undergrowth if one knew where to look. There was no sign of a moat, however, and most of the dry stone walls hereabouts were constructed from stones that had been removed from the castle.

As I drove around the huge place, I found the main gate. There was no physical gate now, just a massive gap in the thick walls, but an entrance tower remained at each side while the opening gave access to the courtyard. Even from my exterior viewpoint, I could see that the courtyard was full of clucking hens and smelly manure heaps – it was now a traditional farmyard. As I looked for somewhere to park, I could see that the towers were occupied, because they had curtains at the windows, chimney pots and modern doors. Even if the original upper floors were missing, the building had been re-roofed at a lower level to provide domestic living accommodation. From my viewpoint, it seemed that all four square towers were in use.

I checked my watch and found it was eleven thirty; I reckoned I had enough time to discuss things with Arnold before his dinner time. Dinner time in the moors and dales was around midday; supper time was in the evening. I found a parking place on some grass beyond the walls, collected my briefcase and set about finding Arnold or some other occupant. He saw me first.

A thickset man in his late forties, he had a round, cheerful face beneath a flat cap that bore signs of having been worn for decades without being cleaned. On his feet were large black leather clogs with wooden soles, a common form of footwear in the farms of this dale, and he had brown leather knee-length leggings beneath his corduroy trousers. A dark grey working jacket covered a thick collarless shirt, and I noticed his trousers were held up by binder twine instead of a belt. This was his working garb, which he also wore when he came to the market.

'Ovver 'ere, Mr Taylor,' he called from the dark green doorway of one of the square towers, the one at the north-east. 'T'missus 'as t'kettle on.'

I went across and he admitted me, showing me into the dark interior, where my first sight was of a stone staircase.

'Up yonder,' he said. 'Fost door on t'fost landing.'

I found myself in a large and airy room at first-floor level; it was fitted out like a kitchen, with a black Yorkist range in which a fire was blazing, and I could smell roast beef cooking. Then I heard footsteps on the stairs and a woman appeared. She was about the same size as Arnold with a cheerful but weathered face, her body concealed by a large hessian apron – a coarse apron, as it was known hereabouts, or, in local dialect, a cooarse appron. Arnold introduced me to his wife, Kitty.

'Sit yourself down, Mr Taylor.' She pointed to a chair at the kitchen table. 'I won't be a minute.'

As I settled down, she placed a knife and fork before me, with two similar settings nearby, got out the salt and pepper cellars, put side plates near my cutlery and then a large pint-sized glass.

'Oh, I don't want to interrupt your dinner,' I began. 'I can come back later . . .'

'Arnold likes to talk while he eats, he says it makes his brain work better, gives it fuel, Mr Taylor, and it's his dinner time anyroad – he allus eats about half eleven, because he has his breakfast at half five, so he gets a bit hungry by this time o' day. So sit yourself there, I shan't be long. You do like roast beef and Yorkshire puddings, do you? And cauliflower, sprouts and potatoes, with a few carrots and a bit o' turnip? You look like a growing lad to me and growing lads need good grub on a regular basis, 'specially when they work hard.'

I knew there was little point in declining this offer; it was an ancient custom in the moors that anyone arriving at meal time, stranger, friend or business acquaintance, would be expected to sit down and join the meal. Quite often, they were never asked – a place was set for them and they were expected to sit there without being invited. Happily, I knew of this custom even though it had surprised me on this occasion by being rather early. While Arnold was washing his hands and preparing for his meal somewhere beyond that room, his wife worked in virtual silence until there were three huge plates of food on the table. Everything was on those plates, there were no tureens or serving utensils, and as the plate arrived at Arnold's place he appeared and sat down without a word.

'Ah'm like a big car when it comes ti eeating, Mr Taylor.' He always addressed me formally even though I used his first name. That was another custom in the moors – people of the professional classes were afforded that kind of respect, and he thought I was of that class, because I wore a suit for work. 'Big cars need a lot o' fuel, Mr Taylor, but they keep gahin langger than little 'uns and go faster an' all. That's me, work 'ard and eat a lot to keep mi strength up.'

And he started to tuck into the meal, which was my signal to do likewise. As he trenched with all the enthusiasm of someone who'd not eaten for a week, he told me about his farm. It had been built sometime during the early eleventh century, with additions and alterations up to the fourteenth. It was similar in design to Danby Castle in nearby Eskdale, but smaller than Bolton Castle in Wensleydale, Gilling Castle in Ryedale and Sheriff Hutton Castle near York, all still in private hands. Arnold explained that each of the four towers of his castle had once borne stone carvings of the coats of arms of all the families associated with the castle – the Latimers, Bruces and De Ros – but they had been thrown aside when the upper walls had been demolished for their stone. These old carvings had been found and were now in his cellar, he told me. The former dungeon, in other words. He told me that all four towers were currently in use as his house – one of them (the one we were now using) was the kitchen, with a lounge upstairs; another tower was their bedroom with a bathroom, the third tower was another bedroom with a bathroom and the fourth was a small single room with an office downstairs, and a toilet with washbasin.

'Hall mod cons as they say nowadays.' He grinned.

He explained that the courtyard was rather smaller than expected for a castle but it made a good place to stack his manure and keep his hens, while the stone buildings around the interior and exterior, such as the castle's former barns, stables and storerooms, were now used for similar purposes – as implement sheds, barns, haysheds, stores, cowhouses, stables and pigsties.

'T'awd kitchin is a henhouse noo,' he said. 'Ah've still got t'original fireplace in there but there's a lot o' staircases that lead up ti neeawhere now that t'top storeys 'ave gone. Ah'd better let thoo have a leeak at t'Great Hall afoore thoo goes. It's t'biggest room in t'house an' we use it for parties and things . . . We allus have oor Kessimas dinner in there, oor yance-a-year family git tigither.'

Whilst he ate, he chattered about the old castle, saying one of Henry VIII's wives lived here as a girl long before she married the old rogue, and it had also been the scene of important meetings between other kings, government officials and members of the local nobility. Another of its functions was to host an early Assize Court and the chair used by the travelling

128

judge was still present in the Great Hall. Arnold had no idea when it had last been used for this purpose, although, he went on, the local Baysthorpe and Gaitingsby Court Leet continued to use the room. Although in their early days courts leet dealt with minor breaches of the peace and appointed parish constables, their powers were reduced in 1887 as the English system of courts and policing was rationalized. Nonetheless, courts leet continued to administer and supervise a variety of local matters, including those concerning common and wasteland, disputes of various kinds, such as mineral or mining rights, and matters of access to greens and commons, repairs to highways and the blocking of public rights of way. One even had an ale-tasting duty. Arnold wasn't quite sure what his local court leet actually did, although its twelve good men and true came to his Great Hall for their annual dinner.

I realized Arnold's plate was empty even though he had chattered almost non-stop, and then he reached over to the breadboard, chopped himself a huge chunk of bread and proceeded to wipe his plate with it, eating the gravy-impregnated slice with obvious enjoyment. Now it was time for his sweet, today apple pie and custard, which would be taken on the same plate. I followed suit, my stomach feeling full to bursting point, and afterwards he slid his chair slightly away from the table, accepted a mug of tea from Kitty and sighed with evident contentment.

'Now then, Mr Taylor, ah've telled thoo summat aboot this awd spot – dis thoo think we have a deal?'

'I'll need some more information,' I said. 'Acreage of the farm, for example, any unusual features or valuable aspects, any particularly valuable items in your house if you want contents insurance, any valuable animals like a bull or stallion. Then I will help you complete a proposal form and, after that, District Office will place a valuation on your property – they might even want to send a specialist to have a look at your farm or impose some conditions if there is something of special value, like that judge's chair . . .'

'It's been there five or six hundred years,' he said. 'Ah can't see onnybody would want to pinch an awd chair like yon.'

'That's exactly the sort of thing somebody would pinch!' I said. 'But it helps if you're not open to the public.'

'We are thinking o' takking in lodgers, holiday-makers, bed-and-breakfast folks. Ah'm telled there's a bit of a demand for an interesting spot in t'countryside now that folks are getting aboot a bit.'

'If I were you, I'd not mention that on your proposal form, Arnold, it might increase your premiums, especially in relation to theft of your belongings. It's never easy getting insurance against theft when a building is used by lots of other people who are virtual strangers.'

'Well, we 'aven't definitely decided to do that.'

'Good. If you're just thinking about it, we needn't make reference to it just yet, but if you go ahead with the plan then we might have to add a special clause to cater for it.'

He seemed to think that because his home and outbuildings had existed for several hundred years without catching fire or being washed away in a flood, they would never suffer such indignities in the future, but I had to point out there was now an increasing use of electrical goods within the home, open fires were still being used, an increasing number of people were smoking cigarettes and cigars (including more women), and there was the ever-present risk of lightning strikes. And those were just some of the sources of fire risks.

I reminded him of storms and pestilence, subsidence and floods, other potential forms of damage to growing crops, like hailstorms, the actions of travelling thieves and vandals, disease and sickness, which could affect him and his wife, livestock risks such as straying on the road and causing accidents, and the possibility that insurance to the old building might be a problem if woodworm existed . . .

I explained much of that as we toured his range of buildings, and, looking across his expansive fields, woodland and moorland, I came to realize he owned a very impressive spread.

His son, he told me, was presently in the army, having joined up for the war and decided to stay in REME, and he still had ten years to serve before leaving, upon which he intended to take over the farm from his parents. Their daughter had married a builder, and was showing no interest in farming, although she would eventually own half the old castle and grounds. Continuity was a good thing, I agreed. I told him there was a basic but all-embracing farm insurance policy, which covered all the normal risks and catered for all the regular problems experienced on farms and by farmers; it seemed highly suitable for his case, albeit with some slight adjustments due to the curious nature of the house and its history. He led me into his office inside one of the towers, and I was impressed by its tidiness and air of efficiency. We completed a proposal form together, and although I could not give him a precise figure he made it known that he had enough money to pay the premiums, whatever they were.

For all his uncultured country manner, I believed him. I said I would despatch his proposal to District Office the moment I returned home and would be in touch once I had a firm indication of the cost. A few days after posting Arnold's very comprehensive proposal form, I received a call from a clerk in our District Office in Ryethorpe.

'Mr Taylor,' said the prim voice of a well-spoken woman, 'I have to query the proposal from Mr Thacker of Baysthorpe Castle. I am sure you will appreciate that our terms for historic buildings, castles and country mansions in particular, are substantially different from those for normal domestic policies. With castles and large houses that are open to the public we have to consider the risks presented by falling tiles, slates and copings, holes in the ground, defective railings and staircases and other factors that may be affected by the age and method of construction of the premises. That adds substantially to the premium.'

'But this is not a castle,' I said. 'It's a farm. He wants farm insurance.'

'But we are led to believe from the proposal form that it is

131

an historic castle complete with a dungeon and Great Hall. Even the address suggests that.'

'It is a former castle, mostly in a ruined state, and part of it is occupied by Mr Thacker and his wife, who use it as a farm. He has just bought it from the local estate, and so far as falling tiles or coping stones are concerned, the public does not have access. That kind of risk is not a factor here.'

'Nonetheless, Mr Taylor, falling tiles and coping stones, or defective staircases and railings could cause injury to Mr Taylor and his wife to the extent that there may be a serious accident and they might be off work due to their injuries. And, of course, a falling tile or coping stone could kill a valuable farm animal or cause further damage to the structure, or even to a motor vehicle or an agricultural machine. And surely visitors do call, such as vets, salesmen, doctors, the postman and so forth. One must consider all the risks – after all, that is our role. I am not saying we cannot accept his proposal, what I am saying is that we need to place the building and its surrounds within the correct category. In other words, is it a castle or is it a farm?'

'It's a farm,' I said with as much emphasis as I could muster. 'With a dwelling house and farm buildings.'

'Then might I suggest you rephrase some of the wording in the proposal? Perhaps you should not mention the dungeon as such – call it a cellar. And the Great Hall could be described as the dining room. The courtyard could be the foldyard or stackyard. And the address might be 'Baysthorpe Castle Farm' which, I would suggest, is more accurate if the castle part of the complex is a mere ruin. I need to get this past our supervisors, you see, and if the present terminology is used, I fear they will levy a very high premium, as they would if the property was a castle.'

'Isn't that cheating?' I asked. 'Or at the least being dishonest?'

'No, the castle is no longer a castle, is it? It is not functioning as a castle, it is not open to the public and it is not being besieged by warring tribes or bus loads of tourists. It's like having an hotel in a former woollen mill. You wouldn't insure the hotel against attacks on the weaving machinery, would you? The fact that the farm occupies the site of a former castle is not relevant; what is relevant is that Mr Thacker's premises are a working farm with a domestic dwelling and outbuildings, and they need to be covered both by agricultural and domestic insurance policies. If you would care to suggest those few amendments, I think you will find Mr Thacker's premiums will be considerably reduced but just as effective.'

I agreed and asked her to return the form to me, when I would have another chat with Arnold. The form arrived by post the following morning and so I rang Arnold to explain the situation and to ask about a suitable time to pay him a visit so that the amended form could be signed. He said either that evening, the next evening or any time the following day would be fine. He also said he thought the Premier was a very good company because they'd suggested making changes which would save him money without reducing the coverage.

'I'll be out in the dale tomorrow evening,' I told him. 'I'm teaching my wife to drive, so I could call round and get the form signed. I can fill it in from the information I've already got, it just needs your signature.'

'Neea trouble,' he agreed. 'Come when thoo likes. Ah might be milking but it dissn't tak an age ti sign a bit o' paper.'

Evelyn's sister, Maureen, said she would look after Paul for a couple of hours while I took Evelyn for a lesson and she added that she didn't mind if we popped into a pub for a drink, just to give Evelyn a break. And so we sallied forth on a lovely evening with Evelyn guiding Betsy along the lanes, down the steep hills and around the sharp corners as if she had been doing so for years. I took her through Lexingthorpe High Street, which was always busy, then into Guisborough for a tour of the town to give her some practice with junctions, roundabouts, reversing into narrow roads, doing three-point turns and even coping with traffic lights, all of which presented no difficulties to her. Then it was time to return home, calling at Baysthorpe Castle on the way.

When we arrived, Arnold Thacker had finished milking and was swilling out the floor of the cowhouse. 'Five minutes, Mr Taylor, then ah'll be with yer. Fetch that missus of thine in, give 'er a leeak roond.'

And so it was that Evelyn was given a guided tour of the interior of the castle walls, first by me and then by Arnold when he joined us. Although he had no knowledge of the formal history of the place, much information had been passed down verbally through his family, who, it transpired, had lived here since the seventeenth century. As we stood in the courtyard, I repeated the suggested alterations and he nodded his agreement and understanding.

'Neea problem, Mr Taylor, neea problem. Mind, t'reet name for t'spot is Baysthorpe Castle Farm, but folks hereaboots just call it t'Castle. T'estate allus called it Castle Farm, but somehow it's gitten shortened.'

'I think the estate would refer to it as a farm for the same reasons as the Premier, to reduce the premiums.'

During our chat, Evelyn was moving around the courtyard, admiring the structure of the four square towers, the sturdy walls and range of outbuildings, then Mrs Thacker appeared and took her into the Great Hall, and through to more of the internal rooms. By the time Arnold and I had finished our business, the women reappeared, Evelyn having thoroughly enjoyed her tour.

We were about to move away when Evelyn cocked her head and said, 'I can hear water. Running water. Is there a burst?'

'Nay, lass, that's t'well. Thoo can only 'ear it sometimes, nut that we use it noo, we deearn't, we've watter on tap, but it was used when this was t'castle.'

I groaned inwardly. If there was a well, perhaps it should be mentioned on the proposal form. A well could be dangerous . . . Somebody or something might fall into it.

'A well?' I asked. 'Where is it, Arnold?'

'Under yon midden,' he said, pointing to a huge pile of

manure. 'It's allus been under yon pile, since we stopped usin' it. We nivver mak use on it nooadays and neeabody can tumble doon because t'covers allus under yon pile o' muck. But there's allus watter runnin' in and oot.'

I had no wish to ignore its presence, because if something did go wrong, such as a child falling into it, or even a pig or cow, at some future date, then the farm insurance would not cover the incident. Both Arnold and the victim needed to be covered against any risks presented by the well.

'How deep is it?' I asked, as I was wondering how best to tackle this.

'Bottomless,' he said with glee. 'Thoo can drop a brick doon there and it taks ages ti hit t'watter. It nivver floods, an' all t'rainwatter from these roofs an' buildings an' t'courtyard all drains inti yon well. It drains oot somewhere doon near that awd bridge on t'river.'

'We should include it in a description of the premises,' I said. 'Under the heading of special features.'

'It's already there.' He grinned. 'Ah put it doon under t'courtyard entry. Ah called it a drain. It is a drain, eh?'

'Yes,' I said, recalling I had mentioned a drain when I had filled in the form. 'It is a drain.'

When we left, Mrs Thacker gave Evelyn a dozen eggs and thanked us both for our attention. A few days later, Arnold was granted his farm insurance for much less than it would have cost to insure the castle, and for that he promised to buy me a drink next time he saw me at the Unicorn.

Evelyn and I had time for a quick drink at the Angel before heading home, and she thanked me for the unexpected tour of Baysthorpe Castle, saying how wonderful it must be to own a house with that kind of character.

'They're not easy to insure, or to maintain.' I expressed my caution at her suggestion.

'But not impossible,' she countered.

'Like you passing your driving test,' I retorted. 'I think you should apply to take your test.'

'Oh, I'm not ready.'

*Nicholas Rhea*

'You're as ready as you will ever be. You can cope with anything on the road and I know you've been swotting up the Highway Code. Once you get the date, you'll have time to take professional lessons to iron out any rough edges, so I think you should get an application form from the post office.'

'I've already got one.' She blushed.

'Then send it off tomorrow!'

# Six

*'I ran over a man. He admitted it was his fault as
he had been run over before.'*
From a claim form

E velyn had not been asked to undertake a large amount of
supply teaching during recent months; those duties she
had been offered had all been of short duration, two or three
days at the most, and were usually requests for her to stand
in for someone at short notice. Although she had not yet passed
her driving test, she had accepted the offers and I'd had no
difficulty transporting her to the schools in question on days
when public transport was not available – some moorland
villages did not have a railway station and many did not have
a bus service. In fact, she drove there and back to get more
experience on the roads and I became the passenger.
Fortunately, we'd had no worries accommodating baby Paul
during those occasions because Evelyn's sister, Maureen, was
keen to have him as he was good company and a playmate
for her own children.

It was inevitable, however, that one day there would be a
clash of commitments, and it began with a phone call at teatime
one Tuesday. The phone rang just before five o'clock as we
were settling down to our meal and I answered it, thinking it
would be a client. It wasn't; it was someone from the educa-
tion department at County Hall and they were asking for
Evelyn.

She took the handset, and I heard her say, 'Just a moment,
Miss Halliday, I'll ask my husband.'

She covered the mouthpiece and asked, 'It's County Hall, they want me to go to St Aidan's School at Annistone tomorrow for two days.'

I knew why Evelyn was asking me. There was no bus or train from Micklesfield to Annistone, which was about eight miles away. It was a remote village, little more than a hamlet really, tucked away in the middle of the moors, literally miles from anywhere. It did not even boast a shop or post office, although it had a thriving Catholic school and two good inns. When I'd agreed to Evelyn accepting these occasional jobs, I'd promised her I would do my best to get her to any of the venues, and I didn't want to let her down. After all, I'd done this kind of run several times already and they always provided a good driving experience for her.

'No problem, I can run you there in the morning and collect you from school afterwards, it won't be difficult fitting it in with my rounds.'

So she returned to her caller and said, 'Yes, Miss Halliday, I can get there. My husband will take me. Starting tomorrow morning. Yes, that will be fine. I'm looking forward to it.'

'I'll have to find something to wear,' she said as she returned to the table. 'And tonight, I must wash my hair . . .'

'Just concentrate on your tea for now.' I laughed. 'You can worry about your appearance later.'

I was pleased that these modest duties came along occasionally for Evelyn, because it gave her a break from the house and child-minding; that was good for her and good for me. I knew that County Hall tried to accommodate her in Catholic schools, because she was a Catholic and familiar with the religious demands of the infant class, where things like religious instruction, attendance at Mass and preparations for first communion or confirmation were important. These jobs provided her with money of her own, which she could cheerfully spend on clothes or whatever took her fancy without wondering whether it ought to be spent on the house or on Paul. We settled back down to our meal, and she was chattering excitedly about her plans for the day, when suddenly she gasped and put her hand to her mouth.

'Oh crumbs, I forgot . . .'

'Forgot what?' I asked.

'Maureen's going away tomorrow, for the day. She won't be able to take Paul.'

'How about your mum?'

'No, it's market day at the Unicorn, she'll be busy all day with meals and things.'

'Cynthia Green? She always told you not to be frightened to ask her if you wanted someone to look after Paul for a few hours now and then.'

'Wednesday is her day for going into Whitby to see her mother . . . she takes her youngest . . . I can't ask her. I'd better ring and cancel it.'

'County Hall will be shut now, it's five o'clock,' I said. 'The staff don't hang about when it's going home time, the place empties faster than it would if someone had found an un-exploded bomb in there. Don't worry, though, I can look after Paul.'

'You?' she sounded horrified.

'Well, it's Wednesday tomorrow so I'll be at home most of the morning doing my books and catching up with some office work and then I'll be going down to the Unicorn for my so-called surgery. I can entertain Paul in the morning, he's no trouble, he might even need his nap about elevenish, and he's got his trains and things to play with. Then in the afternoon he can come with me. I'm sure we can find something to occupy him at the market. I'll take that wooden train set along with all the trucks. He'll play for hours with that, and then I'll bring him when I collect you from Annistone after school. It'll all work out fine, just you see.'

'But I don't want you to be responsible for a small child while you're at work, you can't take him into people's houses when you're talking business.'

'I won't be doing that tomorrow. As I said, it's market day outside the Unicorn so I'll be at home first and then there until I come for you. If I have to make any house calls, I can do them after I've picked you up and got you home.'

And so that is what we agreed. With Paul in the rear seat, Evelyn drove to Annistone, safely negotiating a flock of moorland sheep in the middle of road, and some geese which hissed as we drove past a farm gate.

She coped well and I had no reason to be critical of her efforts. We arrived in good time for her to prepare the day's lessons, and I promised I'd return at quarter to four to accompany her home. Still with Paul on board, I then drove down to the Unicorn with a selection of my leaflets and proposal forms and, among some banter from the market traders, left these in the bottle and jug's hole in the wall. The rest of my morning was spent at home in my so-called real office, where I dealt with some correspondence, completed my various returns and balanced the entries in my cash books while Paul played happily with his toys. He loved anything that had wheels on and liked loading the trucks of his train with wooden bricks and transporting them around the house, even if there was no railway track; he loved his lorries, too, especially the tipper, and could occupy himself for hours. All those sturdy and colourful wooden toys had been made by Eric Newton from Baysthorpe, a farm labourer who produced wonderful hand-made creations in his spare time. I sometimes sold some on his behalf, earning him a useful sum whilst making his skill known throughout the dale, as well as earning myself a little extra cash. Paul had his nap just after eleven and slept for almost two hours, awaking just in time for me to get to the post office to pay in my takings before it closed at one. Then I decided to prepare a light dinner for Paul and myself (I was pretty good at doing beans on toast) before heading back to the Unicorn for my weekly visit to the bottle and jug.

I did not want to abandon my weekly visit today because I knew the system was working – not only was it working, it was working well. Clients and potential clients now expected me to be there. Some would want nothing more than an informal chat while others took a more serious approach, and I felt these very personal discussions about aspects of insurance were important; quite deliberately, I refrained from adopting a 'hard sell' approach. That was an instant turn-off for many Yorkshire folk, although I might indulge in a little gentle canvassing.

Fortunately, it was a fine dry day with warm sunshine and I knew Paul would play happily outside the inn if I took a selection of his favourite trains and lorries; as the Unicorn was owned by my in-laws, they would be on the premises to keep an extra eye on him, but I did not want to hand him over to them, nor did I envisage any problems. I was confident he'd be quite safe without being a nuisance to anyone. In any case, I'd be able to keep a close eye on him because I did not expect to be heavily involved with any clients. I expected I'd have to answer a few questions and issue leaflets, or even help complete a few proposal forms, but I reckoned I would cope. After all, Evelyn and I could conduct our conversations with Paul around, and he was never any trouble when anyone called so I did not expect him to demand attention if I was talking to a potential client.

Although the Unicorn market was small by comparison with others in nearby towns, it was always colourful and well attended, both by traders and customers. The local bus had scheduled its timetable to cater for market attenders and would even wait a few minutes if a passenger wanted only a few items.

I had never thought to count the stalls but there were usually around a dozen, mainly staffed by men who sold domestic produce – meat products of various kinds like sausages, black pudding and brawn, seasonal fruit and vegetables, domestic utensils, tools of various kinds for the home or garage, crockery, clothing and woollens, shoes, second-hand books, fish and cheese on occasion, paintings of the locality and even home crafts, including such turned wooden items as bowls and tool handles. I parked in my usual spot behind the inn and, clutching my briefcase with

Paul following me carrying a train with two trucks, made my way to the bottle and jug.

'What's this then, Matthew?' called out the man on the fruit stall when he noticed Paul. 'A new assistant? Things must be looking up for Matthew's insurance!'

'It's Matthew and Son now!' I responded. 'The beginning of an empire!'

'I hope you've got him insured!'

'How about me getting you insured?'

The good-natured banter continued as I put my briefcase on the ground outside the inn, beneath my hole in the wall, and realized the fish man had not arrived. His empty stall stood on a small concrete patch, which I thought would be ideal for Paul to run his toys round, and it was close to the bottle and jug, which meant I could keep an eye on him. As I assembled his train and placed it on the ground, I realized there was nothing to put in the trucks. Both trucks were about the size of a household brick, hollow with sides, and I considered buying some apples or potatoes, then had a better idea.

I could put some of my leaflets in the trucks and Paul could carry them about, shunt his train and, with a bit of luck, offer them to inquisitive people. I guessed people would go to see what he was doing and I thought this might be a nice, even fruitful, gimmick. So I filled both trucks with a selection of my leaflets, making sure those concerning the insurance of families and especially children were prominent. I asked Paul to give one to anyone who came for a chat with him, but did not know whether or not he understood. After all, he was only two years old.

As I returned to my hole in the wall, I noticed a small car creeping slowly past – a dark grey Standard 10 – and then it turned into the car park behind the pub . . . and I recognized the driver! My boss! Montgomery Wilkins, complete with black beret. Or, to give him his full title, Mr M. Wilkins, District Ordinary Branch Sales Manager – Life. What on earth was he doing here? Would I be in trouble for baby-minding while I was supposed to be working? But I was working, I told myself. This was my job! I was making myself available, making myself known and, apart from anything else, I could make my own hours because much of my income was based on commission. Nonethelesss, his arrival was rather worrying. So far as I knew he'd never made a surprise visit before. Whenever one of my supervisors came to visit me, they invariably contacted me in advance to make an appointment, which in turn allowed me to produce some kind of itinerary. So what had prompted this visit? Had I been doing something wrong without realizing? Was he checking up on me? I was tempted to go and hide somewhere, or to get my mother-in-law to attend to Paul and pretend the child was not with me . . .

As I was dithering, I realized he was heading my way. In spite of his diminutive figure, I could see his black beret bobbing among the shoppers, weaving through them like the fin of a shark cutting through a shoal of fish. I was cornered. Trapped, I could only stand in front of my bottle and jug hole-in-the-wall and hope for the best. Paul, I noticed, was busy with his train set under the fish stall and seemed quite content to shout shoo-shoo and chuff-chuff as he shunted it into a makeshift tunnel and railway station, which one of the traders had produced from surplus cardboard boxes.

'Ah, Mr Taylor, I thought I might find you here,' Mr Wilkins said in his high-pitched voice, grinning. 'I was just passing . . .'

I wondered if, instead of his catching me doing something not quite acceptable, he was the guilty one. Had he spotted the little market whilst on some other expedition, and popped in for a quiet look around? Was he surprised to find me here? It seemed not, judging by his reaction to me.

'Oh, hello, Mr Wilkins.' I must have sounded surprised. 'Welcome to my outdoor office!'

'I had heard about it, Mr Taylor. Word has reached District Office, you know – we have contacts all over the place – and I was most curious to see exactly how it was all working. I have just been to a conference in Guisborough and thought I would make my way home down Delverdale. Such a pretty journey. And I thought I would like to see you in action here.'

'Well, here it is.' I indicated the deep hole in the wall with its bottle and jug window. My leaflets were all neatly laid out and I noticed one or two had been returned; they bore the giveaway letter U that I had written in one corner. I spent a few minutes explaining my system, and how the leaflets were presented for anyone to take away, and then I became aware of a small figure tugging at Mr Wilkins' sports jacket. It was Paul.

'Paul!' I did not know whether I should acknowledge him as mine, as Wilkins looked down to see a small child handing him a leaflet about the benefits of life insurance for children. He accepted the leaflet with a glance at me, whereupon I grinned inanely and said, 'My assistant, he gives out leaflets.'

'My word, Mr Taylor, you do have an original way of doing things. So who is this very efficient young assistant?'

'My son, Paul. My wife has had to go off for the day unexpectedly so I'm looking after him. In fact, this inn is owned by my in-laws, so the family is looking after him really, I'm just using him to deliver my leaflets!' I jokingly made a very weak excuse.

As Wilkins accepted the leaflet, Paul went off with some more, handing them out to stallholders and customers alike. Everyone accepted his offer, some putting them in their pockets or shopping baskets and others standing still to read them on the spot.

'What a wonderful way of presenting our offers to the public!' Wilkins beamed. 'And in a market, too, with people coming and going all the time. Out in the market place, exactly where we should be. Yes, indeed, word had reached District Office about your market day enterprise and we were all intrigued. I said I would endeavour to pop in today – must tell them all about it in the hope some of our other agents will do something equally innovative.'

As he chatted, several of the market traders and some of

their customers came along and helped themselves to leaflets from my hole in the wall. I knew they did not want to take out insurance – I'd already spoken to most of them – but word had obviously reached them that this little man in the beret was my boss, so they were doing what they thought he would like to see. I had directed potential customers to their stalls on occasions and now they were repaying the compliment.

Some chatted to him, and in fact he bought some fruit and vegetables to take back to his wife in Scarborough. After touring the market and, somewhat surprisingly, buying me a cup of tea and a bun from the inn, he said his farewells.

'I've enjoyed this sojourn, Mr Taylor. Most interesting, and a wonderful way of spreading the word without driving for miles and miles. Keep up the good work – and let us hope that young assistant of yours has earned himself a little bit of commission today!'

'I think a visit to the shop is called for, to see what's on the sweet counter!' I laughed.

'Here,' said Mr Wilkins. 'Buy him something with this,' and he pressed a threepenny bit into my hand. 'With the compliments of the Premier!' And so Paul had earned his first commission from the Premier.

When Mr Wilkins had gone, I thanked the other stallholders for their support and they all handed fistfuls of leaflets back to me, all having been given them by Paul in addition to those they had taken in Mr Wilkins' presence, although some did retain one or two of specific interest. I was pleased that they had retained those relating to child insurance! Paul had certainly highlighted the merits of insuring the lives of children. In fact, the Premier offered a wonderful range of low-cost life insurance policies for children and young people, usually taken out by the parents and geared to mature when the child became an adult at twenty-one, or even when they reached the age of thirty or older. Some could even run until sixty-five. These were endowment policies boasting very low premiums due to their long duration, and the returns were quite wonderful, often timed to coincide with an important stage in a young person's life. A handsome cheque when one is twenty-one or getting married or seeking a home of one's own – or retiring – is always most welcome.

At quarter past three, I had to leave the market to go and collect Evelyn. I left my leaflets in the hole in the wall for collection later, although Paul insisted on taking his train set with him in the car, along with two trucks full of yet more leaflets. I felt I had quite a lot to tell Evelyn on the way home.

That night, with Paul fast asleep, Evelyn and I chatted about the day's events and she told me she had applied for her driving test. We discussed the selection of a professional tutor for her final lessons and then she said, 'Matthew, one of the mums who brings her daughter to school at Annistone would like a word with you when you can spare the time. She hasn't a phone but said you can call at any time between ten and three during the week.'

'Fair enough. What's it all about?'

'I don't know. She'd heard I was your wife and just asked me to pass the message on. She's Monica Beachcroft – they live in Keeper's Cottage at Annistone.'

'They?'

'Her husband is Ian, he's the gamekeeper for the Annistone Estate, and they have three children, a nice family. Not very well off, though, not on a keeper's wage, but they do all right for free rabbit meat, grouse and pheasants!'

'Fair enough, I'll pop in. I'm due to collect in the village next Thursday.'

'My spell will be finished by then,' she added. 'A pity, I like Annistone school, the children are lovely, so well behaved.'

And so a week later I knocked on the door of Keeper's Cottage in Annistone. On the eastern edge of Annistone Estate, it was close to the road and was a neat, stone-built house with a very tidy garden. As I eased Betsy to a halt outside the gate, a blowsy woman in her mid-thirties emerged from the green kitchen door to greet me. She was quite large and handsome, with a mop of tawny hair and a round, smiling face. I guessed it was Mrs Beachcroft. She wore an apron and was carrying a mixing bowl in her hands.

'Saw you pull up at the gate,' she called in a loud voice with just a trace of a Scots accent. 'You're not the insurance man, are you? Matthew Somebody.'

'I'm Matthew Somebody.' I laughed, reaching for my briefcase. 'You wanted to see me? Matthew Taylor to be exact, from the Premier Assurance Association.'

'Monica Beachcroft. Come in, the kettle's on. They said I had to call in Matthew's insurance and then somebody said the supply teacher was your wife . . . You're very young to be an insurance man, I expected somebody older.'

'Don't be deceived by appearances!' I joked. 'So how can I help you?'

She led me into the bright and airy kitchen where a kettle was purring on the Yorkist range. She put her mixing bowl on the drainer, washed her hands – I think she had been making a sponge cake – and bade me sit down at the table, which had a blue and white oilcloth upon it. As I extracted my various leaflets and proposal forms from my briefcase, she found a brown teapot, some mugs, a jug of milk, a sugar basin and a plate of scones with butter and strawberry jam. As she poured the boiling water into the teapot, she said, 'You must be wondering why I asked you to call, Mr Taylor.'

'Matthew,' I said. 'Everyone calls me Matthew.'

'So I heard. Well, Matthew, I'm Monica and I'm interested in life insurance but just let me pour the tea and sit down. I hate talking about serious things while I'm doing something else, I can't concentrate on two things at once. When I get sat down, we can talk.'

I waited as she bustled about, and finally she poured the tea and settled opposite me at the table. 'Now we can talk.'

'Life insurance?'

'Yes. I want to know what kinds there are, and whether it is expensive.'

I launched into my sales patter about the options available, stressing matters like the age of the insured person, their general health, their occupation, whether they indulged in any dangerous hobbies or sports and how the length of the term of insurance affected the cost of the premiums.

She listened intently and asked a few pertinent questions, then said, 'You mentioned dangerous sports and hobbies.'

'Yes, it's a consideration when contemplating any type of life insurance.'

'Well, this insurance is not for me or my husband. He's insured through the estate and I'm covered if anything happens to him, like a shooting accident, broken leg, long-term illness or something. We'd get a living wage even if Ian was off work through illness or injury. No, this is for my father. His name is Cooper, Bob Cooper.'

'I'm sure your father doesn't indulge in dangerous sports and hobbies!'

'He's retired but he makes model aeroplanes,' she told me. 'He flies them on the moors – they've got little electric engines powered by batteries and he's made a control box, radio controlled. That's where he is right now, flying two of his Spitfires. I asked you to call when he's out. He lives here, by the way, with Ian and me. Mum died a few years ago.'

'I'm sorry to hear that. So is he living permanently with you?'

'Yes, he sold his house near Berwick and moved in here about a year ago. It's working well. We've plenty of room and lots of outbuildings he can use for his model-making. He likes the country life, too, so we hardly see him – he's out on the moors most days. But it was his model-aircraft flying that prompted me to call you.'

'Really? Not because it's dangerous, surely? Not if they're only models!'

'It's dangerous for him – and for other people,' she said slowly. 'I think he needs some kind of insurance for them.'

'How can that be dangerous?' I puzzled.

'He's not very good at distinguishing his left from his

right, especially in an emergency of any kind.' She smiled ruefully. 'He made his own control box, you see, something he learned to do when he was in the army, he was a radio technician of some sort, but there's been several occasions when he's guided one of his models into the side of a house, or just missed people having picnics on the moor. I've seen quite a lot of his near-misses. You see, Matthew, suppose the plane that hit the house had gone through a window and injured someone. Or what if one of his planes hit a rambler on the head, or blinded someone or killed a dog? Or turned and flew right back towards Dad! He'd panic then, and lose control of it.'

'Life insurance won't *prevent* that kind of thing!'

'I know,' she said. 'But what bothers me is that somebody might claim compensation for injuries or damage, and that could take all Dad's savings. I don't want him to lose all his money – and it's not because I want to inherit it!'

'I'm pleased to hear that!'

'Well, he's worked hard all his life, and saved up for his retirement. He's enjoying his freedom now and I wouldn't want something like an accident with one of his planes to take away his savings. He's a proud man and likes to be self-sufficient; he just wants enough money to allow him to live comfortably and enjoy his hobbies. And it's no good asking him to give them up, because he won't!'

'That's clear enough. So what you're proposing is a type of third party insurance? To cater for the possibility of your dad's aircraft doing damage or injury to something or someone, and his having to pay some kind of compensation?'

'Yes, like the insurance for cars. That's to make sure third parties are covered for injuries and damage, or emergency hospital treatment, isn't it? But I'm also interested in life insurance for him, although he might be too old for that. I can't ignore the possibility he might be injured by one of his own planes.'

'Nothing's impossible!' I had to admit. 'How old is he?'

'Sixty-seven. He's got his old-age pension and a bit from

the army because he was a regular for a while and another small pension from the radio manufacturer he worked for, but we thought an insurance of some kind might be a good idea, especially if he had to pay damages to someone or even pay for his own hospital treatment.'

'Well, the insurance business is noted for being flexible and innovative, and my company is among the best, so I would think our experts could produce something suitable, probably by incorporating one policy with another in this case – a life policy with some kind of model-aircraft accident policy – although at this stage I have no idea what it would cost or what conditions might be imposed.'

'You'll look into it for me, will you? To see if such a policy is available? And let me know, preferably when he's not around. He's not one for spending money on insurance. I'd have to convince him it was worthwhile, and I suppose if he refuses I could pay the premiums.'

'You couldn't take a policy out on his life without his consent, Monica. We'd need his signature, too, and there's another thing that needs to be addressed. This business of him not knowing his left from his right. It seems to me that is the real problem, the root of the danger he presents to himself and others. If he applied for insurance to cover those risks, he would have to declare that incapacity.'

'What would that mean?'

'It could mean the Premier would not accept him as a risk, but if he didn't declare it and it emerged later it would make any policy invalid and stop any claims succeeding. So he must tell the truth, Monica, that's what I'm saying. It might be that my company would accept him as a risk, with certain conditions.'

'So what sort of conditions might they impose on his flying?'

'I don't know, to be honest, but one condition might be that he doesn't fly in places where the public have access. That would reduce the risks considerably.'

'Well, there's just the moors, nowhere else has the space

150

he needs, so I suppose he could go early in the morning, or at other times when the public isn't there.'

'I'm suggesting that as a possible condition, Monica, but truly I don't know what my bosses' reaction will be. Leave it with me. I'll let you know the outcome as soon as I can, but in view of what you've told me, the cost of the premiums could be considerable.'

'He's a Scotsman, Matthew, and he's very careful with his money. It might put him off flying them altogether! It's the only thing that might do that!'

'I'm sure there will be a way around all this, but another matter is the control box he uses. Can we be sure it is properly constructed? I don't want to cast a shadow over your father's skills, but could he, quite literally, have got his wires crossed? In other words, because of an error of wiring or construction or something is it possible that his control box sends the planes to the right when he guides them to the left? And vice versa?'

'He's checked that time and time again, Matthew. There's nothing wrong with his control box. He's had it checked by a friend, it's in perfect working order. It's him who gets confused!'

'Has he tried to correct those errors? It must make things difficult for him.'

'He's tried all sorts. He painted a red mark on the control box to signify "right", and wrapped a red ribbon around his right forearm so that he would know which way was right, but that didn't work. He's all right when he has time to think about it, it's only when there's an emergency and he has to do something in a rush.'

'So what about driving his car? Doesn't it cause problems?'

'It never has done. He copes with steering, he writes with his right hand, everything else is absolutely normal. It's just when he gets into a flap when he's trying to correct a plane's flight. The lever he uses is like the joystick on a plane – just the one lever, which he uses to make it go left or right, dive or climb.'

151

'It would take a cleverer person than me to sort that out,' I had to admit. 'OK, one other point, Monica. You said he goes up to the moors to fly his planes, so surely he can find somewhere very quiet where there are no people and dogs, no houses and cars, nothing he could harm? I would have thought the moors were ideal for that.'

'So did he, Matthew, that's why he goes there, but during the years he's been flying up there people have started to visit the moors at weekends, and even during the week. They have picnics, take walks, go bird-watching or looking for rare flowers, leave their cars while they head off into the heather or just sit in them and read their Sunday papers. It's very difficult now, finding somewhere peaceful and quiet without a human being in the middle of it, especially at weekends.'

'And he thinks he should have rights over them?'

'He's never said that but there are times I think he feels he was there first. He grumbles that they're in his way now, and says he should be able to fly his planes where and when he wants. He knows he can't, of course, and I do know he's worried about them injuring someone or damaging something when they get out of control or go the wrong way. But there's nowhere else he can fly them. He needs a lot of space, these are not little toys, they're quite large-scale models of famous aircraft, some with a four-foot wingspan. The cricket field is too small, farmers' fields are too small as well, in addition to having livestock around them . . . There's just the moors, and now they're getting too crowded and busy.'

'Right,' I said. 'I'll have words with my District Office in Ryethorpe to see if they have any experience of this kind of insurance and I'll try to get some indication of the likely costs from them. Then I'll return, hopefully with a proposal form for your dad to sign. Now, Monica, in the meantime is there any possibility that you could put the idea of insurance to your father? Soften him up a little?'

'I've tried before, but I'll try again,' was all she would promise.

When I rang District Office to discuss Bob's problem, there

was a good deal of umming and ahhing from various members of staff, all of which ended with a promise to contact Head Office because they'd never encountered this kind of proposal. The general consensus was that Bob Cooper should stop flying his planes in places where the public had access or where they might cause damage to property, but I received an assurance that enquiries would be made of experts in London. Eventually I received a letter outlining an attempt to reach a compromise. Clearly, the Premier wanted this business, however modest it was, because they did not reject Mr Cooper outright. The letter said it was not company policy to allow random proposals like this to be garnered by their competitors but because of Mr Cooper's admitted problems and his insistence on flying in places open to the public, the company felt the overall risks may be too great.

The letter made it clear that the Premier did not want to finance any claim that might be substantial, bearing in mind the probable effect of an aircraft that had crashed or gone badly out of control, even if it was merely a model. It was pointed out that such a heavy object crashing into a person could prove fatal. However, there was a compromise suggestion. The matter would be reconsidered if (a) any such insurance was linked to or taken out in conjunction with a policy on Mr Cooper's life; (b) Mr Cooper did not fly his models in places frequented by, or open to, the general public unless it was in association with a properly organized and supervised display or competition of model aircraft, whether upon payment or not; (c) he avoided places with buildings and other structures or vehicles in close proximity unless it was during a properly organized and supervised display or competition of model aircraft, whether upon payment or not; and (d) he joined a properly constituted club formed for the building and flying of model aircraft. Such a bona fide club could then apply for a block insurance for all its members.

When I read those conditions I thought it heralded the end of Bob's hobby, although, of course, he could continue as he was doing now, albeit with all the risks attached. There was nothing to stop him, but if his models caused any damage or injury then he could be personally liable. Armed with that letter, I went back to see Monica and put the contents to her in detail; clearly she was disappointed because she was genuinely worried about her father's liability and felt he would never agree to the conditions imposed by the Premier. And, of course, the cost of the premium had not been determined at this stage.

She made me a cup of tea as we chatted and then turned the subject away from her father, asking how Evelyn's driving tuition was progressing. I updated her on Evelyn's progress and then suddenly remembered something. Being from the Borders and fairly new to the district, he was probably unaware of the existence of the place.

'Monica, I've just had a flash of inspiration. While teaching Evelyn in the early stages, I found an old airfield. It's near Stonethorpe – that's less than half an hour away by car – and it's not used by the public. It's huge with old runways still there. I got permission from the farmer who owns it . . . Why doesn't your father see about using it? It's ideal for flying; it was a wartime airfield, the control tower is still there but no other buildings except a pair of old hangars, and they're all battered and falling to pieces. There's not much damage he could do there!'

And so it was that Bob Cooper and Monica went to look at Stonethorpe Airfield. They managed to locate the owner, and he said Bob was more than welcome to fly his models there. Because of that, Bob felt there was no need for any kind of insurance, and in the weeks and months that followed he seemed cheerful and pleased with the way things had turned out. A real airfield for his models!

It was several months later when he rang and asked if he could speak to me sometime. I agreed and said I would call during my rounds the following day. When I arrived, I found an affable man with a lovely Scots accent, iron-grey hair and blue eyes, which twinkled with a deep humour.

'I wanted to thank you for all you did for me,' he said.

'Sorry we've not met until now but I know Monica did all the batting on my behalf, without my knowledge I might add, but I am grateful for the suggestion about the old airfield. It's ideal. Now, while I've been flying there, I've had several people, men, women and children, calling to ask if they could join me. So I've formed a club, Matthew, a model-aircraft flying club, based on the old airfield. And you can guess what's coming next!'

'No,' I said, rather stupidly.

'We need to be insured, Matthew. As a properly constituted club, we need to obey all the rules and one is to be insured against all risks. So how about it?'

'Yes.' I smiled. 'Yes, I am sure we can find something suitable.'

I did win the business for insuring Stonethorpe Model Aircraft Club (SMAC). But I never did find out whether his right/left problem had been rectified. Fortunately, the Premier never raised that question when they insured his club.

Evelyn's work as a supply teacher provided another tale that was somewhat curious. She had completed three days at the County Primary School at Lexingthorpe, and she had enjoyed the work. Afterwards we were chatting over a cup of cocoa before going to bed and she said, 'Oh, by the way, Joseph Hudson asked to be remembered to you. He's the father of one of our pupils, a six-year-old boy. Sam.'

'Hudson? He's one of my clients, isn't he?

'Yes, he's got several policies with you, car, house, accident, life. He reckons he's your best customer!'

'I remember now, he renewed some of them one evening recently, he's the chap who works for ICI at Wilton near Middlesbrough.'

'Yes, that's him. He's a scientist of some sort. He was off work, catching up with some overtime due to him, so he brought little Sam to school. The head said he was one of the famous Hudson twins.'

'Famous Hudson twins?'

'Famous in Delverdale, perhaps, but not very famous anywhere else.'

'So why are they famous?' I was puzzled now.

'I don't know. Mrs Rose told me he was one of the famous Hudson twins but I couldn't quiz her about it because one of the children came up to her with a question.'

'So who is the other Hudson twin?'

'I don't know, I didn't ask.' Evelyn laughed, knowing she had presented me with a puzzle I couldn't ignore.

Before going to bed I checked my list of clients and the names in my collecting book, but found no other Hudson. Joseph was the only Hudson on my books and he was listed with his home address and policies, with their serial numbers. I thought Evelyn had perhaps misunderstood. But the matter was not pressing so I let it rest there and went upstairs to bed. By the following morning I had relegated the famous Hudson twins to the back of my mind and thought no more about it until spots of soot began to fall down our chimney.

'It needs sweeping,' announced Evelyn with the wisdom of a wife. 'We've no idea when it was last done, so while you're on your rounds today can you find a chimney sweep?'

My first call that morning was Roger Crossley in the village shop at Micklesfield. Roger's store contained almost everything one could wish to buy, from groceries to fruit and vegetables by way of kitchen utensils, cycle repair kits and decorating materials. He also had a noticeboard on the wall just inside the door, to which were pinned lots of postcards bearing local adverts. He displayed them for a fee of sixpence a month and it was a useful guide to tradesmen such as plumbers, electricians, chimney sweeps and window cleaners or people with things for sale.

'G'Morning, Matthew.' Roger was a cheery fellow with a shining bald head bearing lots of thin white wisps of hair around his ears. Although he was only in his late forties, he looked nearer sixty.

'Not a bad day for the time of year, Roger,' I responded.

Roger and I had an arrangement whereby we would get

156

together at the beginning of each week, or at any other convenient time, to discuss our routine for the days ahead. If I was visiting a remote village where he also had a solitary delivery to make, I would take his order with me and deliver it; it often saved him from making a special journey. Likewise, if he was heading for a village where I had just one collection outstanding, probably something like a shilling sitting on someone's outdoor toilet window ledge, he would collect it for me. It was a good arrangement that helped both of us.

'Looking for something in particular?' he asked when he saw me peering at the assorted postcards, some of which were pinned on the top of others.

'A good chimney sweep, we've had a fall of soot.'

'Michael Hudson's your man,' he said. 'He lives at Arnoldtoft, he'll be out on his rounds now but you can leave a message with his wife, or call in if you're going that way. He does all these villages.'

'I'll head that way, I might come across him on my rounds.'

'He's reliable and efficient. He's one of the famous Hudson twins, you know.'

'I've heard of the Hudson twins, Roger, but why are they so famous? I've met the other one, Joseph, but had no idea he was a twin until my wife mentioned it.'

'They're identical, like two peas in a pod.'

'Is that all? It's hardly enough to make them famous – there's lots of twins who are identical.'

'I don't think they're famous away from Delverdale, but hereabouts everybody calls them the famous Hudson twins. It's because they look alike, but act so differently. Everybody used to talk about them when they were younger.'

Roger told me that the twins' parents, who now lived in retirement at Whitby, had been determined that their sons would not be identical even if they looked alike. Throughout their young lives, the parents had dressed the twins in different clothes, given them different hairstyles, different toys for Christmas and birthdays and different makes and colours of bike to ride, as well as ensuring they didn't habitually go around together. The parents' argument was that the lads should grow up to be independent of one another, to lead their own lives and not to be permanently burdened with a shadow-like double, which was the fate of some identical twins.

The lads had made different careers – Joseph had won a scholarship to a boarding school while Michael had left school at fourteen to learn the trade of chimney sweep, eventually launching his own business when his former employer retired. Joseph had become a scientist and was now a leading figure in ICI at Wilton, near Middlesbrough. Each, according to Roger, was happy with their lot in life and they remained good friends, often visiting one another at their homes. However, there had been some odd coincidences, hence the description 'famous' whenever anyone who knew them spoke about them.

Roger gave me some examples. On one occasion, each twin had been playing cricket on the same Saturday, Michael for the village team of Arnoldtoft and his brother for ICI Wilton. Both had scored 63 runs before being caught at slip, even though the matches were some thirty miles apart. On another occasion, both had been struck on the head by a cricket ball on the same Saturday, even though they were playing miles apart. Then both had won money on Littlewoods football pools on the same weekend, Joseph winning £28 15s and Michael £364. Both had had tiles blown off their roofs during a gale and both had married girls called Susan. Those coincidences were especially curious because Mr and Mrs Hudson senior had made such a determined effort to ensure their sons would lead separate and quite different lives.

'I've got Joseph as one of my clients, but not Michael,' I told Roger. 'I didn't even realize Joseph had a twin until Evelyn mentioned it.'

'That's typical of them: if one was insured by you, the other would go elsewhere and find another insurer, just as they deliberately buy different makes of car, different best suits, different coloured carpets for the house and live in different villages. They really try hard to live completely separate lives and do

158

different things, but these weird events keep happening to remind them they really are identical twins.'

I was pleased Roger had spent time explaining about the Hudson twins, because I felt that this kind of local knowledge was important in my business. After chatting about the routes of our prospective collections and deliveries, we decided we could not help one another today with our mutual aid scheme. For me, it was time to try and locate Michael, the chimney sweep.

Arnoldtoft is little more than a hamlet lying on the floor of Delverdale midway between Gaitingsby and Baysthorpe. It does not possess an inn, a church, a shop or a post office, although there are several farms and lots of cottages, some occupied by farm workers, others by commuters and some owned by small businessmen like Michael Hudson's. I had a few clients living there but it was probably the smallest community within my agency and certainly the most quiet. From the postcard in Roger's shop, I knew that Michael lived in Ivy Cottage at the eastern end of the village. I had discovered his wife was called Susan, but knew nothing of any family they might have.

Ivy Cottage was at one end of a row of six small terrace cottages, all facing the road and all built of local stone with blue slate roofs. Ivy Cottage had a clean white front door, and as I approached I could see the kitchen area, which protruded from the rear and also had a door. As it was customary on these moors to enter by the back door, I parked on the verge and went to knock on that door. There was no reply. I hammered again, louder this time, and waited, but there was nothing. As one did on these occasions, I tried again and then tested the door handle, but it was locked.

It was clear no one was at home so I would either have to stick a note through the letter box or ring when I returned from work unless I encountered Michael Hudson somewhere on my rounds.

As I turned to leave, however, an elderly lady appeared and asked, 'Are you looking for Mr Hudson?'

'Yes, I am, I need my chimney swept.'

'He's had to go to hospital. His wife is there with him.'

'Oh dear . . .'

'Yes, a child ran headlong into his ladder this morning when he was in Baysthorpe. He was climbing up to a chimney pot, the ladder fell and he tumbled down and broke his arm. His wife's taken him to Whitby Cottage Hospital – she's a good driver, you know. Is there any message?'

'I can wait. I'll contact him when he's fit and well, it's not urgent.'

'All right. Who shall I say called when Susan gets back?'

'I'm Matthew Taylor from Micklesfield. I need my chimney swept but it can wait a while. I'll contact them again, at a better time.'

She nodded and said she would tell Susan I had called.

Then I decided to collect some premiums in Baysthorpe and, if I had time, do likewise in Gaitingsby, on the way home. On my rounds, I asked about other chimney sweeps in the area but it seemed there was none. Either I would have to do it myself by dropping a live hen down from the top, its flapping wings doing a wonderful clearance job, or sending up a dry twig of ivy that had been set on fire. It would roar up the chimney with the updraught and clear most of the deposits. Or I could wait for Michael to recover. I hoped he had sufficient insurance to guarantee him an income during the time he would be off work. But it was not my worry – he was with another company. I must admit I wondered which company he was with and whether his returns would be better than the Premier's. I hoped he would be well looked after– it is never easy when a self-employed person can't work through illness or injury.

When I got home, Evelyn had tea ready, and as we ate we discussed the day's events, and I told her about Michael Hudson. There had been no further falls of soot during the day, so the problem did not appear to be urgent, although, of course, the chimney would have to be swept without much delay. An accumulation of soot could lead to a chimney fire if we weren't careful, particularly as we burned a lot of logs, and we had no idea when the job had last been done. In an urban area, such a chimney fire could lead to a fine of ten shillings, but, happily, that law did not apply to rural districts.

When Paul went to bed, I read him a bedtime story and settled down to listen to the wireless. Then the telephone rang. I lifted the handset.

'Oh, hello, is that Matthew's insurance?' asked a woman's voice.

'Yes, Matthew Taylor speaking.'

'Ah, good, it's Sue Hudson here . . .'

'It's good of you to ring back,' I said. 'It's not all that urgent, and I must say I'm sorry about Michael.'

'Michael?' the voice reacted. 'What about Michael? My husband is Joseph.'

'Oh, I'm sorry. You must be the other Sue. I called at Michael's today, to see about getting my chimney swept . . .'

'So what's happened to him?' she demanded.

'Well, he fell off a ladder this morning and had to be taken to hospital with a broken arm.'

'I don't believe it!' she cried. 'My husband was knocked down by a car in Middlesbrough this morning. It swerved on to the footpath and he's been taken to hospital with a broken arm. I was ringing to ask if you would call sometime. The police dealt with the accident and are talking about a prosecution for dangerous driving but we need advice about the driver's insurance and how to claim from him.'

'Another story of the famous Hudson twins!' I said.

'It's one I can do without! You'll call when you can?'

'You'll be my first customer tomorrow morning,' I assured her.

# Seven

*'A lamp-post bumped into my car, damaging
it in two places.'*

From a claim form

E velyn received a note saying her driving test would be in
four weeks' time on a Thursday afternoon at 2.15 p.m.
There was an accompanying leaflet, which outlined the various driving techniques on which she would be tested, along
with a reminder that she would have to answer questions from
the Highway Code in addition to displaying some simple technical knowledge such as how to refill the radiator, check the
oil and change a tyre if she got a puncture. She was reminded
to take a current provisional driving licence with her, duly
signed, and to make sure the vehicle bore the statutory
L-plates back and front, that the car was in a legal and roadworthy condition and that she was accompanied by a qualified driver when she presented herself and her vehicle for the
test. That qualified driver was me.

It was clear that Evelyn would benefit from as much driving experience as possible before her test, and we discussed
whether she might drive me on my daily rounds, but eventually rejected that idea because she would have to tolerate a lot of waiting and hanging about as I visited my
clients. There were times Betsy might be parked in a village
for a couple of hours or more as I completed several calls
and, as a learner, Evelyn could not drive unaccompanied.
We felt this was too restrictive and counter-productive.
Instead, I promised Evelyn I would do my best to complete

my daily work in good time to take her for a drive each evening.

I thought it important she drive every day, even if it was for only a short while, and I also felt it necessary for her to gain experience in towns like Whitby and Guisborough. And, of course, there were always the weekends, when she could drive further and for longer while practising things like three-point turns and hill starts.

Getting Evelyn through her test dominated our lives to such an extent that we continued to thrust to the backs of our minds, momentarily at least, our thoughts of buying a house, although I did casually examine several that had come on the market in various parts of my agency. None was suitable – either they were too small or too large, or not in the right place or too close to noisy business premises or lacking in privacy. There was always something that was not quite to our taste – but the driving test had now assumed far greater and much more immediate importance.

Even if the test dominated our lives for those few weeks, my work could not be ignored. I needed to earn more commission to pay for Evelyn's driving lessons and for the amount of petrol we were consuming. We could manage on our ration – just!

Much of my work was routine and distinctly lacking in excitement, even if it did provide me with a useful income, but then, one Monday evening, I got an interesting call from a man in Crossrigg.

'Now then,' said the Yorkshire voice. 'Is that the insurance man?'

'Matthew Taylor speaking, yes.'

'Stan Paxton from Crossrigg, Mr Taylor. I need you to fettle some insurance for me.'

'No problem,' I said. 'When can I come and see you?'

'I'm on shifts at the brickworks, late turn for the rest of this week, starting tomorrow. I'll be at home most mornings until Friday.'

'Tomorrow then? Ten o'clockish?'

'Champion, I'll see you then.'

'What sort of insurance do you want, Mr Paxton? It might help me make sure I bring the right information and proposal forms.'

'A boat,' he said. 'A cabin cruiser. I built her myself and she needs insurance if I'm going to take her out.'

'I've never insured a boat before!' I told him, and, after he'd given me his address, I promised I would see him the next morning. I knew that the insurance of ships and boats was very specialized, mainly due to the fact they transported people and goods into foreign seas and distant countries, with some larger vessels being insured for each voyage rather than on an annual basis. The cost of their insurance would depend largely upon where they were going and what they were carrying, and in some cases the hulls alone were covered by special insurance. Most marine insurance cover would include risks like collisions and what were termed 'other liabilities and marine perils'. This sounded very wide and all-embracing, rather like a fully comprehensive car insurance. Marine insurance, which could be both expensive and complicated, was still governed by the Marine Insurance Act of 1906, although some large modern claims had led to the Act's provisions being subjected to interpretation by the courts, probably due to their having been overtaken by modern developments.

I wasn't quite sure how Mr Paxton's boat fitted into the general scheme of things or what kind of marine perils he would confront in a home-made boat, especially if he sailed it on the River Delver, or even in the North Sea off Whitby. Although Monday was my usual day for visiting Crossrigg, I decided this potential client was worth a special trip. At ten o'clock that Tuesday morning, therefore, I arrived at his home in Byland Terrace. It was an end-terrace house located among a network of closely packed terrace properties on a site very close to the north bank of the River Delver. Indeed, the front gardens of at least one row of houses led down to the river bank – ideal for those who were fishermen, although some also used the fast-flowing water to get rid of questionable rubbish. Each terrace bore the name of a ruined Yorkshire abbey such as Rievaulx, Fountains, Whitby, Easby and Roche. The houses had been constructed late in the nineteenth century to accommodate brickyard workers. In fact, they were rented from the brickworks company.

As was the local custom, I walked around to the back of the house, intending to knock on the kitchen door, but was confronted by the sight of a large boat in the backyard. It was resting on a wooden ramp of the kind one sees in shipyards, and supported by struts. A ladder stood next to it, reaching up to the deck rails near the glass-windowed cabin. With a large propeller at the rear, it looked very new and smelled of fresh paint or varnish; it was a lovely blue and white, with the name *Bluebell* painted on the rear panels and the Whitby registration WY 187 on the bows. *Stanley Paxton, Crossrigg, Yorks*, was painted on the flat stern.

The combined height of the boat and its ramp was almost that of the two-storey house, and greater than the walls of the yard. Clearly Mr Paxton had gone about this in a professional way, and it appeared his craft was now registered; from my very limited knowledge of boats, it looked exactly like those holiday craft one sees sailing in our canals, estuaries and harbours. It was a boat in which to cruise, sleep and eat, rather like a water-borne caravan.

Although it was small by the standard of fishing boats and canal boats, it was of considerable size and I wondered how he was going to get it out of his backyard. The door was far too small. Knock down the walls, perhaps? He couldn't take it directly into the river, because it was on the other side of the house.

As I was admiring the craft and puzzling about its mode of exit, Paxton emerged from the kitchen and came to greet me.

'What do you think of her, then?'

He was clearly very proud of his creation and had realized who I was. He was a stout man in his mid-fifties with a large beer belly and a head of thin ginger hair; his face and fore-arms were also rather red, but he modified the effect by wear-ing green overalls and black wellington boots.

'She looks wonderful,' I had to admit, remembering to use the feminine form. 'You built her yourself, you told me?'

'I did that. It's taken me nearly four years working in my spare time, but now she's just about ready to go. A few inter-nal things to sort out and that's it . . . And once she's out of here, me and the missus will be going off on a cruise. The Norfolk Broads, mebbe, or down to the Isle of Wight or even up to the Western Isles. Who knows? The world will be our oyster, or summat.'

'I wish you luck.'

'Well, we haven't got a car and our outings have been on trains and buses, so we thought how about a boat . . . We couldn't afford to buy one, so I set about building this lovely lady. There were times I never thought I'd get her finished but, well, that day's come.'

'She looks all ready for action.' I smiled. 'She'll hold her own among all the others, I'll bet!'

'She will that! By the time I get the insurance sorted out, she'll be ready for off. A bit like a favourite chick flying the nest, I suppose.'

'Right,' I said. 'Let's get down to business.'

'The missus is at work, she's the invoice clerk in the Co-op, but I can make a good cup of tea and she's left some biscuits out. Come in, Mr Taylor.'

He led me into the very dark kitchen, which had a small wooden table under the window, and showed me a chair. I settled down and began to draw various leaflets and proposal forms from my briefcase. He busied himself with an electric kettle and soon had a full pot of fresh tea, milk, sugar and some buns.

'Help yourself,' he invited. 'She made 'em herself.'

Once he was seated opposite me, I began to detail the specialized nature of maritime insurance and the ocean-going perils it had to cope with, and said the Premier had its own

166

maritime specialists, which meant that his rather modest case should not present a problem.

'Oh, I'm not thinking of that just now,' he said. 'I've a mooring promised just in front of my house on the River Delver, for nowt. It's estate water and they don't mind me mooring her there for a while, then I can take her down to Whitby when the time's right. It'll do her good to sit in the water for a while, make sure she's stable, swell the timbers and so on, find any leaks.'

I now knew what he had meant on the telephone when he said he wanted insurance so he could to take her out. He meant out of the yard, not out to sea!

He went on. 'I might need a low-loader for that, the river's not navigable up here. I've got her registered in Whitby, so all that's done and dusted. I shan't be making any voyages just yet, Mr Taylor. She'll sit in the beck just behind us until I'm read to shift her to Whitby – there's a deepish pool there. No, what I want from you is some insurance that will cover me getting her out of my backyard.'

'I wondered how you were going to do that.'

'It's not going to be easy, I can tell you.'

'You've made enquiries?'

'All over the place, believe me! Then, last weekend, I happened to meet this chap in a pub in Whitby and told him all about it, and he said the job would need a crane. He told me he knew a firm who did this sort of thing, but they would demand I got myself and the house insured, just in case summat goes wrong. They'll be insured for their side of things, but I need to be insured for the boat causing accidental damage to my house and property, and other folks' houses or cars or sheds or whatever, while she's being shifted. I've been on to the firm and they can do the job, they do a lot of this kind of thing, working with boats, but they said I had to get my boat insured for accidents of all kinds before they'll even think about coming to lift her out. Once I can prove that I'm fully covered for things at my end, they'll come out and have a look at the job, then give me an estimate and a timetable if I want to go ahead.'

167

'I understand. Then once she's afloat you'll need another insurance to cover her against things like theft, fire, accidents, collisions, damage and so forth. Rather like you would with a car.'

'Right, Mr Taylor, but let's take things one at a time. Right now all I need to do is get her out of that backyard and on to yon river.'

'So where will she go when she's first lifted out?' I asked, wondering about the small space beyond this backyard. It backed on to a narrow tile-floored alley that was too narrow even for cars to drive along. The piece of land at the end of the terrace also seemed too small to accommodate a crane, or a low-loader with a cabin cruiser on board. How would a crane manoeuvre itself in such a small area?

'I reckon she'll be hoisted out of my yard and over the wall, then around the end of the house,' he said with confidence. 'The usual method of shifting boats from places like this is to run strong slings under the hull with chains up to the crane. I think that's what they'll do – I know other boat-builders who've had that sort of thing done. That's why I need to have this insurance, to cover all that, in case of accidents and damage, because it'll probably swing very close to the house end. That's why the job can't be done on a windy day.'

'Well, I'm sure we can do something for you,' I said with confidence. 'I'll need to know the value of *Bluebell*, the method of removing her, the name of the proposed contractor, although that can be altered if necessary, a list of properties along the route between your house and the mooring, including your own premises, and anything else that might be damaged during transit. Then I'll submit your proposal and get costings for you. It will be a one-off policy, issued for this single special occasion, and I'm sure a company as large as the Premier have done this kind of thing countless times before. They will know that the crane operators are also fully insured for their part in the operation and that will help keep down the cost of your premium.'

And so we got to work. It took about half an hour to

complete the proposal form and then I went out for another more critical look at the backyard. The bulk of the boat filled it, which explained why the kitchen was so dark. The yard was enclosed, and the means of entry was a single doorway, so the snag was that, so far as I could determine, there was no space to permit a crane or a low-loader to get anywhere near Mr Paxton's backyard. I began to wonder whether he'd ever get the boat out! I had heard tales of people building things like gliders and boats in confined spaces, and then being unable to shift them. They remained for ever unused, no more than showpieces or talking points.

But I was sure Mr Paxton had researched that kind of problem before embarking on his boat-building exercise, and, in any case, experts have the capacity for confounding all gloomy forecasts and coping with tasks that others believe to be impossible. I had to tell myself this was Mr Paxton's problem, not mine. I felt sure my company would provide the necessary cover for the operation. I would refer to the limited space when I submitted the proposal, and told Mr Paxton I would submit his proposal form and inform him once I had any news.

Very soon, I received a written acknowledgement of Mr Paxton's proposal, stating that his application had, as a matter of routine, been despatched to the maritime branch at Head Office for consideration of its feasibility. A couple of days later, a further letter arrived, saying that the proposal had been accepted on condition that a 'Premier approved' crane operator was used to lift the boat. A list of such operators accompanied the letter, which included the one selected by Mr Paxton. I later learned that this kind of operation was quite common along the north-east coast, where small private craft were home-built in backyards and gardens and then hoisted out by crane, and there was a group of very skilled operators who regularly fulfilled this role. However, I must say it was not very common in inland villages like Crossrigg.

The one-off premium was modest considering the risks to both the boat and the house, but this was due to the fact that only approved and heavily insured crane operators were used.

They knew their job. All that was required for the policy to become effective, therefore, was confirmation of when the removal of *Bluebell* would take place, and the payment of £7 10s for the premium, to be paid in advance. I rang Mr Paxton with the good news and he said he would relay that information to the crane operator and he'd let me know the date of the operation as soon as he was notified. I said I would collect the premium when I was in Crossrigg the following Monday, and deliver the policy documents to Mr Paxton so that he could show them to the crane operator if required as proof. Everything was in place – all that concerned me now was how on earth anyone could remove that cabin cruiser from Mr Paxton's backyard.

A day or two later, Mr Paxton rang to say he had a date; the crane operator had confirmed the job would be done on Thursday next, commencing at 8 a.m., weather (gales in particular) permitting. I told him I would telephone District Office, who would activate the insurance policy, but if for any reason the job was postponed he should let me know as soon as possible. The insurance policy could be carried forward to a new date at no extra cost.

Fortunately, there was no postponement, and I thought it would be fascinating to watch this operation, provided I did not get in the way. I could leave my car in the village and walk down to Byland Terrace. I guessed other spectators would turn up, too, with whom the experienced crane operators would know how to deal.

When I arrived, at about ten minutes to eight, there was a small knot of spectators, and Stanley Paxton was moving among them, assuring them they would be all right provided they stood in the alley to the rear of his premises. From there they would be able to see everything because all the action would take place above the walls of the yard. When he saw me, he ushered me past the group, saying I could join him in the backyard if I wished and offering to explain what was going to happen. I said I did not feel happy about remaining in the yard while the boat was being hoisted out – if it slipped

170

or fell I did not want to be anywhere beneath it! – and I would find some other observation site. He assured me it would be very safe and told me what was going to happen.

On the upper beams of the ramp were several indentations, which were now immediately beneath the timbers of the boat. Strong chains, covered in leather to protect the woodwork of the boat, would be passed along those and linked to the crane's huge hook when it was positioned above the boat. He said the effect would be rather like a hanging basket of flowers – the boat would be like the contents of the basket, safely enclosed in a hammock of several strong chains as she was hoisted off the ramp. Once the crane began its hoisting operation, the chains would tense and take the weight; there would be a short period of reassessment, checking things like the balance of the boat, the clearance available and any danger points, and then *Bluebell* would be lifted smoothly out of the yard. Once she was above the height of the wall, the crane would slowly turn and swing its cargo past the end of the house. Then there would be some adjustments to make sure the boat was placed gently into the appointed place on the river. No problems were anticipated, particularly as the day was fine and dry with no appreciable wind – there were breezes off the river but nothing too serious.

Paxton was saying, 'Once the chains are fixed to the hook, the word will be given and up she'll go, right over the wall. She'll be slewed around the end of the house, at about the height of the rooftop, like a football in a string bag, and be deposited straight into the river. The chains will be dismantled and that'll be that. She'll sit in the water at the bottom of our garden for a week or two, when I'll be checking for balance, manoeuvrability, leaks and so on, then I'll take her a few yards downstream where there's access for a low-loader and she'll be taken to Whitby on the back of that.'

'It must be a colossal crane if it can reach above the house!' I commented.

'It is, and it needs to have a very heavy and solid base with good balancers if it's to cope with Bluebell's weight, but these

171

chaps are experts, Mr Taylor, they know what they're doing
. . . Ah, this sounds like him now.'

The sound of an approaching slow-moving machine of immense size broke the peace of the morning and we all turned to watch its arrival. It was a very heavy motor vehicle, sturdy and solid with its counter-balancing weights and retractable stabilizers. The hammerhead crane was extremely powerful. Manned by an experienced crew, hammerheads were widely used in dockyards and shipyards and were capable of lifting loads up to 250 tons while extended horizontally over a great distance. Some operated from stations on the docks, others from rails and some, like this one, from motor vehicles.

Mr Paxton went off to guide the driver on to the site from where it would operate and within minutes the place was alive with activity. It seemed to take very few minutes for the chains to be passed beneath the boat by three of the crane's crew; while this was being done, the crane's jib appeared above the house and then swung around to lower its hook directly above the boat. The chains were attached, the crane driver started the motor, which would retract the hook to take up the tension, and the moment he saw the chains were taut he halted. The boat was now about an inch off the ramp, its woodwork creaking and groaning quite alarmingly as the crane took its weight. The boat was not crushed by the power of the chains being tightened, the struts had eased from the sides of the boat and everything seemed to be going to plan.

A signal was given by a man on the ground to the crane driver, then, slowly, and with a lot of shouting and engine noise accompanied by clanking and other strange sounds, including groans from *Bluebell*'s woodwork, the little cabin cruiser was very slowly lifted higher and higher, leaving its ramp behind and allowing the supporting struts to noisily fall away.

Although the jib had extended over the roof, *Bluebell* was going to be lifted almost as high as the roof, to be sure of clearing any obstacles, and then swung around the end of the house and eventually into the river. Everything was going very slowly but very well; I watched as she was carefully swung across the small patch of wasteland at the end of the terrace, next to the Paxtons' house. By now, *Bluebell* was about the height of the roof ridge and some two or three feet away from the end wall. The crane driver was working within a very confined area and his caution was evident as he undertook every move at a very slow and very careful pace. I watched, heart in my mouth, as the boat was being slowly moved past the end of the house, now at chimney-pot height. Then something unexpected happened.

The almost imperceptible breezes from the river suddenly erupted into a brisk wind and I saw the boat move; it swung like a massive pendulum towards the end of the house and part of the hull touched the chimney pot. There was the sound of crashing pottery as the pot tumbled from its place on the chimney stack and rolled down the roof, rattling down the tiles to vanish from our sight.

Work halted immediately amidst much shouting and cursing, and the boat had swung back in that slow pendulum motion, swaying a little with ever-smaller movements until it was finally sitting steady in its big chain basket. A visual examination showed no damage to the hull or to the roof and the call came to continue. Slowly the boat was carried towards the river, when luffing commenced. Luffing is the lowering of the jib, which in turn lowers the load. At this point I lost sight of *Bluebell* as she disappeared out of my view at the front of the house. There was no restriction on the spectators hurrying to the riverside so long as we stood well clear of the operational area, so we all ran forwards and were in time to see *Bluebell* being lowered gently into the water. The chains were removed; Bluebell did not sink but sat sedately in the water as if she had done so for years. At this sight, everyone cheered.

Suddenly, it was all over – except for the matter of the smashed chimney pot.

'Thanks for coming to watch,' said Mr Paxton. 'I'm pleased you saw everything that happened, so mebbe in a week or two

I'll be in touch about insuring *Bluebell* for all risks. Sorry about that chimney, though it doesn't bother me – I shan't be making a claim off anybody for that small thing, and *Bluebell*'s not damaged, but I know the crane operator was upset. It made him look a bit silly.'

'I don't think so. He couldn't help it – it was due to an unexpected puff of strong wind at exactly the wrong time. If you do decide to claim for it, I was a witness and can say it was a pure accident. There's no reason why you shouldn't claim, that's why you took out the policy.'

'I shan't bother,' he said. 'We make chimney pots at the brickworks so I can get one at cost, only a few pence, and I can fix it myself. No tiles were cracked, either. It's not worth claiming for. Thanks anyway, Mr Taylor, it's been a good day in spite of that. I can't wait to get into that little boat now she's afloat at last . . .'

And so I went home to tell Evelyn all about it, but I did wonder whether Mr Paxton might change his mind and submit a claim for repairs to his chimney. If he did, I could well imagine the hilarity and puzzlement in District Office if they read on the claim form that 'my chimney pot was damaged when it was struck by a passing boat'.

One of the problems of insurance is the accurate valuation of goods and property, and, for that reason, people with collections of any kind are strongly advised, for insurance purposes, to have them revalued at fairly regular intervals. These might include stamp collections, collections of toy soldiers or teddy bears, rare books, glassware, pottery, jewellery or even larger items like horse-drawn vehicles or classic cars. Anything, in fact. That advice is not restricted to collections, however. Quite often a person will buy, say, an oil painting, only to find that, with the passage of time, the artist has become better known and the value of his work has increased. A painting for which one paid £50 might later be worth a hundred times more than its original purchase price. Similar things happen to antiques.

# Rest Assured

What might be second-hand junk one day might unexpectedly be found to be a valuable antique, so it is always wise to be constantly alert to the possible value of one's belongings. Precious objects should be insured for their true value.

I encountered a problem of this nature with a man called Reuben Thornthwaite. Reuben farmed at the appropriately named Hill Top Farm at Walstone and he was forever short of money. He had eight children, a very hard-working wife and a farm well stocked with cattle, sheep, pigs, poultry and horses. Unlike many of the farmers in the dale, he owned his property, having inherited it from his father, who was now dead. It was a remote but beautifully situated farmstead on the lower edge of the moors; rising above it were acres of heather and moorland where Reuben ran his flocks of black-faced sheep while on the lower slopes were more acres of pastureland, ideal for his milking herd and beef cattle. The farm derived its name from its location on the summit of a small mound midway between the moors and river, which gave it stunning views down the dale and across the river.

Even though Reuben was always short of money, he believed in insurance for his family and so did his long-suffering wife, Lucy. They had taken out endowment policies for each of their eight children, whose ages ranged from three to sixteen. Each policy had been taken out at birth and was due for maturity when the respective child reached twenty-one. There was also a house and contents insurance, a farm buildings insurance and insurance for his car and farm machinery. There was, however, no insurance for his livestock. Quite simply, Reuben could not afford to insure his animals.

His shortage of cash meant that he was frequently unable to find the money for the various policies he held, and when I called each month to collect the premiums, I usually left with something in lieu of cash. Fresh eggs were a regular substitute for smaller premiums, or perhaps a side of bacon or leg of ham, and on one occasion I even took home a smart oval mirror of the kind one would find in a fine hallway. Over the months from Reuben I had accepted a pair of riding boots, some ships' lanterns, several chisels and a carpenter's plane, a five-gallon can of petrol and sundry other items which I could either sell or use myself. I don't think I was ever out of pocket through my bartering efforts with Reuben, although I know he did not have such a friendly relationship with the Rural District Council so far as his rates were concerned, or with the Inland Revenue authorities.

Reuben, in his late forties, was a likeable fellow. He was very short in stature, almost like a jockey but much more solid in build with sturdy and slightly bowed legs. Some local people joked he would have difficulty stopping a pig running along a passage. He had very dark brown skin, which was not due to sunburn or weather; some said he had an interesting family background, while others maintained there was a lot of Irish or even Cornish blood in his veins. His hair was curly and dark, his features quite marked, with heavy lips, and he had dark brown eyes. Most of his children bore similar characteristics although his wife, Lucy, was quite tall and slender with light brown hair and a very pale skin. She was from a local farming background, her parents working a busy spread in nearby Lexingthorpe.

The entire family worked hard on the farm even if they did not earn much money – certainly they earned their own keep, but producing sufficient cash for their everyday needs seemed to present constant difficulties. There never seemed to be enough money to run the farm, maintain the premises or pay the bills. Even if they had difficulty paying their many creditors, however, they ate well from their own resources, and the children were always well fed and neatly clothed. All of them had specific jobs around the farm – even the tiniest, a little girl aged three, collected the eggs and helped to feed the hens. Indeed, with the farm being so isolated, the older children had little else to occupy them. And all the children loved horses. Horses seemed to dominate life at Hill Top Farm.

Perhaps that was a fault. The fault, if it can be so described, lay with Reuben, because he had an obsession, which, it was claimed by most of the people who knew him well, he spent

*Rest Assured*

far too much time on, instead of working with the farm animals and earning regular money through good husbandry. Reuben was obsessed with National Hunt racing, otherwise known as steeplechasing, which was obvious to anyone who went to visit him at the farm. One of his larger fields was laid out in the form of a National Hunt racecourse, complete with a range of jumps of the kind one might find at the Grand National, including a water jump and some huge hedges. Behind the main buildings, he had constructed a quadrangle of stables so that the premises looked very like those of an established race-horse trainer.

Reuben was desperate to breed the winner of the Grand National, something that had so far eluded him in spite of years of trying. Reuben, of course, did not regard this as an obsession; for him, it was an ambition. To those who said he spent too much time with his horses instead of earning a living from the farm he said that to win the Grand National would set him up for life. He talked of breeding from the winner, upon which the future of his family and of his horses would be assured for generations. He bred lots of horses, all for steeplechasing, and certainly some had secured good wins on courses throughout Britain, but the kudos and fame that went with winning the Grand National, the world's finest steeple-chase, remained a dream.

He knew, though, that one day he would produce the winner. One day. It was that total belief in himself and his destiny that drove him to ignore troublesome and incidental matters like paying his bills, taxing his car, paying his rates and income tax or even milking the cows or shearing the sheep. During the winter months, when horse racing was 'over the sticks' as it was known, Reuben would attend as many National Hunt meetings as possible, either to race one or more of his horses or to discuss the finer points of winning the greatest race of all. He became steeped in steeplechasing legend and lore. It is said that the term 'steeplechasing' derives from an incident that occurred around 1803 when fox hunters in Ireland decided to race their horses in a straight line across country, the end of the race being a distant church steeple. The race was remark-able for the number of obstacles en route, such as hedges, ditches, lanes, rivers and open fields.

To help her husband achieve his ambition, Lucy, his long-suffering wife, managed as best she could, albeit with the aid of the children and with a good deal of help from her own younger sister and brothers. I think she believed in Reuben's dream, otherwise why did she tolerate what, to an outsider, looked like selfish behaviour? Did she honestly believe that, one day, one of his horses would win that race and earn the family a fortune? I think she did, because she appeared to tolerate much of their income being used on the horses.

Against this background, therefore, one Sunday evening when I was meeting a friend in the Unicorn for a quiet drink, Evelyn received a phone call from Reuben asking if I would pop in to have words with him when I was next in the Walstone area. On my behalf she promised I would, although he gave no indication of the subject he wanted to discuss. The following Thursday, I was collecting in Lexingthorpe, which was only some three miles from Reuben's farm, and decided to pay him a visit. No premiums were due at that time so I would not have to mention money that was currently due, although I knew sufficient about him and his affairs to realize he might be in financial trouble of some kind, and may be seeking to cut his losses by surrendering some of his policies.

It was a cool day in June as I motored up the rough track to his farmhouse, and, as I had now come to expect, I found him in the stables. It was almost three in the afternoon; the horses were all out in the field behind the stable block and he was mucking them out, restocking their interiors with fresh bedding and filling their feeders with oats.

'Ah, Matt.' He always called me Matt. 'Glad you could make it.'

'Nice to be here, Reuben. I got your message.'

'Give me a couple of minutes to finish this one and I'll be with you, then I can say I've finished this job. We'll go to the house and have a cup of tea and a cake. I'm ready foɪ a break.'

While he was finishing that stable, I wandered down to the rails and watched his horses in the field. I counted eight, all magnificent animals within my limited judgement, all calmly nibbling at the grass, although one or two stopped when I arrived and looked towards me, then continued. To me, they were merely horses; to an expert, I am sure they were beautiful, interesting and even valuable.

Reuben joined me after a while and said, 'Nice, aren't they, Matt? All my own work, I'm proud to say.'

'Thoroughbred racehorses, are they?'

'Not thoroughbreds, Matt. Thoroughbreds are usually to be found racing on the flat, my horses are for the jumps. I use mixed breeds to gain extra stamina – thoroughbreds can be a bit temperamental, like pure-bred dogs. Sometimes in a dog a bit of the mongrel can work wonders and I reckon it's the same with horses that need stamina rather than speed. Now, see that one over there, to the right, the far right? That tan-coloured beauty?'

I indicated that I knew the one to which he was referring and he told me he'd bred it with an Anglo-Arabian stallion upon a Cleveland Bay mare, and the result was a powerful and very fast hunter.

He said it could be ridden during the hunting season as well as being raced over the sticks. All this horsey jargon meant nothing to me but I could see he was delighted with the animal, saying it had proved itself both as a hunter and at several race meetings, all National Hunt events.

'He's four years old, Matt, which means that in two years' time, when he's six, I can enter him in the Grand National. His name's Jeremy Joy. Remember that.'

'Jeremy Joy? After a relative?'

'No, after a missel thrush. It was singing on top of a tree behind the stables in a howling gale when he was born. Jeremy Joy is the local name for a missel thrush. Some call them storm cocks, but I didn't think that was a very nice name. Jeremy Joy is much better. An omen, I thought.'

'I agree, It's a really good name, but isn't six rather old to be racing in a tough event like the Grand National?'

'No, Matt, no. Until 1930 only those horses who were five years old and over were eligible, but in that year the age went up to six. A high percentage of the winners are nine-year-olds, so time's on his side. I want him to enter when he's six, though, if only to get experience of the Aintree course. And he can win, Matt, he can win. I know it. I just need a bit of good luck on the day.'

He turned away and began to walk back towards the house and I fell into step at his side as he chattered non-stop about his horses with all the enthusiasm in the world. I could see they were his life and that he was besotted with them, and I wondered why he did not specialize in breeding or training horses. Perhaps that was his ultimate dream. A win at the Grand National would place him in a very strong position to develop his present stable of steeplechasing horses.

When we went into the kitchen with its huge central table, large enough to cater for all his children, we found the youngest playing with her dolls in a corner while the others were all at school or working. Lucy, a quiet and very pleasant woman, had put out a plate of cream buns and some chocolate biscuits, and as we entered she poured the hot water into the large brown teapot.

'Hello, Lucy.' I smiled.

'Nice to see you, Matthew. What's he up to now, my husband?'

I did not know how to respond but Reuben prevented my embarrassment by saying, 'It's about Jeremy Joy, we need to start thinking seriously about insurance for him.'

'You and that horse!' she castigated him gently. 'You think of nothing else!'

'He's going to be our lifesaver, Lucy, you mark my words. He'll put our name on the map, you can bet on that! You'll be thanking me for all this one day.'

She raised her eyebrows as if to the heavens and said, 'I'll leave you two alone to talk business. Come along, Linda, we'll go and see if there are any eggs.'

As the three-year-old child trotted out with her mum, Reuben bade me sit down and poured me a mug of tea, then pushed the plates of buns and biscuits across the table, with an exhortation to help myself.

'So you want insurance for Jeremy Joy?' I put to him after he'd provided more accounts of his theories and the results of his horses' outings at race meetings. He'd been breeding and racing his horses as a preparation for his assault on the Grand National; in Jeremy Joy he had produced exactly the sort of racehorse he wanted. And he was winning races.

'You've got none of your other horses insured, Reuben, nor any of your flocks of sheep or herds of cattle or dairy cows. And why? It's too expensive. You can't afford it. I know that, Reuben, that's why I take other things in lieu, to help you. If you're going to insure Jeremy Joy, it could cost a lot of money. I can't see how you can insure him while not insuring your dairy herd, for example. They're providing your daily bread and butter. I reckon they're more valuable than just one horse.'

'Now, maybe. But think ahead, Matt. As a potential Grand National winner, he could be worth a fortune, a lot more than just one cow. I can afford to lose one cow out of a herd, but not one horse like this one. You can see why I want him insured. There's money tied up in that horse, Matt, big money.'

'And it could all go up in smoke if he broke a leg,' I put to him.

'Don't I know it? Look, Matt, here am I, on the threshold of the greatest thing that has happened in my life, the thing I've been dreaming about ever since I knew what a horse looked like, and I'm asking for help. It's a bit like somebody coming up with a new invention and not having the ability or the wherewithal to do anything about it. I don't know how I can pay the premiums if they're very big – I was sort of hoping you might come up with some ideas.'

'We're not talking of me taking a dozen eggs in lieu of the premiums on a child's endowment policy, Reuben. We might be talking big money; it all depends on what Jeremy Joy is worth, for a start, and how comprehensive the insurance needs to be.'

'I realize that, but I do need the best. Fire risks while in the stables, disease and illness, broken legs, accidents on the road travelling to race meetings, lightning strikes in the fields, injuries through ramblers leaving gates open, nutcases nobbling him, all risks when at the racecourse or even while racing . . . There must be a choice of policies for that kind of thing.'

'I am sure there are, and I am sure there are specialist insurers who will cater for your needs. Specialists often work on a mutual basis – in this case all their insurance might be of racehorses – which helps to spread the risk. It strikes me you need to have words with a racehorse trainer, Reuben, someone who knows the risks and can help to find a reliable specialist company.'

'I wanted you to be involved, Matt. You've been good to us in the past. All my other insurance is with you, which is why I've come to you first. I know you'll help. If I'm dealing with some faceless insurance clerk at the end of a telephone in Newbury or somewhere I'll not get the same understanding.'

'It's good of you to think like that. So, for starters, how much is Jeremy Joy worth?'

'Now, or when he wins the National?'

'I can't arrange insurance for what might be, Reuben. I can only work on what we've got.'

'But I need to be insured for what he's going to be worth, don't I? That's what's at stake for me. That's what all this is about. It's my future – well, my family's really.'

'We insure things at their current value, Reuben. It is possible to have items revalued year by year, and that would occur if Jeremy Joy won the National, or started to win big races before then. But there's no way I can put a value on your horse based on what he might do in the distant future. In spite of your confidence in him, there's no guarantee he'll win the

National, is there? He might be capable, he might be the new superhorse, he could be another Sheila's Cottage, or a local winner like the lovely Teal from Middleham, but there are no guarantees. As things are now, I could arrange to have him insured for all the normal risks that attend a racehorse, and the policy could be based on a current value agreed between you and the Premier. As his value increases, so you could have the policy amended to keep pace with the changes. I'll be honest, there is no other way with the Premier, or with any other company, I shouldn't imagine. Not even the specialists would value him for what he *might* be worth if he wins the National.'

'So what do you recommend?' He looked defeated.

'You must consider what you can afford.' I tried to stress that point. 'I'm sure the Premier will look favourably upon your proposal, even if it's to insure Jeremy Joy alone, although they might be more favourable if all your horses were covered, and the premiums might not be all that much greater for including them all. It might even be possible to include Jeremy Joy's insurance on the farm policy we already have for you. But I stress the value of the horse must be as it stands today, not what it might be at some future date.'

'You know, Matt, I'm so sure he's going to win the National that I was even considering selling my dairy herd, just to raise the money to make sure he's properly trained, cared for, given the best veterinary treatment and so on.'

'You've never felt like this before, have you? About any of your other horses?'

'Not to this extent, no. I've recognized winners in some of them, but not National winners. I've always wanted to breed a National winner, as you know, and I've never been so sure about a horse in my life. Never. He's going to do it, Matt, I know it. That's why I thought about putting the dairy herd up for sale.'

'I wouldn't do that, Reuben. Relying on racehorses to do what you want is notoriously insecure, just ask any punter. What's your bank manager think about all this? Have you talked it over with him?'

'I'm always talking things over with him, Matt, invariably with me asking either for more money or more time to raise more money . . . That's when I thought about selling the dairy herd or possibly some sheep. I'm so absolutely certain, you see. I *know* he's going to be a great steeplechaser – the best in the country.'

'I respect your judgement and admire your confidence, Reuben, but people in the financial world have heard it all before and they know things have a nasty habit of not working out as planned. Look, shall I submit two proposals for you – one proposal for an all-risks policy on Jeremy Joy alone, based on his current value, and the other for all your horses, just to see what the difference is? Then we'll have some idea what the premiums will cost you. I'll also float the idea of including Jeremy Joy on your existing farm policy, at his current value. I can come back to you once I get some feedback from my bosses, and take things a stage further if you feel we should. At least this will get things moving for you.'

'You've kept me going when I've not had a penny to my name and other insurers might have given up on me.' He sighed ruefully. 'I do appreciate what you've done for us, Matt, you've gone out of your way to be helpful to us so, yes, I respect your advice. Do what you think is right.'

'OK. So, how much is Jeremy Joy worth now? If you sold him, what would you expect to get for him? That's always a good way of placing a value on something.'

'I'd be asking something between two hundred and three hundred guineas, I reckon.'

'Shall I say two-fifty for the insurance? As a starter?'

'If you think that's a good idea.'

'I do. And the others?'

'A hundred guineas each, Matt. All seven of them.'

And so I compiled two proposal forms, only one of which would be used, and I got Reuben to sign them. I knew he was somewhat dejected by this, but equally I knew he now understood the folly of insuring something for a future value it might never achieve. I left him with a promise I would be in touch the moment I had obtained the reaction from my District Office. I told him that when I submitted the proposals I would include a personal letter in which I would try to impress upon the faceless people who determined such matters that, in the opinion of its highly experienced owner, the horse known as Jeremy Joy was rather special and potentially a winner of future steeplechases, or even the Grand National. I guessed my letter would not have any effect but it was something I felt I should do for Reuben. At least he would know I had done my best for him.

My first task the following morning was to write that letter and include it with the proposal forms along with a suggestion that the horse might be included on the general farm policy. I added my own opinion that the horse was worthy of special consideration.

I was very surprised a few days later to receive a telephone call from Head Office in London. It was nine thirty in the morning and the secretary asked me to hold the line for Mr Alfred Rogers, the Deputy Chief Actuary, who wished to speak to me.

After a few crackles on the line, a well-spoken voice with a distinct southern accent asked, 'Mr Taylor?'

'Speaking,' I responded in my best voice.

'I am calling about the proposal for a policy relating to a racehorse in your agency,' he said. 'A most interesting case, I feel. You recall it?'

'Mr Thornthwaite's horse, yes. Jeremy Joy.'

'Is the gentleman already a client of yours?'

'Yes, he's got several policies with us. He believes in insurance. His children, the house and farm buildings, car and agricultural machinery.'

'Good. Now, Mr Taylor, is the likelihood of that horse being a National winner realistic, do you feel? Or is it merely a dream in the mind of a no-hoper?'

'I'd say it was very realistic, Mr Rogers.' And I gave my reasons, based on what Reuben had told me about his methods of breeding and the knowledge he possessed. I stressed

185

that Reuben had never made such a strong claim about any other of his horses; I added that, in my view, this was a rather exceptional case because Reuben had clearly recognized the potential of Jeremy Joy.

Mr Rogers listened and when I'd finished he said, 'I would like to send two of our experts along to see Mr Thornthwaite. One is a specialist in racehorse insurance, a Mr Browning, and the other is our public relations manager, Mr Steele. I would like you to be present too, so perhaps you could agree a date with Mr Thornthwaite – any Tuesday during the next three weeks. Our men will be working in the north around those dates and so they can meet wherever is suitable. Perhaps a nice hotel for lunch? You, them and Mr Thornthwaite. At company expense, of course. Can you arrange that and give my secretary the details once you have made the arrangements?'

'Good heavens!' I was amazed. 'Can I ask what this is about? Mr Thornwaite is bound to ask.'

'And so he should. We want to expand our sponsorship activities, Mr Taylor. We find sponsorship linked to major sporting events is an excellent way of getting our name known, and if this horse is as good as you suggest it would be nice to see it carry the Premier's name and logo as it wins the Grand National. We are willing to take risks, of course – that's what insurance is about. We would like to discuss a sponsorship package, probably spread over two years or perhaps three, during which any winnings would be his to keep. We would benefit from the nationwide publicity even at some lesser meetings but especially if his horse won the Grand National. Clearly we would discuss the details with Mr Thornthwaite, and we'd like to see the horse and the general set-up of his enterprise. And if we did sponsor Jeremy Joy then, of course, we would pay any insurance costs.'

'I don't know what to say . . .'

'Just go and see Mr Thornthwaite and tell him of our interest so that he can be prepared for the matter to be discussed in detail. You may tell him of our outline plans;

before meeting my colleagues, it will enable him to consider the type of support he would like us to provide. We are always open to suggestions. So go and see your client, Mr Taylor, find a good hotel for lunch for four then ring me back as soon as you can.'

I couldn't wait to tell Reuben and drove to his house immediately, where I found him working in the stable block. He was beside himself with excitement at the idea of a nation-wide company like the Premier sponsoring one of his horses, but confessed he had no idea what it entailed or what kind of deal he should attempt to negotiate. I suggested he have discussions with one of his racing friends, who had won a similar sponsorship deal from a large brewery – that particular horse-owner had been given a horsebox bearing the brewery's name and logo, he wore their colours during races, he received a cash retainer each month and every time the horse appeared in public, or was named, the name of the brewery was featured. I said that the Premier might want something along those lines, plus some kind of slogan for display, such as 'You're on to a certainty with the Premier'; 'There's no gamble with the Premier'; 'You can't lose with the Premier'; 'Lengths ahead with the Premier'; or something along those lines.

I told Reuben that this possible sponsorship was not a gift: it was a hard-nosed business arrangement. The Premier was making an offer that would benefit them as a form of advertising, although the scheme was also a type of partnership, with possible long-term commitments and benefits for both parties. After discussing it at some length with him, we agreed to meet on Tuesday week at the Crown Hotel, Lexingthorpe, at midday; from Reuben's house, I telephoned the Crown to book lunch for four, and they said they would provide us with a small private room. After lunch, the men from the Premier would be invited to look around Reuben's stables and meet his horses. I then returned home to ring Mr Rogers' secretary in London to confirm the details.

To cut short a long story, the Premier agreed to a very good sponsorship deal over three years, which included the provision of a new horsebox bearing the company's name, logo and slogan (yet to be devised); payment of all Reuben's expenses for attending National Hunt race meetings; clothes bearing the Premier's logo and colours; horse insurance and a retainer paid monthly as a form of regular income. In return, Reuben would carry the company colours, name and logo on *all* his horses when they were racing or appearing in public over the next three years; he would make sure the Premier's name was included in all publicity material and on race cards and, of course, it would always be shown on his horsebox, which must be maintained in a clean and serviceable condition. Everyone, including me, was very happy with the deal even if Jeremy Joy could not compete in the Grand National for at least another two years.

Jeremy Joy had a good year and won a race at Cheltenham. Then, on his first outing in the Grand National two years later, he came a very creditable second. The following year he romped home the winner by seventeen lengths, and the Premier renewed its sponsorship for a further three years, chiefly because Reuben had another likely winner in his expanding stable.

No longer did I accept Reuben's bartered goods in lieu of premiums, although he did give me one of the horseshoes that Jeremy Joy had worn while winning the world's greatest steeplechase. He said it would bring me luck, and it hung on my office wall below a slogan which said, 'The Premier – a winning choice'.

# Eight

*'If the other driver had stopped a few yards
behind himself, the accident would never
have happened.'*
From a claim form

With Evelyn spending so much time practising her driving skills with me at her side I seemed to be busier than ever. My telephone was proving invaluable because people were ringing up to seek my advice about all kinds of insurance, much of it involving motor vehicles. That form of insurance alone made me busier, because more and more people were buying cars, just as more and more were buying electrical goods for use in the home, such as washing machines with small fold-up mangles on top, vacuum cleaners, television sets and kettles. Some people worried about the fire risks these electrical items might create, even if their concern was largely misplaced. Most of these modern devices were quite safe, but it meant I won considerable business in domestic fire insurance. Much of it was from people who'd never previously considered that kind of insurance, which I felt rather odd among people brought up with open fires, oil lamps and candles.

Television sets were becoming increasingly popular at this time, in large part due to the anticipated Coronation of Her Majesty Queen Elizabeth II, due to take place on 2 June, 1953, which would be televised. There had been a lot of debate about this, some people believing that such an historic and solemn religious event should not be cheapened by being shown to the masses on television. Some detractors thought

189

it might be regarded as little more than a piece of public entertainment, although most welcomed the idea because it would give the public a wonderful opportunity to observe this moving and historic ceremony.

The Queen, then only twenty-seven years of age, had given her approval, which meant that almost everyone would be able to watch the progress of this most wonderful of British events. This was something quite unique for people living at a distance from London, and even if they couldn't afford a TV set, or if, as in parts of the country, there was no reception, TV set owners would offer open house for the occasion. Family, friends and neighbours would all be invited to watch – it would add to the party atmosphere.

There were other reasons for increased well-being at this time. Petrol was no longer rationed and people felt able to make more and longer journeys in motor cars. This resulted in yet more cars being bought by people who would usually have travelled by train or bus, with those cars being increasingly used for both leisure and work. Clothing was de-rationed, too, meaning that the ladies in particular were becoming more fashionable.

During that summer of 1953, therefore, there was a feeling that massive social changes were occurring. And so they were. The great sense of adventure that had followed the end of the war was now developing into the anticipated time of peace and happiness.

People were experiencing better incomes, increased security and a more relaxed way of life – and the Coronation was a vital part of that.

Back in Delverdale, it was the approach of the Coronation that prompted the formation of the Micklesfield Village Orchestra, the idea being to bring together talented people from the local community and neighbouring villages and weld them into an efficient and tuneful orchestra that would play during the Coronation festivities. It was the brainchild of Major Charles Broadley and his wife Gertrude, the major being retired from the army, where he had been involved with military music-making in some unspecified capacity. No one was quite sure what he had done during the war because the major liked to create an air of great mystery about his military activities. Some thought he might actually have worked in the cookhouse, because he was quite skilled at roasting beef on Sundays and at producing rhubarb with custard.

As far as his music was concerned, he let it be known that he was a talented oompah player although he would rather deploy his real skills, in leadership, than display his prowess with a wind instrument. Thus, he claimed, he would mould the players into a first-rate orchestra fit to play for the Queen at her Coronation, even if the venue was to be Micklesfield cricket ground.

I did not volunteer because I had no particular musical talent, even if I had been taught the basics of playing a violin and blowing a recorder, and, besides, I was too busy at work and too busy each evening taking Evelyn for driving lessons. Nonetheless, I knew that musicians were being recruited, because posters appeared in the shops, post office and village hall, with the result that one enthusiast would speak to another, each acting as a very proficient recruiting agent. Eventually, some thirty-five hopefuls, clutching a bewildering array of instruments ancient and modern, turned up at the village hall one Friday evening for the very first gathering of the MVO – Micklesfield Village Orchestra.

Major Broadley took to the stage to outline his ideas, one of which was to arrange the volunteers into relevant sections, such as strings, brass, woodwind and percussion, before getting down to the actual act of making music. It was while the major was pontificating that the village hall caretaker, Jack Black, otherwise known as Black Jack, appeared from backstage. Jack, often nicknamed the Führer behind his back, was a former army drill sergeant, whose daily dress in civilian life included black boots with shining toecaps, trousers with creases so sharp they might have been moulded around a razor blade and a long-sleeved shirt with similar creases in the sleeves and down the breast. In his fifties, he was thickset and

191

muscular. He made sure he remained fit for active service by performing weird exercises in his garden and taking long runs up to the moor and back each morning, but, with his drill-sergeant mentality still very much alive, he would not tolerate any kind of sloppiness in the village hall. Woe betide anyone who did not wipe their feet upon entry, or who dropped chewing gum on the floor or who brought beer bottles or cream buns into the building.

And, being a former 'other rank', rather than a commissioned officer, Jack did not particularly warm to the retired major. Now, though, the two men were civilians which made them equal, except that Jack was king of this particular midden. When he appeared before the fledgling orchestra, he halted on stage in a silent pose to gain their attention, then put his hands on his hips and stared at the gathering as if seeking some kind of fault in their dress, footwear or haircuts. They saw him and lapsed into an uncertain silence, most of them having crossed swords with Jack on previous occasions.

In the telling silence, he said, 'I hope you lot are insured for bringing those instruments in here. It's the rules, you know.'

'Insured?' boomed Major Broadley. 'The secretary said nothing about insurance when I booked the hall.'

'The hall has insurance, Major Broadley, but that is for its own purposes. If a tile fell off the roof on to a person, or if somebody left a tap running in the kitchen or a cloakroom and we got flooded, then we'd be insured. It's that sort of insurance. Public liability and so on.'

'Naturally. One would expect that in a well-run organization, Mr Black.'

Jack ploughed on. 'Or if we had a loose floorboard and somebody got hurt if it shot up and hit them on the nose. We have to have public liability insurance, it's in the rules. But if one of your orchestra members stuck the pin of a double bass through somebody's foot during rehearsals, then the person would not be insured under our cover. Or if a violin string broke and took out an eye, or somebody dropped a euphonium on somebody's foot and broke a toe . . . And I hope you will not be sticking those pins of double basses and cellos into my floorboards, or pushing that piano backwards and forwards just when I've polished the floor for dancing.'

'My orchestra members are responsible people, Mr Black, and they do not go about assaulting one another with cellos and euphoniums, or should that be euphonii? I see no need for special insurance cover during our rehearsals here.'

'Then I shall have to show you it in black and white,' snapped Jack, who marched off to find his rule book. Jack was very knowledgeable about the rules of everything, including the village hall.

In trying to ignore the unseemly interruption, pretending it didn't really matter, the major returned his attention to the budding orchestra. They had formed themselves into sections as he had asked and it was now time for the next stage, so he decided it would be sensible to seat them in some kind of order, as if they were about to rehearse.

'Find yourselves a chair each, and there are music stands under the stage, that door on the left. Settle down in formation just as if this were a rehearsal, and then we can go into more detail.'

As they were noisily finding their chairs and music stands, then being precisely positioned by Gertrude, Jack returned with a red-backed rule book and handed it to Major Broadley, open at a page.

'Rule 46 (a),' he said, stabbing the page with his finger. 'Read it.'

The major read aloud. 'Organizers of special events within the hall will be responsible for arranging their own insurance cover. This will be in addition to the general public liability insurance which prevails.'

'There,' said Jack. 'There's no doubt about that.'

'I don't think we can be regarded as a special event,' countered the major. 'We are a group of villagers who are using the hall for what it was intended. A group activity of a very normal sort. Recreational and instructional. There's nothing special about what we are doing.'

'You are special because you are different,' snapped Jack. 'A whist drive is not special, nor is a WI meeting or even the monthly tea dance, but if we had a display of antiques in here, they would have to be specially insured, and so would sword dancers or somebody showing his craft work . . . Special shows need special insurance, the secretary should have told you.'

'So what if I disagree and do not take out special insurance cover for our visits?'

'Then I won't let you in,' said Jack with an air of finality. 'It's not that I'm being awkward or obstructive, but rules are rules. You should know that, Major.'

'Rules are for the obedience of fools and the guidance of wise men, Mr Black,' retorted the major with more than a hint of venom. 'But I shall check the situation, for I would not wish any of my members to be uninsured if something unexpected happened to them.'

'Good, then you may remain today and I trust that before your next visit the matter will be resolved.' And Black Jack walked away.

Major and Gertrude Broadley completed that evening's work with the musicians and even managed to produce some sort of a tune from them, but afterwards Major Broadley went immediately to speak to the secretary of the village hall committee, Jacqueline Pollard. Jacqueline was also secretary of the parish council, and involved with many other village activities.

'We've had trouble before with Jack,' she told the major. 'I'm afraid he does insist on people sticking rigidly to the rules, and there is no doubt the rule he quoted does mean that something like an orchestra should be specially insured during their time in the hall. I know we had to get insurance when the folk dancing classes were being held – danger from swords you know – and it was the same when we had that variety show with the fire-eater and lion-tamer. He did the same with the children's show of pet animals, just because he discovered one lad was going to bring a snake. And when we had an antiques fair. Jack is very insistent, and he knows the rule book from cover to cover.'

'Well, if that's the case, I'll have to go and have words with Matthew Taylor,' said the major. Which is how I came to be involved.

Major Broadley arrived at my house shortly after nine next morning and explained what had transpired. I listened, and felt that Führer Jack had a point. I could not take sides here, because I had to be realistic and consider the wider issues.

'Let me get this right,' I said. 'You'll be using the village hall for practices and rehearsals until Coronation Day, when you'll be playing on the cricket ground?'

'Right,' said the major.

'Then what? Will the orchestra disband or do you envisage further concerts?'

'I would hope they will remain together and continue with weekly practices in the hall, then I would wish them to play at concerts, either in the village hall or elsewhere, maybe in Whitby Spa or on the seafront at Scarborough. There is always a demand for a good quality orchestra with a wide repertoire, particularly on special occasions like village shows or galas.'

'In that case, I think Jack has done you a favour. If you are taking the band on the road to a variety of venues, you will need insurance – some of those instruments will be valuable and you need to consider theft and damage to them at the very least, especially if you are travelling.'

'But won't the instruments be covered by their owners' household insurance?'

'It's possible, only the owners will know that, but you might find that some insurers' household policies don't cover the use of instruments at commercial events. As founder of the orchestra, you might find yourself held responsible if something when wrong, say if a valuable violin was lost, stolen or damaged while on Scarborough seafront.'

'So what do you recommend, Mr Taylor?'

I suggested comprehensive insurance cover for all instruments, players and officials in the orchestra while playing as a group in both in the village hall and at other venues, and also during the journeys to and from such venues, whether by coach, trailer, train or private car. I could arrange for such a policy to run initially for a year with an option for it to be renewed annually. A lot would depend upon the future success of the orchestra. I knew the Premier had a suitable policy, because this had been discussed during my induction course when someone had raised a similar question about brass bands. I emphasized that this insurance would be for the orchestra as a group, not for individual members. I stressed that individuals' instruments would have to be insured in their own right when not being used in the orchestra.

The major then told me that the orchestra, at this very early stage of its development, had no funds, so I suggested he either open a bank account and arrange an overdraft until it began to earn money from its appearances, or that members themselves pay for the insurance as a group. After all, it was for the benefit of all.

I advised him to complete a proposal form immediately, and he said that by the time I had received approval from District Office, along with a note of the cost, he would have made arrangements for paying the first premium. It meant that all members and instruments would be comprehensively insured during all rehearsals, practices and concerts irrespective of their location, and also during travel to and from such events.

One would have thought that would have been sufficient, but we hadn't bargained for fifteen-year-old Hugh Berriman and his trumpet. Hugh's grandfather, Desmond, had been a keen member of the prize-winning Skinningrove Silver Band, and upon his death his treasured silver trumpet had been passed down to Hugh. Hugh's father, Raymond, had his own instrument and was also a keen player, and so it was logical that Hugh would be expected to continue the family's silver band tradition.

At first, Hugh was quite keen, although he preferred football and cricket, but his family had persuaded him not to abandon the long-standing family tradition. For a lad of fifteen, however, with no band to encourage him, and no band hut in which to practise or have fun with his mates, trumpet-playing was an increasingly solitary occupation, which he found more and more boring. The foundation of Micklesfield Village Orchestra changed all that, because Sylvia Newberry, the gorgeous fifteen-year-old from the top of the village, whom Hugh had long fancied, joined the orchestra to play the violin. Hugh suddenly realized that trumpet-playing might turn out to be very interesting indeed.

The snag was that when he presented himself to Gertrude Broadley that first night, she insisted he demonstrate his skills with a few bars, but he made rather a mess of things, whereupon she suggested he practise his scales and fingering and gain more experience. Sylvia Newberry, on the other hand, was immediately accepted as one of the first violins, so Hugh decided he would practise until he was perfect.

That's when another snag presented itself. Hugh's sister, Jennifer, was swotting for her O-levels and when he began to practise at home, he was told to either stop or go elsewhere. Jennifer could not concentrate on her French, English, geography, maths and religious studies with a trumpet blasting away in the next bedroom, so Hugh found himself wondering where and when he could practise to acquire the skills necessary to place him close to Sylvia and her violin. Then he remembered an old disused barn down Swang Lane on the edge of the village.

It was small but very isolated, and a large field separated it from any other village building – in fact, the only building remotely near it was the village hall, and that was at the opposite side of the field. It was at least a hundred yards away, and far enough for the trumpet music not to be heard by anyone using it. Not even Jack Black would hear it, even if he did live in the caretaker's house that adjoined the hall. And it must be said that Hugh knew that he would have to pass Sylvia's house on the way to that deserted barn.

Carrying his precious instrument in its case, along with some simple music to practise on, Hugh embarked upon his mission the following Saturday morning. He passed Sylvia's house without catching sight of her, but full of hope and determination he entered the barn, which had no door, hooked his music to a nail in the wall and began to practise. The barn smelled rather bad, because it was often used as a shelter by the cows that inhabited the field, but at that time they were all out munching grass, as was their habit.

The sudden blast of a trumpet, probably amplified by the hollow emptiness of the small barn, had an immediate impact upon the herd. In terror at the awful noise, they stampeded away from the din. It was perhaps unfortunate that the first obstacle they reached was the rather flimsy fence between the field and Jack Black's vegetable patch; it was perhaps more unfortunate that he happened to be in his garden at the same time, tending that very same patch.

Upon hearing the thunder of hooves he looked up in amazement as the first line of cavalry was urged rapidly forward by those behind; within a matter of seconds, they had demolished his fence and ended up among his cabbages and carrots. Their heavyweight feet did little for his crop and produced a mass of deep hoof marks in the soil.

It was some time before the reason for their stampeding terror was discovered, and that is when Jack arrived at my house.

'I want to claim off the orchestra's insurance,' he said. 'For damage to my garden fence and growing crops. It was that lad of Berriman's, frightening the cattle by playing his trumpet.'

'He won't be insured for that,' I had to tell Jack. 'The orchestra's insurance only covers members as a group while they are rehearsing, practising or playing in concert. It doesn't include individual members practising or playing, unless they were playing a solo in the hall.'

'Then I'll have to claim from him direct.'

'You can try, but he's only fifteen, remember. I doubt if you'd succeed, Jack, not against Hugh individually, his being a minor in law. I doubt if anyone would agree he was negligent. You could ask if his dad has some kind of policy that might cover the damage. But doesn't your own insurance cater for that kind of thing?'

'I'm not insured for herds of cows smashing down my fence and trampling all over my garden.'

'Doesn't the hall insurance cover you? Your house is part of the hall premises.'

'Not my garden – it's private premises, it's not on the hall's insurance. I have to make my own arrangements for private insurance.'

'So why not try the cow owner's insurance?'

'I have, and he's not insured against his cattle damaging my fence and garden.'

'I'm sorry I don't appear very helpful, Jack, but you know how it is – rules are rules. But if you want to cater for similar things happening in the future, I might be able to offer a suitable policy.'

He stomped away, glowering and muttering, but so far as I knew he never attempted to claim any kind of compensation from Hugh's parents or Hugh himself. For the orchestra, of course, this was but a minor blip in its determination to be highly competent and fully entertaining on the day of the Coronation.

Perhaps I should add that Hugh's determination was rewarded. He was accepted as a member of the orchestra and was soon going steady with Sylvia.

Over the months preceding the Coronation, a hard-working committee of volunteers had been planning celebrations in Micklesfield. Similar events were being planned for other villages throughout Delverdale, with some of the very small communities joining nearby larger ones instead of celebrating alone. In most cases the celebrations would follow a well-tried pattern of street parties, garden parties and galas with singing, music, dancing, food and drink.

In Micklefield's case, there would be events on the cricket ground during the day, commencing at 10.30 a.m. and continuing until 5 p.m., followed by a grand party for the children in the village hall with food and drinks from 5 p.m. until 9 p.m., then, rounding off the day, a dance for the adults during the evening until 1 a.m. The celebrations on the cricket ground would cater for all ages and would include a gymkhana, a show of livestock and pets, various stalls and fairground activities such as roundabouts, shooting galleries and dodgems, sports contests, which would include races, high jumps, long jumps and a cross-country race, and many other competitions such as guess the weight of the pig or cake, duels of strength and skill, fancy-dress competitions for adults and children, with the inevitable teas and soft drinks. All that was to be enhanced by the well-rehearsed music of the Micklesfield Village Orchestra, who would later play for the dancing in the hall. At midnight, on the cricket field, there would be a fireworks display that would be seen for miles around.

There would even be several television sets around the ground and some in the marquee if anyone wanted to watch events in London. Many would watch in the comfort of their own homes, but for those without a television set and with no access to one this offered a unique opportunity to witness a part of history. The organizers had made it possible thanks to a helpful TV shop, some local engineers, lots of extension cables and tall masts upon which to position the familiar H-shaped aerials. The six-hour-long television broadcast, and the two-and-a-half-hour Coronation ceremony in Westminster Abbey, commented upon by Richard Dimbleby, would be the highlight of the day. Fifteen million viewers were expected to watch the ceremony on television and pictures could even be beamed across to America within six minutes.

It was appreciated that many would prefer to watch the ceremony on television rather than take part in other events at that particular time, and the day's activities were arranged so that people could come and go as they wished. There would be something for everyone, young and old, royalist or not, right through the day and into the night. For Micklesfield, it would be a memorable occasion.

Arrangements for the Coronation Day celebrations were

being undertaken by a committee of local people, all of whom had expertise in areas likely to be of value on the day, and the secretary was Jacqueline Pollard. So it was that she came to see me one morning before I set off on my rounds.

'Matthew,' she said as I led her into my lounge-cum-office. 'It's about the Coronation Day celebrations. As you know, the parish council is heavily involved in the arrangements for Micklesfield's celebrations, and the county council has told me that because of this, the county insurance policy, which normally extends to parish councils and their work, will be extended to our Coronation Day celebrations at no extra cost. It's a celebratory gesture by the county council, and it means we need not worry about getting insurance for people who are taking part in sports and games, or working on the gymkhana, erecting the marquee, working with animals, helping on the stalls or whatever. It's a very wide-ranging insurance, which means all risks are taken care of.'

'That's a load off your mind,' I said.

'It is.' She smiled mischievously. 'But our chairman has come up with another idea, something the county council insurance cannot cater for.'

'Go on,' I said. 'This sounds ominous!'

'Pluvious insurance,' she said. 'He's asked me to explore the possibility of getting pluvious insurance for the events on the cricket ground and for the fireworks display afterwards.'

I had to admit I had never arranged that kind of cover, providing insurance against an event being cancelled due to heavy rain. This was never an easy insurance to negotiate, owing to the vagaries of English weather, and although many insurance companies did operate a pluvious policy of some kind, they tended to differ widely.

For example, one company would only agree to a pluvious policy if the event was to raise money for charity. Their logic was that if the event was cancelled due to rain, then the charity would be the loser, not the organizers, and so it was a condition of that policy that the insurance payout was handed over to the charity, less expenses incurred by the organizers.

That seemed a very good idea. In another case, a company agreed to issue this kind of insurance only for events where an entry fee was charged, and would only pay out if the entire event was cancelled due to heavy and persistent rain before the official opening time. If the event had opened and even just a few paying visitors had arrived then there would be no payout. The event would be deemed not to have been cancelled. In addition to these variations, the premiums could be substantial, again due to the uncertainty of English weather. In most cases, a mere shower of rain was not a reason for activating such a policy – the outcome of the rain had to be so devastating that the entire function was cancelled and money lost.

After I had explained how this cautionary approach was exercised by most insurance companies, Jacqueline felt it was perhaps not such a good idea, because, she felt, even if there was heavy rain our event would not be cancelled, and another factor was that entry was free. All that would have to be paid for was food and drink, and games such as the shooting gallery or tombola. The television sets were inside a marquee, and in addition there were stalls and amusements also under cover, as well as the tea tent, and the cricket pavilion was being used as an office, first-aid centre and lost property office.

Rain would be a nuisance, she said, but we both agreed that even the heaviest of downpours would not wash out our Coronation Day celebrations.

Although she had made up her mind that pluvious insurance was not feasible for our celebrations, I said I would explore the situation with my District Office. It might just be possible that a large company like the Premier had produced a pluvious insurance especially for Coronation Day events, and I said I would ring while she waited. I called my District Office at Ryethorpe and when I explained the purpose of my call was put through to John English, the District Sales Manager.

'Yes, Mr Taylor,' he explained after listening to me, 'the Premier's Head Office has authorized a pluvious insurance for

Coronation Day celebrations. They will apply the policy to any bone fide outdoor Coronation Day celebration which is formally organized with a committee and chairman, and which is cancelled prior to the official starting time due to heavy and prolonged rain. But the premium is high – in spite of a huge variation in size of Coronation Day events, they feel that this is a case for more of a mutual approach and so a flat rate of £150 will be the cost of the premium irrespective of the nature of the celebration, and the payout on proof of cancellation will be a maximum of £250. That will prevent small street parties and such from claiming if they get rained off.'

I thanked him for this information and said I would get back to him if our village committee decided to proceed. But they did not. They thought the premium was too high and, in any case, they felt that no rain, however heavy, would deter Micklesfeltonians from celebrating Her Majesty's Coronation. They were right. It poured down throughout the day, but Micklesfield people ignored it. Everyone wished all the very best to the new Queen and lots of champagne was drunk out of very wet glasses.

Very shortly after the headiness of that time, Evelyn passed her driving test, and when we arrived home that day, minus her L-plates, we found our neighbour, Mr Browning, waiting for us. He was a quiet man in his late seventies who lived alone, and we hadn't seen a great deal of him since moving into our modest terrace home. We were the second in a row of terrace houses, and he lived in the first, a large house with a spacious garden around the front, back and eastern side. He was the gentleman who had loaned us his garage at no cost to accommodate Betsy.

'I wanted to catch you,' he said. 'I saw you put the car in the garage. Well done, Evelyn, by the way; I see you've discarded your L-plates. What I wanted to say was that I have decided to go and live with my daughter in Leeds, and so the house will be coming on the market very soon. I'd like you to have first refusal. Would you be interested?'